TRAPPED

AN EVERYDAY HEROES WORLD NOVEL

Kristina Beck

EVERYDAY
HEROES

Published by KB Worlds LLC.

Cover Design by: Jody Kaye

Cover Photo by: depositphotos

Editing by: Rachel Overton, Wordscapes

Proofreading by: Helen Pryke

Published in the United States of America

ISBN: 978-3-947985-15-9

Dear Reader,

Welcome to the Everyday Heroes World!

I'm so excited you've picked up this book! Trapped is a book based on the world I created in my *USA Today* bestselling Everyday Heroes Series. While I may be finished writing this series (*for now*), various authors have signed on to keep them going. They will be bringing you all-new stories in the world you know while allowing you to revisit the characters you love.

This book is entirely the work of the author who wrote it. While I allowed them to use the world I created and may have assisted in some of the plotting, I took no part in the writing or editing of the story. All praise can be directed their way.

I truly hope you enjoy Trapped. If you're interested in finding more authors who have written in the KB Worlds, you can visit www.kbworlds.com.

Thank you for supporting the writers in this project and me.

Happy Reading,

K. Bromberg

To all of those who have suffered during the Covid crisis, this book is for you.

1

CHARLI

Fake smiling sucks the ever-loving life out of me. But it keeps your facial muscles tight, right? Anyway, that's what I try to convince myself, since I have to do this day in and day out. Pretending to be happy and in love. How did I get to the point where I'm trapped in a life I thought would be a total dream but, in reality, is a never-ending nightmare? Relief is coming—I'm escaping for Thanksgiving weekend. Alone.

"That's a wrap, everybody," the director calls. "Happy Thanksgiving!" At least he still loves his job.

He doesn't have to say another word. I'm out of here. I head down the sidewalk toward my car, wobbling in ridiculous four-inch heels, wishing a happy Thanksgiving to the crew and staff I pass along the way. No one's following me, so I think I can sneak out of here without anyone knowing. I'm not even giving this hideous outfit back.

"Charlize—wait!" Jordan shouts from behind me, pretending he cares. He deserves an Emmy. Unfortunately, he can walk faster than I can in these damn heels. He grabs my elbow and tugs until I stop.

"I told you I was leaving right after the shoot was done.

And you know how I hate being called Charlize outside the show," I snap. My mom was obsessed with Charlize Theron when I was born. It is my name, but most people call me Charli… at least back home. Not on the set.

"You know that I should be going to your mom's with you." He leans in and whispers, "It's not good for my, um, *our* image if we don't spend the holiday together. We're engaged."

Ugh. As always, only thinking about himself. He rubs his hands up and down my arms, then glances over his shoulder to see if anyone is watching. I shiver in disgust. It's hard to believe there was a time I loved his touch. I step back and unlock my silver BMW.

"I need a break from acting and all this bullshit. Engaged… what a fucking joke." I say it under my breath so only he can hear me. My assistant, Lizzy, catches my attention in the distance. Her eyes are wide, and she shakes her head slightly. That's her cue that people are watching.

He wraps his arms around me and mutters in my ear, "Until this house is finished, you're wearing that rock on your finger, and you're still my fucking fiancée. So hug me like you used to when you were in love with me. The camera's always rolling." Ha! That ship sailed a long time ago.

I squeeze him tightly out of frustration and anger, but all I want to do is kick him in the balls. "Some people might think you care about me, but we both know you're only worried about your image. You don't give a shit about me or anybody else." He stills in my arms because he's not used to me speaking to him so harshly. "Let me remind you, I'm the reason your career is such a success."

I pull away from him and pat his cheek sweetly. *Gag.* "I'll miss you so much," I say loud enough for someone to hear. Maybe no one does. Maybe they aren't even paying attention anymore. *Wishful thinking.* He remains mute and steps away from the car.

I yank off my ridiculous shoes and toss them along with my handbag on the passenger side, then grab my favorite silver ballerinas from the side pocket of the door. I put them on and close my eyes. It's like stepping onto a cloud compared to those toe pinchers.

I slip into the seat, and Jordan closes the door for me. He taps the roof, then waves as I drive away.

Once I've gone a couple blocks, I pull off to the side of the road and park to gather my thoughts and to breathe. I pull down the sun visor and observe myself in the mirror. *Processed.* That's how I look. I rip off the fake eyelashes I'm sporting and flick them out the window. I know it's not environmentally friendly but right now, I don't care. I grab the package of makeup remover towelettes from my handbag, pull one out, and start scrubbing. Slowly, the ugly red lipstick disappears off my mouth. I should clean my face too because I could probably carve my initials into the crap on my cheek.

Jordan and I star in a home renovation show called *Fast-Track Renovation*. We renovate houses with a quick turnaround time. I'm an architect and interior designer. He's also an architect, and we both have construction experience. Every time I see an episode, I want to throw my TV out the window. Who in their right mind walks around a construction site in four-inch heels and a short skirt? They've turned my image into a joke. I should be wearing a tool belt, not a Gucci one. Do I really need fake eyelashes and tons of makeup? And how am I supposed to do physical labor with long nails? Oh, I'm not. I'm only there as eye candy. This is not what I signed up for.

It is. You should have read the fine print. Maybe my name was Naivety in another life.

When I look at my reflection, the only thing I like is my hair. I was born with blond hair and naturally loose spiral curls. That's the one thing they haven't changed about me. And only because I wouldn't let them.

I slap the visor closed and groan. The drive home through beautiful Napa Valley wine country should relax me before I get to Mom's. It has in the past.

I'm about to put the car into drive again when my phone pings. Do I really want to know who it is? Probably not, but maybe it's Mom.

I dig through my bag and pull it out. A smile grows on my face. It's a message from my sister, Sandy.

Sandy: I can't wait to see you tomorrow. We have a lot to catch up on. I have so many things to tell you and a couple of important questions too. See you soon!

Me: Can't wait either. It'll be like old times. I'm on my way to Mom's now. See you tomorrow!

The tension in my shoulders slowly decreases. I need to forget my real life and focus on my family for once. Holidays haven't been the same since Dad died three years ago. Sandy didn't take his death well. None of us did, really, but we haven't seen her since a couple weeks after the funeral. After that, I've spent most of the depressing holidays with Mom and sometimes Jordan. Thanksgiving and Christmas have been the worst.

Sandy was the hippie of the family—we were used to her disappearing without warning or explanation, but this time has been different. We received postcards from France and Switzerland a couple of months after she left, but few phone calls. She sent text messages once in a while, letting us know she was still alive. But recently, nothing.

So when she called Mom earlier this month and said she wanted to spend Thanksgiving with us, we were floored. Until she called, we didn't even know she was in California again. She promised she'd explain everything and said she'd be bringing someone special for us to meet. Maybe she's bringing a boyfriend. I couldn't miss out on this. Maybe we'll finally have a fun-filled holiday again.

I just wish something would happen to make me stay there longer than the holiday weekend.

2

KELLAN

Shit, I missed the exit. "Pay attention!" I yell at myself, smacking the steering wheel. My thoughts are all over the place with the number of project deadlines we have to meet before the end of the year.

Construction signs blink in the distance, warning traffic to slow down to fifty miles per hour. I decrease my speed and merge into the farthest right lane on the highway to take the next exit. My phone rings, and my construction manager's name flashes on the display.

"Hey, Jay. I'm in my truck and have you on speaker." I turn up the volume. "Hasn't anyone told you it's Thanksgiving? What's up?" Like I should talk? It's almost eleven thirty, and I'm supposed to be on my way to my aunt's for Thanksgiving, but here I am, stopping at one of the houses we're working on.

He chuckles. "My wife has reminded me several times, but I wanted to let you know that I got a message that the custom-made bathroom tiles for the Duncan house will be delayed. They've been damaged en route. I had to reorder, but they're making it a priority so we won't have to wait too long. I should get a call tomorrow or Monday. I'll have the adjusted timelines to you as soon as I can."

"I swear, there's never a dull moment with that house," I growl. "Nothing but problems. I'll contact the Duncans tomorrow. I don't want to ruin their Thanksgiving... or mine."

"Yeah, I wouldn't want to be you."

"Thanks for the update. Now go enjoy your time with your family and the long weekend."

"Will do. Talk to you on Monday."

When the call disconnects, I look in the side mirror of my pickup and gasp, squeezing the steering wheel. A massive truck loaded with long, wide steel pipes is speeding in the lane next to me. Suddenly it's like watching an action film. Instinct has me slow down. The truck jerks sharply into my lane three or four cars ahead of me but doesn't see the beige sedan next to it. The sedan swerves and tries to stop, but it's too late. It collides with the truck and spins, sparks shooting everywhere. The truck's brakes lock up, causing smoke to plume as the tires skid along the asphalt. The car behind doesn't stop in time and smashes into the sedan too, pushing it forward. The truck swerves again, back into the sedan, and its tail slides to the left, hitting several other cars. Crumpled pieces of plastic fly through the air, and glass shatters around me as more cars collide. I brace myself and look in the rearview mirror, waiting for someone to rear-end my truck. But traffic behind us has slowed down.

I look ahead at the smashed sedan that now stands still, parallel to the truck. And then, if I didn't think it could get any worse, the pipes break loose and topple onto the roof of the sedan, crushing it, blowing out the windows, and flattening the tires before rolling off and onto the ground. One huge, steel pipe remains in a trench down the middle of the car. Everything around us comes to a stop.

"No!" I yell. "Holy fuck." I throw the truck into park, turn off the engine, and grab my phone. Then I jump out.

People get out of their cars too. Some already have their phones out. "Call 911," I command as I run toward the sedan. Smoke, the smell of burnt rubber, and panic permeate the area. Several people run to the other crashed vehicles and the truck to help.

I slow down as I get closer, trying to grasp what I see. Someone reaches the flattened sedan before me, then runs to the side and pukes. I push myself to go on, knowing that the passengers probably didn't survive. But as I get closer, I hear a baby screaming.

I whip around, waving my arms. "There's a baby trapped in here and it's alive," I shout.

I make it to the front passenger door and freeze. I no longer see the blood and destruction around me. All I can focus on are the empty turquoise eyes staring at me. I shake my head vigorously, and a singeing pain rips through my chest as if a hot piece of metal from the truck is lodged in my heart.

"No, no!" My stomach clenches, and I gag. "Charli! No!" Tears threaten to blind me, but then I see the brown hair and relief spreads through my body. *It's not her.*

It's her sister, Sandy. Charli has blond hair, and Sandy has dark brown. Shock. Despair. Relief. And then crippling guilt takes over because I shouldn't be relieved for someone else's death.

I snap out of the trance I'm in and feel her neck, even though I know it's too late by the way her head is angled. No pulse. *Fuck.* All I can think about is her mom, Tricia. And Charli. I turn away and bend over, bracing my hands on my knees. My lungs constrict, letting little air in. *Relax. Inhale. Exhale.*

The baby shrieks, and my head shoots up. Sandy's baby! "Noelle!"

"You know her? Them? Is the woman still… breathing?" A big biker dude yanks at the back door, trying to get it open to get Noelle out.

I drop my head. "Yes… And no, she didn't make it."

"Fuck. It's jammed," he yells. He reaches inside the door and checks the lock. Yanking again, it doesn't budge.

"Did someone call 911?" I bellow to the bustling crowd of people watching us, pulling on my hair.

"Yes. Help is on the way. I told them a baby is involved and people are trapped in their cars," an elderly woman responds from afar.

Adrenalin takes over, blocking my rage. The biker and I try to get the door open again, but nothing works. I look inside and notice some glass on the blanket that's covering Noelle's legs. It's a relief that she's wearing long sleeves and a hat. I don't see any blood on her. One after the other, I pick off the glass and toss the pieces outside until I can't find anymore, barely noticing I've cut my finger along the way. I gather the edges of the blanket and remove it carefully, shaking it outside the car to remove any smaller shards of glass. Then I drape it back over her jerking arms and legs. The baby's face is scarlet from her screaming cries. But that's good—it means she's alive.

"We have to get her out of the car seat," the guy shouts. "This roof could cave in even more any second."

I stick my head in the window and check the size of the car seat against the window opening. It's a small, rear-facing seat for younger babies. It's attached to something.

"I think I can get it through the window. I need to figure out how to detach the damn thing from the apparatus." My fingers graze the surface, searching for some kind of button or lever.

I push and pull until I feel the latch. "Found it!" Then I press the side buttons to push the handle back, over the baby's head. "Okay. I need your help. I don't want to jostle her too much in case she's hurt."

"I'm here."

I lift the seat gently and maneuver it through the window. It clears the frame only by centimeters. "Take it," I tell the guy. "I'm caught on something." Once he has her, I yank at my shirtsleeve. A jagged piece of glass makes a long tear in it as I pull free. Then I take the baby from him and rush her away from the car to the side of the highway where two women crouch next to her, trying to calm her down.

I return, trying hard not to look at Sandy, and someone asks, "What about the driver?"

"I'll go check." I run around the car, jumping over the pipes. My boots skid on the pavement slick from oils and antifreeze and who knows what. When I see the condition of Sandy's wife, I turn away, tears pooling in my eyes.

The things I've just seen will haunt me for the rest of my life.

I don't go any closer to check for a pulse because I know there won't be one. The biker guy comes around the car and inches up to me. I throw my arm out.

"Turn around. You don't want to see. There's nothing we can do."

He rests his hand on my shoulder. "You going to be okay, man? I'm sorry that you know these people, but the baby is safe."

Grief weighs heavily on my chest. Of all the accidents, why did I have to witness this one? People I know. People I just saw a couple of weeks ago for the first time in years. Why did I have to miss that exit?

Together, we walk away from the car toward the women who are taking care of Noelle.

"I can't believe that baby survived when the car is wrecked like this," the guy says. He's sweating; his hands are shaking. He's obviously as disturbed as I am.

"It was a miracle, that's what it was. Angels protected her. That baby was supposed to survive," one of the women with Noelle says, clasping a necklace on her chest. Then she does the sign of the cross. "That poor family."

I pace back and forth, getting more pissed off by the second that no ambulances or police have shown up yet. I want to go to Sandy and comfort her even though she can't hear me. I want to promise her that her daughter will be taken care of. But I don't know if I can stomach seeing the condition she's in again. I feel helpless because there's nothing else I can do.

Finally, sirens blare in the distance, and in minutes, emergency vehicles flood the accident scene. I wave them over to us. Almost immediately, they push me away so the firefighters can extract the victims from the car. Grady Malone is among them. Our eyes connect for a few seconds, and then he gets to work.

Two EMTs rush over to Noelle and take her to an ambulance. The firefighters analyze the situation for the driver and Sandy. If I'd had any doubt, their body language and the shaking of their heads make it clear that neither survived.

I drop my head in my hands and wish I could turn back time. If only I'd taken the right exit! Or if I could somehow have slowed them down or... something. I never would've witnessed this. How can I tell Tricia and Charli that I was here? How will I look at Charli without being consumed with guilt because I was thankful it was Sandy and not her?

The answer is... I can't tell them anything.

3

CHARLI

Not Sandy! My body shakes like a leaf and the taste of my salty tears makes my stomach turn. Mom sobs in my arms as Officers Jacobs and Wicker from the Sunnyville Police Department tell us that Sandy and another woman died in a car accident this morning. Thanksgiving morning.

Our Thanksgiving table was decorated festively, a massive turkey was in the oven, and we'd added extra place settings. We baked Sandy's favorite pies. We watched Macy's Thanksgiving Day parade on TV while we waited for her to arrive. But then she didn't show up at twelve like she'd planned.

I called her phone several times, but it kept going to voicemail. Mom said it was Sandy being Sandy. I hoped she was right, but a niggling feeling in my stomach was telling me something was wrong. Then the officers showed up to tell us about the accident.

"I'm sorry for your loss," Officer Wicker says, sympathy dripping from his voice. Officer Jacobs nods his head in agreement. "There was nothing the paramedics could've done. It was a miracle the baby survived."

Mom stills next to me, and I drop my arms, stepping forward. "Wait, what? What baby?"

Officer Jacobs' eyebrows shoot up, but he remains silent. Wicker responds, but he's obviously surprised at our reaction.

"There was a six-month-old girl in the back seat. A couple of witnesses removed her from the car. She's at the hospital now."

"But whose baby is it? My sister doesn't have any kids." *At least I don't think so.* Is the baby the someone special she wanted us to meet?

"There was a bag with documents in the back seat, including the baby's birth certificate. Her last name is Brannon. And her parents are your daughter and Abigail. They were married. Their purses were also recovered from the car."

"So you're telling us that my *daughter* is—was—married to a woman, and they have a child?" Mom's eyes are wide.

Sandy had a wife? I didn't even know she was a lesbian. Well, we haven't seen her in forever, so I guess anything's possible.

"Yes, Ms. Brannon," Officer Wicker confirms.

Mom grasps my arm as if she's going to pass out. I wrap mine around her waist and walk her to the couch, then we both sit down.

"Are you okay, Mom?" I motion to the officers to sit down across from us.

She nods and grabs a tissue from the box on the coffee table.

I wipe the tears from under my eyes and take a deep breath. Mom squeezes my hand. "I'm sorry, officers," I say. "This is a bit of a shock. We didn't know that Sandy was married or that she had a daughter."

Mom nods in agreement. "We haven't seen her in years. We don't even know where she lives now. *Lived…* We were so excited when she asked to come for Thanksgiving. It was supposed to be a reunion."

I shake my head. "Were they the only ones who died in the accident? Was the driver drunk?"

"So far, yes. But there are a couple who are in critical condition. As for the driver, the cause of the accident is under investigation."

"You said the baby's okay. What's her name?" Mom interjects.

"Her name is Noelle, and she's perfectly healthy. Not a scratch on her. Truly a miracle with the severity of the accident," Officer Wicker says. "Now, Ms. Brannon, we have to ask you to pick up Noelle at the hospital. Or is there someone else we should contact? We couldn't get hold of Abigail's family."

What? I stiffen and my chest tightens. Mom squeezes my knee.

This is too much. How are we going to take care of a baby? I live hours away, and I'm only here for the weekend. And Mom has a one-bedroom apartment.

"All of their personal items from the car are at the hospital with the baby."

"Where did they live?" It pisses me off that I have to ask a stranger where my sister lived.

"Her driver's license said Margo Grove. An officer went there, but no one answered the door or telephone."

Mom gasps, and I spring from the couch. "*Margo Grove?*" I explode. "The town twenty minutes north of here?"

Calm down, Charli. Am I sad right now or downright pissed? She was living twenty fucking minutes away and didn't tell Mom? Sandy and I weren't really close as we got older, but she could've told Mom. She's worried about Sandy for years.

"Charli, sit down." Mom tugs gently on my hand.

I pinch the bridge of my nose and try to compose myself, then sit on the edge of the couch. "Sorry." I push my hand through my hair. "I feel like you're talking about the wrong person. This has to be a horrible mistake."

The officer's eyes are kind as he shakes his head. "I can't imagine what you are going through. Maybe once you pick up their personal items, things will become clearer."

"And the baby," Mom and I say in unison.

"Yes, the baby too."

I park my car in the hospital lot, then turn to Mom. "Are you okay to go in there with me? I can do it alone if it's too hard for you."

Once the officers left Mom's place, we held onto each other and cried. Heavy tears full of sadness, regret, and a touch of anger ran like a waterfall. Over and over, we tried to figure out what we could've done wrong to make Sandy feel like she couldn't come to us or share those special moments. We would've welcomed Abigail and Noelle with open arms.

Then the shock set in that I'm an aunt and Mom's a grandma. And now that little girl has no parents. But she won't be alone. I know the idea was shocking, but she has us now.

Mom grasps my hand. "No, honey, we'll do this together. I can't let my emotions rule me right now. We need to be there for Noelle. And like you said, once we have her, we'll drive to Sandy's house. We have to—we have no baby items other than the diaper bag and the car seat they took from Sandy's car. It's not like we can take her back to my apartment without anything."

She's the strongest woman I know. She's had her share of sadness and tragedy when Dad died suddenly of a stroke. But she always makes her way through it. They were the perfect example of soulmates. Something I wished for... but sadly, I settled for something less.

A year after Dad passed away, Mom changed everything. It was the only way she could finally move on. That's what she kept telling me anyway. She sold the four-bedroom house in Marimount where I grew up. Then she sold Dad's shares of his highly successful construction company to his partner, Kellan Kierney.

Sexy, arrogant Kellan. The one man I begged myself to hate but couldn't.

She rents a large one-bedroom apartment in an active adult community. Now she has a small group of friends and has become a yoga queen. She invested the rest of the money, so she's comfortably set. But how will she deal with Sandy's death? There's nothing else for her to change. Maybe Noelle?

And me... After what I wished for... Yeah, I wanted something to get me out of the disaster called my life, but this isn't what I meant.

Mom pats my arm, then smiles softly. "Let's go. I want to meet my granddaughter."

Time drags by as we sit in a narrow, private waiting room. The strong scent of disinfectant seeps into our clothes. Every time someone passes by, Mom and I perk up in our chairs. It's been twenty minutes already.

A ton of emotions are surging through me. I don't know which one is dominant. I'm scared shitless of babies, or children in general. Sandy was the neighborhood's favorite babysitter when we were teenagers. Having children of my own hasn't been on my radar. My career has always been my main focus.

My phone buzzes for the millionth time, distracting me from picking at my acrylic nails. I want to rip them off. I pull the phone out of my pocket, even though I know it's Jordan or maybe Lizzy. I have no desire to speak to either of them or to tell them about Sandy. I've been ignoring Jordan's calls since I left yesterday. He doesn't seem to have understood when I told him I needed a break.

A baby cries in the distance, and Mom jumps from her chair. A nurse walks in, cuddling Noelle, trying to soothe her. An aide follows her, carrying several bags and a car seat.

And then Noelle turns her head and looks at me. She stops crying, but then it's my eyes spilling tears. She's absolutely gorgeous. She has the Brannon women's big turquoise blue eyes and peach-fuzz blond hair. Sandy and I were often mistaken as twins. Her nose was a little bigger and she was three years older than me but really, the only obvious difference was that she was a brunette like Dad. Maybe Noelle thinks I'm Sandy because my hair is pulled back. That makes me want to cry even more.

For some reason, I move to take her from the nurse before Mom can. To my surprise, Noelle lets go of the nurse and opens her arms to me. I take her and hold her in front of me with her little legs dangling, like I don't know what to do with her. Well, I don't.

Her eyes roam my face, and then her lip starts to quiver.

"She has our eyes, and she looks like you did when you were a baby," Mom says between sniffles. Her voice is surprisingly cheerful. "My turn. Let me hold her."

I twist toward Mom and extend my arms carefully, but Noelle starts crying again. I pull her back and hold her properly… I think. She lays her head on my chest and sticks her thumb in her mouth. My heart swells up with an emotion I've never felt before.

Unconditional love.

The navigation system says it's the next house on the right. It's late, and there are no lights on the street. It's kind of eerie here this time of night. I pull into the driveway marked with the number twenty. My headlights light up the front of the house. I turn on the high beams to see it better. It's a decent sized white brick ranch with a covered front porch and a double garage, probably built in the late seventies. I can see it needs some work by the way one of the black shutters on the front window is hanging askew.

"Ready, Mom?" I say over my shoulder. She wanted to sit in the back so she could be near Noelle. "Do you have the key ready? I'll get Noelle. Once we're inside, I'll come back for the other things."

She gets out of the car, so I guess that's a yes. We didn't talk much on the way here. I know our heads are spinning and we're exhausted. But we have to be strong for Noelle. I open the back door to get her. She's fast asleep with her thumb still in her mouth. My heart melts but also cracks open a little bit more. Why does an innocent baby have to go through something so traumatic? But at this age, will a baby remember what happened? I don't know. The doctor said she'll probably sleep a while after all the stress she's been through.

A sensor light turns on as we approach the peeling black front door, making us inhale sharply. Mom tries a few keys from the keyring we found in Sandy's purse. We both sigh when one clicks. Mom opens the door and steps in.

"Eww." I swallow hard.

"It smells in here," Mom complains. The musty odor sinks into our pores. Cold, damp air fills the house, creating a grue-some atmosphere. Why the hell would they buy such a rundown house?

She finds a light switch and turns it on. I follow her in. We're in a long corridor with floral wallpaper and dated brown-brick linoleum flooring. Quietly, we move down the hall until we come upon a long, narrow living room. Its peeling golden-yellow patterned wallpaper and brown shag carpet have seen better days. The gray sectional in the middle of the room looks comfortable but doesn't match the style. I spot an old radiator under the picture window and an electronic air filter near the fireplace. Mom moves ahead of me and finds more light switches.

"I feel like we shouldn't be here. We're invading their privacy." I whisper, as if Sandy and Abigail might hear me.

She glances over her shoulder. "I know. But what other options do we have?"

To the left of the living room is a narrow kitchen with dark wooden cabinets. The yellow-and-green vinyl flooring is worn and lifting in some areas. The pea-green Formica countertop and backsplash is overkill. This would be the first room I'd gut.

We come upon Noelle's room. It's in no better condition than the rest of the house, but the radiator works in here. Another air filter hums in one corner. The white furniture and pink accents give the spacious room a warmer feeling.

"Do you think I can put her down in the crib?"

Mom shrugs. "Try it. Maybe we'll get lucky, and she'll sleep for a while. Then we can get more familiar with the house."

I lay her on her back carefully, as if she's fragile like an egg. Yet today has proven she is stronger than either of us. We stand there watching her to see if she stirs. Nothing. Keeping the light on, we tiptoe out of the room.

There are boxes stacked throughout the house as if they moved in recently. We find Sandy's bedroom and stand at the door like we're waiting for someone to welcome us in. I nudge Mom forward. The house might need a bit of special care and boxes are in every corner, but the rooms are neat and tidy. Sandy was the neat freak in our house.

I follow Mom in, then turn in a circle. She stops by a nightstand and picks up a picture. She covers her mouth with her free hand and the arm holding the picture begins to shake. A whimper escapes her.

"Mom, what is it?" I walk quickly to her side and wrap my arm around her shoulder. She doesn't have to say anything. It's a picture of Sandy and Abigail on their wedding day. The building behind them looks like a town hall. They're both dressed in beautiful white sundresses. Their left hands are up, and they're pointing at their wedding rings. Their smiles are contagious. Abigail is just as beautiful as Sandy.

I pick up another picture on the nightstand. My shoulders sag. It's one of Sandy and Noelle in the hospital. Most likely minutes after she was born.

"Why didn't she tell us? *Why?* It's like with your father—I didn't get the chance to tell him how much I loved him before he died. Now Sandy too."

"Aw, Mom. They knew. You showered all of us with love. No one ever questioned that. But Sandy was different. She chose her lifestyle. I don't think she did these things to maliciously hurt us." She nods and puts the picture back down on the nightstand. I do the same. Without another word, we leave the room.

We walk through the rest of the three-bedroom house, but not the basement. It's too spooky to go down there in the middle of the night. I've seen one too many horror films. We're shocked that they lived in these horrible conditions. Half the radiators don't work. The bathrooms have rotten carpets and tiles that are cracked and loaded with mildew.

If Sandy were here, I would beg her to let me renovate this house. But she's not. So what will happen to this place? Mom yawns, and Noelle whines in her room.

Mom rubs my arm. "Don't worry, Charli," she says. "We'll figure this out together. Why don't you go get the rest of the stuff we left in the car. I'll take care of Noelle. You and Sandy were babies once. I know what to do." She cracks a little smile.

Thank God for Mom because I have no idea what the hell I'm doing. I wish I could pass out and wake up to find today was only a bad dream.

4

KELLAN

It's already dark by the time I park the truck in front of my sister, Dara's, house. With my head resting against the seat, I try to compose myself before I face my sister. I called her earlier, once I'd calmed down, but she heard the tremor in my voice anyway... and the sirens. I didn't give her details but made it clear it was a horrific scene and that I'd tell her what happened when I saw her tonight. She ended up going to our aunt's alone for Thanksgiving. Lights are on inside, so I'm pretty sure she's back. Being alone is the last thing I want right now.

Traffic was at a standstill for hours while they cleaned up the highway. Then the police pulled me aside as an eyewitness. I told them what I saw happen, but I asked to remain anonymous. I was stuck there for hours, watching victims being medevacked out, ambulances speeding away, and witnessing Grady and other first responders get Sandy and her wife out of the car. It was such a nightmare. I don't know how I'll get the images out of my head. How could anyone?

Thanksgiving. A day to be thankful for what you have. But this? It's not right to celebrate when people are mourning the deaths and injuries of those involved in that accident today.

Especially the Brannons. What's there to be thankful for? Noelle?

As I walk up the driveway, the front door swings open and Dara stands there waiting. She turns on the outside light, and her eyes zone in on my face. "Man, you look like shit."

"*Pfft*. Thanks. Love you too. You wouldn't look any better after the day I've had."

She moves to the side to let me in. Her black-nosed white cat, Jinx, saunters up to me and rubs his pudgy body against my leg, meowing away. For some reason, this cat loves me. I think animals sense when something is wrong because they try to cuddle with you even more.

Other than the cat, I'm greeted by the North Pole. Every year at Thanksgiving, she decorates her house like she's in a Christmas contest. It looks like Santa Claus threw up in here. I don't think I'll be in the holiday spirit anytime soon.

Her eyes bulge when she sees the blood on my shirt and the bandage on my hand. "Oh my gosh! Are you hurt?"

I shrug. "It's no big deal. I cut my hand on some glass. I've had much worse at the construction sites. The paramedics were overzealous. I didn't even need stitches."

"Seriously, whatever you wouldn't tell me over the phone... It must've been bad. It's written all over your face. But I thought you only witnessed the accident. The bandage says something else. How did you get cut?"

"Before I answer your questions, I need something to drink."

"Go sit on the couch and relax. I'll bring you some water."

"No," I blurt. "Something stronger. Whiskey. Please."

She nods, then unlocks her liquor cabinet and grabs a bottle. She goes to the kitchen and fills a tumbler with ice. Then she brings it and the bottle into the living room and sets them on the table where I'm still standing. "So tell me what happened."

I listen to the ice crackle and pop as I pour the whisky over it, then take a big gulp. The burn is welcomed, so I pour some more and empty the glass. She sits on the couch and pats the cushion next to her. I place the glass on the table, then drop to the couch, putting my head in my hands. Jinx jumps up next to me and meows as if he's asking what's wrong.

When I remain quiet, Dara pokes me and says, "Come on. I'm listening. When I was on the way to Aunt Lorna's, I heard about the accident on the radio and that the highway was blocked off."

"I think every firefighter, EMT, and police officer from the Sunnyville area was called in. Several of the injured had to be medevacked out and at least two people died. A semi lost control at high speed… right in front of me. I saw *every… fucking… thing.*" I squeeze my eyes shut, trying to block the replay in my head.

"Oh, shit."

"It was bad. So bad. The worst thing I've ever experienced. I keep seeing her face, the blood, and those trapped bodies. And the baby screaming."

"A baby? Whose face?" Dara rubs my shoulder gently.

"Sandy Brannon and her wife." Bile pushes at the back of my throat as I say the words.

She freezes, eyes wide. "No! Sandy? No! Please tell me they're okay." I close my eyes and shake my head. "They *died*? Their daughter too?"

"From what I know, the baby's fine. Me and another guy were able to get her out of the car. Sandy and her wife—I think they died instantly. They were trapped." I describe what happened. "How their daughter survived is something I'll never understand. Those pipes flattened that car, except where she was. It was like there was a protective bubble around her. It wasn't just her car seat."

She rests her cheek on my shoulder and sniffs. "And you

saw them recently. They bought that old house and hinted about you helping them renovate it. I don't understand how life can be so cruel. Charli and her mom must be a fucking mess… and now that little girl has no parents."

"They might not even know yet." I draw in a frustrated breath.

I ran into Sandy a couple weeks ago at the grocery store. She introduced me to her wife… I can't remember her name… and their daughter, Noelle. The baby's name stuck with me because she reminded me so much of Charli, or at least what Charli probably looked like as a baby with the blond hair and big turquoise eyes.

And Sandy had mentioned wanting to discuss renovating the house they'd bought recently. I told her to call me. Then she also said she wanted Charli to be the architect and interior designer. When I heard that, my stomach flipped with anticipation at the thought of seeing her again.

Mr. Brannon, Mickey, died three years ago, but I've stayed in touch with his wife, Tricia. I needed to keep the connection I had to the Brannon family. Since I was with Mickey all the time, she and I were pretty close too. She felt like a mom sometimes. My own mother has been living in Florida for years. Tricia and I still call each other randomly, and sometimes I drop by for a quick coffee or beer. She tells me about Charli and her TV show. I die a little more inside every time. As for Sandy, Tricia thought she was off in Europe somewhere.

I was pretty surprised to see Sandy at the store. When she found out I was still in contact with Tricia, she asked me to keep it a secret that she'd bought the house in Margo Grove or that I saw her. She said they'd be spending Thanksgiving with Tricia and Charli, and that's when she'd ask Charli about helping with the renovations. I have a gut feeling Sandy has been hiding a lot. Tricia would've told me Sandy got married and had a baby.

Mickey owned a successful construction company, ColMa Professional Construction. The houses his company built were beautifully unique and had an excellent reputation for quality. He took me under his wing when I was eighteen and, as the years went by, he asked me to be his partner. He treated me like the son he never had. Or maybe I treated him like the father I never had. In some ways, he was my best friend. My dad took off when I was ten years old, and that was the last time I saw or heard from him again. I remember the day Mickey offered me a job like it was yesterday. That's when I met Charli for the first time and I knew my life would never be the same.

I spring from the couch, startling Dara and Jinx, and pace the living room, guilt and rage building in my gut. "I could see the passenger was trapped. She was bloody and... I knew it was hopeless. But once I got close enough to really see her, all I could focus on were her eyes. Empty. Blue. And I recognized them. Well, I thought I did. Except—my stomach dropped, and my heart split open because... because I thought it was Charli." My heart pounds rapidly and crippling pain overwhelms me again. "And then I saw she had dark brown hair and—" my voice drops to a whisper, "and I realized it was Sandy. Oh, God, I'm a pathetic asshole."

"Kell, I don't understand. Of course you'd be upset. We've known Charli and Sandy since we were teenagers."

"No. You don't get it. When I realized it was Sandy, this massive sense of relief rolled over me. *Relief!* And then that transformed into this overwhelming guilt that makes my skin crawl. I was *thankful* that it was her sister who died, not Charli." I have the urge to kick the rotating Santa that's in front of me. "I'm vile, Dara."

She stands up and steps in front of me, taking hold of my arms. "Kell, I don't know what to say because I'm not in your shoes, but I haven't seen you this distraught before. I'm worried about you. You're talking about Charli like... I don't know. You've always acted like you didn't like her. Now you're talking about her like, like—"

I yank my arms away and stomp over to the table. I pour another whiskey to distract myself from blurting out something I've never told anybody. *That I've always wanted Charli more than any woman I've known.* Well, I did tell one person, but he took it to his grave.

Dara continues, "I think you need some time to work through what you saw. I can't imagine what it was like. Was Grady Malone there? Or Gray?"

Grady and Gray are brothers. Grady is a firefighter for the Sunnyville Fire Department, and Gray works for Mercy-Life as a rescue pilot. The Malone family is well known in Sunnyville. I've helped out with some renovations at both their houses.

"I saw Grady," I confirm, swirling the whiskey in the glass. "We acknowledged each other, but it's not like there was time for a chat. He was part of the team that got them out of the car. I wouldn't be surprised if Gray was flying one of the helicopters." I down the rest of the amber liquid.

She nudges my upper arm, then takes the bottle and glass from me. "Slow down or you'll be hungover for days. God forbid, you'd miss a day of work," she says sarcastically. "All work and no play."

"That's not true. I started making wooden garden furniture."

"*Pfft.* Oh, yeah, that bench I asked you to make two months ago? I have yet to see it. That hardly screams *hobby*."

Okay, I'll admit it. I work more than anything else. Something changed in me when Mickey died. I felt empty inside. And in ways, I still do. We had a deep conversation that morning, and I remember every word. Not business related but very personal and from the heart. One that I buried away and haven't spoken about to anyone. I've vowed to keep the legacy of his business alive, but if I'd had the chance, I would've fulfilled another promise I made to him that day. I've never had the opportunity.

Most of my friends are married and have kids. I meet up with the guys a couple times a month for drinks. Lately, I find myself a bit of a loner. Dara tries to keep me busy when I have time, but sometimes I don't mind being alone.

Not long after Mickey's funeral, my long-time girlfriend, almost fiancée in fact, Chelsea, moved out of my house because she couldn't stand competing for my time or heart. When she left, she said she'd always known that I loved her but I was never *in love* with her. She was right, and she deserved more than I could've given her. She married someone else a year ago.

"Events like these reminds us how things can change in a blink of an eye." Dara interrupts my thoughts again. "It's important to appreciate everything we have and to enjoy life." Her eyes bore into mine. "We shouldn't wait to tell someone that we love them or how much they mean to us. Or to live our lives to the fullest. You should know this better than anyone, after the way Mickey died so suddenly.

"Let's keep our eyes open for funeral arrangements or... maybe I'll call Tricia myself. You're in no shape to do it. We need to pay our respects. I haven't spoken to her in a long time, but I think I should be there. Sandy and I were close friends when we were younger."

"I'll let you know if I hear anything. Please don't tell anyone, especially Tricia, that I witnessed the accident."

She frowns. "Why the hell not?"

"Think about it. They'll ask questions and... they'll get answers they don't want to hear. It's to protect them. I'm sure it'll be on TV or in the newspaper tomorrow, but I hope they don't see the condition of the car. I wouldn't be surprised if there was a story about Noelle."

"And what if they have a picture of you pulling Noelle out of the car? Then you'll have to tell them."

"I'll deal with that if it happens. For now, I'm staying quiet."

She glowers at me. "I strongly disagree, brother. It's a big risk. But it's your decision."

"Yep. So let's drop it."

Suddenly, I'm being dragged into the kitchen. Dara pulls out a chair from the table. "Sit down and try to clear your head for a little while. I brought some leftovers for you from Aunt Lorna's. She made your favorite pumpkin crumble."

My stomach turns, thinking of food, but I have to suck it up. My thoughts drift to Charli and Tricia. I saw how devastated they were when Mickey died. Now they're mourning the loss of a daughter and sister.

But the sick fuck in my head is excited, knowing he'll get to see Charli again.

5

KELLAN

19 Years Ago

"Whose house is this again?" I ask, pressing the doorbell. It's not just a house, it's a mansion. More beautiful than any I've ever seen or been in before.

"You never listen to a word I say. *Teenagers*," Mom groans, shaking her poufy hair. "This is Dr. Gable's new house, and it's a housewarming party... barbecue."

"And it has a swimming pool," Dara chimes in, chomping like a cow on a huge piece of Hubba Bubba.

"Maybe he should increase your salary instead of building a house like this," I say snidely under my breath.

Ever since Dad took off years ago, Mom's been working two jobs to keep us afloat. One is working in Dr. Gable's Eyes, Ears, and Throat practice. The other is working at the local grocery store on the weekends. I've been taking odd jobs in construction since I was sixteen and figured out that I loved it. I graduated high school a couple weeks ago and have been searching for a full-time job to help out with the bills. Starting in the fall, I'll be taking business and project management classes at the community college.

"Kellan Kierney, watch your mouth while we're here. Do not embarrass me."

I shrug. "You know I'm right."

"Drop it," she says through gritted teeth.

"Yeah, drop it," Dara repeats annoyingly. I roll my eyes.

How long does it take for someone to answer the damn door?

"You said Mickey Brannon should be here, right?"

"At least you heard me that time. Yes, he'll be here with his family. His company built this gorgeous house. He's all Dr. Gable talks about."

The only reason I wanted to come today is because there'd be a chance he'd be here. His construction company is the biggest one around. I want to somehow ask him if he has any job openings.

Finally we hear talking behind the door and it opens. From that moment on, we're sucked into the party. I'm introduced to a lot of people I probably won't see again. To avoid more small talk, I head into the house, pretending to search for the bathroom. Instead, I end up exploring the first floor as much as I can without looking like I'm trying to steal something. The angles, the curves of the double staircases, the marble floors throughout. I wouldn't want to live here, but the craftsmanship is amazing. I trace the smooth wood of the staircase railing. When I hear voices, I pull my hand away like I touched fire.

Dr. Gable comes around the corner with a man, pointing at the massive crystal chandelier hanging in the middle of the foyer. It probably cost more than Mom's annual salary. They see me standing on the steps.

"Hi, Kellan. Did you get lost?" Dr Gable chortles. "Let me introduce you to Mickey Brannon. He's the reason I have this new home. Isn't it beautiful?"

"I didn't do it myself," Mr. Brannon responds, extending his hand to me. I shake it firmly. "Nice to meet you, Kellan."

The man looks nothing like I thought he would. I pictured him all business, stone-faced, and intimidating. But his smile relaxes me as soon as I see it. He's a tall, broad man with dark brown hair. His hands are rough like he still works on the sites and doesn't sit in an office all day telling people what to do.

"Nice to meet you too. This house is amazing. I was just admiring the design."

He props his hands on his hips, smiling brightly. "Thanks. I'm proud of this house. It's the first one we've built like this."

"Kellan, your mom was saying you work in construction and are looking for a job. Maybe Mick can help you out." *She did?* I'll have to thank her for that.

Dr. Gable's wife walks up behind them and places her hand on his forearm. "Sorry to interrupt, but there's someone who'd like to talk to you before they leave."

He pats her hand. "Okay, dear." He turns back to us. "Sorry, gentlemen. I'll talk to you later, Mick. Help yourselves to the food and drinks. And the pool."

A girl comes running over to us, giggling and out of breath, with a boy chasing from behind. She hides in front of Mr. Brannon. She pushes her back up against him and looks up at me with her finger over her mouth full of braces, begging me not to give her away. Her bright eyes light up her entire presence. Their unique color of turquoise would stop anybody in their tracks. Bluer than any ocean. Frizzy ringlets of golden-blond hair frame her round face that has a cute dimple on full display.

She squeals when the boy finds her, then runs off toward the living room with him on her tail.

"And that crazy girl is my eleven-year-old daughter, Charli. She's the tomboy of the family. She's going to keep me on my toes when she gets older."

Eleven? Great. Now I feel like a total perv because my first thought was how beautiful she'll be in a couple years.

"So why don't we go grab ourselves a cold drink, and you can tell me what kind of job you're looking for." *Really?* I follow him back outside. "You know, I started like you and worked my way to the top."

Now I'm sitting on a lawn chair by the pool, basking in the sun, sweating my ass off. The beating sun couldn't melt the smile off my face. Mr. Brannon offered me a job for the summer, and when it comes to an end, he'll evaluate if he wants to keep me on board. Just like that. It was almost too easy. While we talked, he introduced me to his wife, Tricia, and his other daughter, Sandy. She's around the same age as Dara.

Water's splashing everywhere from all the kids in the pool, cooling me off in the process. I was stupid not to bring swim shorts. Dara seems to have hit it off with Sandy. They're sitting together watching some teenage boys splashing around at the far end. I look to the left and see Charli jump into the crowded pool, holding hands with the boy who was chasing her before. She comes up for air, but suddenly another girl pushes backward off the edge and dives into Charli's face. I jump off the chair and watch as Charli sinks into the water and doesn't come back up. The girl swims back to the edge, rubbing her head.

"Mr. Brannon!" I yell to him, kicking my shoes off. He turns my way. "Charli!"

I jump in and swim toward her. Blood swirls through the water. "Move out of the way!" I shout. I get to her as fast as I can, pull her head above the water, and move us both to the side. Mr. Brannon waits there with a towel and pulls her out. Blood is dripping from her nose, and she's coughing.

After that, it's kind of a blur. Her parents thank me profusely for saving her and then rush her to the hospital.

Days like these remind me how quickly things can change. Both good and bad.

6

CHARLI

Katherine Panter's face drops when she sees me and Mom standing on her front doorstep. Her eyes glisten, then focus on me. "Wow. I can't believe how much you look like Sandy. And you all have the same eyes." She lights up when she sees Noelle, then a tear trails down her cheek. "I'm sorry. Please come in." *Sniff.* "I hope you don't mind that I asked you to come to my home. I wasn't only Sandy and Abi's lawyer; I was Abi's best friend. We went to college together."

Katherine leads us through her large condo. It's impeccably decorated—looks like something from *Romantic Homes* magazine. She directs us into a cozy living room accented with shades of purple, white, and green. The color combination is brilliant.

"You have a beautiful home," I tell her sincerely.

"What a compliment coming from you. Thank you." She admires the room. "It was redecorated a couple months ago. I'll tell my decorator you liked it."

I bounce Noelle on my hip as I scan the room. There are plenty of little things a baby could play with and break... or maybe even choke on. I've never noticed things like this before, but now I'm a nervous wreck. I'm so worried that she'll find something that could hurt her if I look away for two seconds, and she doesn't even crawl or walk yet.

"Please make yourselves comfortable. Would you like coffee or tea? Or water?" she offers.

"No, thank you," I respond. Mom declines too.

I sit on a violet-colored couch with white and leaf-green throw pillows. Once comfortable, I place my handbag and the diaper bag on the polished cherry wood floor. Mom takes Noelle from me and Katherine takes a seat on a matching armchair across from us.

"Is it okay if I let Noelle sit on the floor?" Mom asks.

"Sure. She's been here several times. Here's a blanket for her to play on. I'm sure the floor is cold." She pulls a lilac throw blanket from the armchair and spreads it out on the floor. "Don't worry if she spits up or anything. It's washable."

She sits back down and says, "I can't express how sorry I am. It's hard to believe it's real. I've called as many people as I could think of. Everyone sends their condolences." She looks up at the ceiling, blinks several times, and dabs at the corners of her eyes. "Bear with me if I start to cry."

"As long as you don't mind us doing the same, we'll get along just fine," Mom says. Katherine and I chuckle. If I start crying now, I probably won't stop.

"How are you two holding up?" She glances at me and then Mom.

"We're doing the best we can. It helps that we have Noelle to focus on. I don't think it's hit us fully yet." I let out an embarrassing yawn.

Mom and I are living on very few hours of sleep. Last night was hard because Noelle kept waking up every couple of hours. We weren't sure if she was sick, hungry, or maybe missing her parents. Noelle's functioning a lot better than I am today, but she can nap whenever she wants. Then again, maybe she shouldn't sleep so much during the day. I don't know. On top of that, I can't stand the condition of their house. It's depressing and very dark. I'll have to suck it up until I can find a better solution.

Mom sighs and looks at Katherine. "My daughter lived a life we weren't aware of or even a part of. We thought she was living in Europe somewhere. And then we find out she lived not too far from me. We're hurt, frustrated, and mostly devastated. There's so much we don't understand or don't know what to do. On top of that, we have to focus on Sandy's funeral and belongings."

"Ask me anything you like." With folded hands, she leans forward and says, "I want you to know that Sandy was really looking forward to introducing you to Abi and Noelle."

Then why did it take so long for her to call us? And why did she make it sound like we were only meeting one person instead of two? Well, Katherine said to ask questions. I dive in.

"How did Sandy meet Abi?"

"They met in Paris at a café almost three years ago. Abi was there for a medical conference. They told me it was love at first sight. But Sandy was in a bad place because her father had died recently. They kept in touch and then Sandy moved back to California to be near Abi. I think maybe two years ago? They got married soon after that in a private ceremony at the town hall. They didn't tell anyone until after. Not even me," she huffs.

"So she was living in California all this time, when we thought she was in Europe?" Mom presses her lips together, trying to stay calm.

"Yes. I'm sorry to be the one to tell you," she confirms with a sympathetic gaze.

I want to hate Katherine because she knows more about them than we do, but she has such a welcoming personality that I can't help but like her. And she's our only lifeline to Sandy. It makes me feel a little better that no one attended their wedding.

I open my bag and pull out some documents I found among the things that were removed from Sandy's car and her office. I haven't had the chance or the energy to read them all. "I noticed in one of the documents that Abi was a doctor. Out of curiosity, what was her field of practice?"

"Reproductive endocrinology. A fertility doctor among other things."

"Oh, so that's how Noelle is with us today? Artificial insemination?" I ask. "She looks too much like a Brannon to be adopted. Or is there a father somewhere who we need to worry about?"

"Artificial insemination," Katherine affirms. "They really wanted kids, and Sandy wanted to carry the child." That's no surprise with the way she loved kids when we were younger. She used to say she wanted to be a stay-at-home mom. It's like it was what she was made for. And now she can't do it.

"Do you have any clue why she didn't say anything to us? It hurts to not have been a part of their lives. We can't think of anything that we could've done to make her feel she couldn't talk to us. Was she afraid to tell us she was in love with a woman?" Mom flutters her hand. "Don't get me wrong, it was a shock for both of us, but we wouldn't have treated her any different. We just wanted her to be happy. She was very close to her father and when he died, it felt like a part of her died with him." *That happened to all of us.*

"Sandy said that Abi made her happy again. She knew she was bisexual but wasn't sure how to tell you. When Abi came out to her family at nineteen, they disowned her. She tried for years to contact them, but they wouldn't respond. So Sandy was worried that would happen to her too. I've tried to contact Abi's family about her death, but all the numbers and emails I could find were no longer in use."

Mom and I glance at each other. This makes me so furious. More for Mom than me, but why would she think we'd disown her? Especially Mom. This is all so unbelievable.

"Abi urged her to tell you both everything sooner rather than later, especially when they bought that house in Margo Grove a couple months ago. She finally made the decision to tell you on Thanksgiving."

That still doesn't explain anything. We'll probably never know, and we'll always wonder why. Could we have done more? Maybe I was too absorbed in my own life, but Mom's always made us her number-one priority and encouraged us to be brave and spread our wings.

"They were so in love and died happier than most. If we could all be blessed with that kind of love… And Noelle completed them. They were adorable parents." Her voice cracks. "Sorry. It's so unfair."

"Thank you for telling us that. It'd be even harder if she had died unhappy and alone." Mom sighs.

"We're staying at their house until things settle," I tell her. "I'll be honest, I don't know what the hell I'm doing. Among the documents were things about the house and blueprints. The house is falling apart. Why would they buy something like that when I'm sure Abigail was making good money as a doctor? They could've had one built or bought a newer one."

"I know. I was there one time after they moved in." Another pang of jealousy sweeps over me. Katherine leans over and straightens the pile of documents in front of us.

"Abi was successful but lived very modestly. She wasn't one for expensive things. Sandy was the same and suggested they buy a house to renovate. They couldn't wait to do it. All they wanted was to make the perfect home for Noelle to grow up in.

"That was one of the things she wanted to talk to you about, Charli. She bragged a lot about you being an excellent architect and interior designer. They watched all your renovation shows. And so do I." She smiles. "They wanted to ask you to help them renovate it. Sandy mentioned a couple weeks ago that she ran into a man who used to be your father's partner. She wanted to talk to him about helping with the house too. He had a unique name." She taps her cleft chin. "Kell something. Does that ring a bell?"

The knot in my stomach twists tighter, and I sit up straight. I'll be lucky if I don't develop ulcers from this. Kellan! I had a crush on that gorgeous specimen of a man for years, but he hardly noticed me. When he did, he treated me like I was a pain in the ass. He was a mystery to me, and that made him even more attractive because he always had a scowl on his striking face. Why? Was it me? His eyebrows were a constant furrow and his jaw was clenched so tightly that I thought his teeth would turn into powder. There were only a few times when I saw a slip in his façade, making me think the attraction was mutual. Those heated moments were rare but unforgettable.

Mom smiles affectionately. "Kellan Kierney. He was part-ners with my husband for years. When Mickey died, I sold Kellan his side of the business. We're still in contact. Not as much recently. He's a good man with a huge heart." *Huge heart?* Are we talking about the same guy?

"You've seen him?" I ask Mom. This is new to me. Why didn't she tell me? But I guess it isn't all that odd. It's almost a given since he was close to Dad. Mom and Dad were a pack-age. I was the one he avoided like the plague.

"Of course," Mom says. "He's been different since your dad died. Quieter. He hasn't said it in words, but I think he misses Mickey a lot." Her voice drifts off. "Anyway, since Sandy was so close to her dad, Kellan would've been the perfect choice for their new house. And he lives in Margo Grove too."

"Still? Something else I didn't know," I mumble. "So this explains why Sandy had a lot of information about the house with her. There were even pictures of living rooms and kitchens from magazines. We still have similar tastes. A country style home with a colorful open living space, creating a happy, welcoming atmosphere." I close my eyes and ideas for the house gather in my mind. "Of course, I would've loved to have been a part of it. If we only had the chance. It has a lot of potential."

Katherine stands up and walks over to a wooden desk behind the couch. "There's something else we need to discuss; the obvious adorable elephant in the room." We all look at Noelle, who's happily playing on the floor with the couple of toys we brought with us. She looks up at me, shaking a set of plastic keys, and gives me the biggest smile, her chubby cheeks on full display. A few days or maybe a few minutes, that's all it took for her to win my heart.

"Around two months ago, Sandy and Abi discussed who they'd want to take care of Noelle if anything would ever happen to them. As I said, Abi had no relationship with her family." She clears her throat. "Charli… they were planning to ask you to be her legal guardian." She walks back around the couch and places a document in front of me on the coffee table.

"Oh my gosh. That's wonderful," Mom gushes, leaning over the table to look at the paper.

"What?" I yelp. I don't think my nerves can handle any more surprises. My body vibrates from the hammering of my heart.

"Charli, calm down. You're going to scare Noelle," Mom says firmly.

"Calm down? I don't have a clue how to take care of a child! I don't even live here. My job takes up most of my time." *A job I hate.*

In reality, who else would take care of Noelle?

It doesn't matter because I wouldn't want anyone else to get custody of her.

What? That thought came out of the blue.

"I know it comes as a surprise and it's a lot to take in right now, but Sandy was adamant that you get full custody of

Noelle and inherit their belongings, including the house they own outright and other assets. They also each had very lucrative insurance policies. Some specifically for Noelle. We can talk about them later."

I leap from the couch and pace around the room. Katherine goes and sits next to Noelle on the floor. Giggles fly as Katherine plays peek-a-boo with her. Mom stands up and gets in my way.

"Honey, look at me." My eyes connect with hers. "Remember what I said? We'll get through this together. Over my dead body is a stranger taking care of my granddaughter."

Let's not talk about any more dead bodies.

I massage my throbbing temples. "They wanted me to have everything. Why? I don't even know how I could do this. What about my job, my life?"

"You mean the job that's sucking the life out of you?" she snarks.

My eyebrows pinch together and my mouth drops open. How does she know that?

"Uh oh. Looks like someone's diaper's full," Katherine coos. "I'll change her in the next room. You can talk in here as long as you want." She slings the diaper bag over her shoulder and picks up Noelle.

We wait until they're gone.

"Don't forget, I'm your mother. I know you're unhappy. Something has changed over the last year or so. You're not even enthusiastic about the show anymore. No one knows you like I do, and I know your heart isn't in it. You aren't you. And what's going on with Jordan? You haven't spoken about him since you got home, and I haven't seen him since June. I noticed you're not wearing your engagement ring either. You haven't talked about a wedding in I don't know how long. Have you even told him about Sandy yet?"

"Mom, this isn't the time or place to talk about this. I

don't want to have a mental breakdown in front of a stranger," I mumble desperately.

Am I strong enough for all of this? It's so much pressure. In the last few days, my sister has died, I've become a mother or legal guardian, and I've inherited Sandy's house, her belongings, and her money.

You wanted something to change. Wish granted. Deal with it. I struggle to catch a breath.

"Didn't you say your contract is up when the current house is finished?" Mom asks. "Has your agent presented you with any new offers yet?"

I prop my hands on my hips and stare at the floor. "No. Not yet."

"Maybe it's meant to be this way. Everything happens for a reason. Maybe Noelle is that reason."

Deep down, I know she's right, but the fear of change and failure won't let me admit it.

7

KELLAN

12 Years Ago

I balance the phone between my shoulder and chin as I slide the electric sander farther into the cargo bed of the truck. "Hey, Mick. What's up? I thought you were taking this afternoon and weekend off. Doesn't that mean no phone calls either?" I joke with him.

"*Pfft.* You'll find out some day that when you own a business, you never get a day off. By any chance, are you at the office?"

"I'm at the Tuscan house, but I'm leaving now to go back to the office. Is there something you need?" I close the tailgate and check that it's secure and locked.

"I think I left a large manila envelope on my desk. I can't find it anywhere. If you see one from Lightning Architecture, would you mind dropping it off at my house on your way home? I'd go pick it up, but I know I'd end up staying at the office. Today's Charli's prom. What kind of dad would I be if I missed that?" He laughs.

I lean against the side of the truck and wipe dust off my

left hand. "A bad one for sure. I wouldn't want to be you." I chuckle. *Yeah, right.* He couldn't be a bad father or husband even if he tried. He's the best man I know.

"I'd really appreciate it. Why don't you stay for a beer if you don't have plans?"

I catch myself before I respond. Charli dressed for the prom is asking for trouble. I shrug. "Maybe one. I'll call if I can't find it. If I do, I'll be there in about an hour."

"Perfect. But don't mind the chaos when you get here. A bunch of Charli's friends are coming over to take pictures with their dates before they leave. It's not easy being the only man in the house. With you there and some of the fathers, I won't feel so outnumbered." It's impossible to say no to him.

"Then I'll definitely take you up on the beer. See you soon." I yank the door open and kind of hope I don't find the envelope Mick's looking for.

A while later, I turn onto their street with the envelope lying on the passenger's seat. There's no getting out of this one. The grip I have on the steering wheel gets tighter and tighter. I don't know if I'm tense, nervous, or frustrated. Seems I'm one or the other when I'm around Charli.

She turned eighteen a couple weeks ago and is becoming quite a woman. Not that it matters. Our age difference will constantly be an issue. She's at our jobsites all the time, but I make sure I only admire her from afar. I don't want anyone to know how taken I am with her. As beautiful as she is in steel-tipped work boots, jeans, and a tank top with a hammer in her hand—I can't imagine what she'll look like in a prom dress. But I shouldn't be looking at her the way some of the asshole workers do at the sites. Mickey's asked me more than once to watch out for her and to warn the guys to stay away. I assume that includes me too.

In all the time I've known Charli, I've hardly spoken to her. If I have, it's very short and to the point. I know I probably come off as a dick, but it's the only way I can keep the wall up between us.

I approach the house and see two girls in their colorful prom dresses, posing on the manicured front lawn. Tricia and I guess other moms are taking pictures. Charli's nowhere in sight. I park my truck in the street and walk up the long driveway, then continue onto the sidewalk to the front door.

"Hey, Kell," Tricia says, running up to me. "I didn't know you were coming." She embraces me warmly like she usually does.

"Mick needed me to drop off this envelope. I'll be out of your hair in a minute."

"No rush. Go on in. Mick's out back, having a drink with the other dads." I walk up the stairs and pull open the screen door as Tricia adds, "Oh, can you please tell Charli to get her butt out here. The limo should be here soon with their dates."

"Will do."

I turn to face the entrance and breathe. Forget the beer. I'm not going to stay. In and out of the house, quick and easy. That's all. Maybe I could put the envelope on the kitchen table and sneak out of here.

I walk into the open foyer that I recently helped Mick redo. My eyes scan the adjacent rooms. Nobody. Then Charli's tense voice echoes from upstairs.

"What a nightmare," she complains. "Sandy, my hair looks better down like this. Let's ask Mom. I need her opinion."

Just when I think I can escape to the kitchen, Charli starts down the stairs. I do a double take. Fuck, I've never seen her hair down before. She usually has it in a ponytail or some sort of bun. *Whatever you do, do not look down.* Too late.

She takes the stairs slowly, holding her dress up a little, revealing one of her long, tanned legs. My mouth goes desert dry and my pulse skyrockets. *Walk away.* But I can't because my feet are cemented to the floor. She's fucking gorgeous.

Once she's off the stairs, she grabs the railing to balance herself on her high heels. Definitely sexier than work boots.

She scowls when she sees me. "What are you doing here?" she snarls. I deserve her nasty tone.

I wave the envelope in my hand. "Got something for your dad." My voice croaks. *Keep your eyes above her shoulders.*

"Figures. He's out back." She turns to observe herself in the floor-length mirror I hung a couple days ago. Her perfect ass faces me while I see her full reflection in the mirror. Our eyes connect for longer than they should. Her mouth quirks up, revealing the dimple that I love, as if she caught me admiring her backside. I look away, wanting to leave, but freeze when she asks, "Have you seen my mom?" I glance back at the mirror. She bends over slightly to mess with something on her dress and my eyes follow the movements of her hands. *Bad idea.* The air in my lungs evaporates, leaving me breathless. The powder-blue strapless dress makes her eye color pop and clings to her luscious curves like it was sewn on. *Fucking breathe.* I look up again, and she definitely caught me watching her this time.

"Outside. She said to hurry up," I respond with my practiced lack of interest. Hoping that she doesn't notice how unsettled I am or how the sight of her lights me on fire.

Sandy runs down the stairs with a brush in her hand. "Oh, hey, Kell! You're a guy. You'll have to do. Tell us, which looks better on Charli?" Sandy points to her hair. "Down or up?"

"Kellan? Why would he care?" She huffs. "He still looks at me like I'm twelve. Besides, what would he know?" *So maybe she didn't notice.*

"Oh, be quiet. We're desperate here." Sandy steps behind Charli, angles her toward me, and pulls her hair up off her neck. "I like it up like this."

"No! My neck looks like a freakin' giraffe's," she protests. *Ugh, she doesn't want to know what I think about her neck.* "I like it down, with maybe one side pushed up. What do you think?" Charli pushes one side up and looks at me for approval. The curiosity in her eyes stops my heart.

"Come on, Kell. Hurry. Which way?" Sandy pushes, checking her watch.

I swallow the cotton ball in my throat and stuff my hands in my jeans pockets. "I'm the last person you should be asking."

"Seriously, man. Spit it out. We're running out of time," Sandy huffs. Charli stands there with one hand on her hip, observing me.

My eyes shoot back and forth between them, then focus on Charli. "Down. You always have it up." It looks beautiful flowing over her shoulders in natural curls.

A genuine smile grows on her face. Why? I didn't compliment her. She'd be late to the prom if I told her all the things that I like about her and what makes her beautiful.

"Wow. Okay." Sandy digs through her pockets and pulls out a hairpin or something like that.

"No." My voice has a tone to it I don't recognize. "Leave it. She looks beautiful just the way she is."

Sandy turns in my direction with a crinkled forehead. "Really?"

My eyes fix on Charli's again. Her cheeks are aflame, and she tosses some of her hair over her bare shoulder. The typical thing girls do when they're nervous.

"Yes… Perfect."

We all startle when the limo horn honks, dispersing the thick air around us. Sandy looks out the front door and claps her hands. "They're here," she squeals. "Jeff is going to drop dead when he sees you."

Time to disappear.

"Kellan, you're here!" Mick's jolly voice comes from behind me. He claps my back. I hand him the envelope, and he lays it on the foyer table. I greet the other men. "Thanks for bringing it. Come out front with us. We're going to threaten the boys to keep their hands off our daughters. It'll be fun. Or maybe I should walk out with a baseball bat in my hand." They all laugh.

"Dad, do *not* embarrass me in front of my friends," Charli growls, pulling her long locks forward over one shoulder.

"Look how beautiful you are, Charli." He kisses her cheek. "Let's go outside. I still haven't met the boy who better keep his hands to himself."

She rolls her eyes. "Go outside with Sandy. I'll be there in a second."

Charli stands to the side with her hands clasped in front of her while everyone files out the door. Then it's only me and her in the house. *Awkward.*

"Thank you, Kellan," she says softly with a sweet smile. One I haven't seen directed toward me before and it makes my skin warm. "That meant a lot coming from you." She gives a slight wave, then walks out the door.

I press my hand against my chest. If I were seven years younger, I'd be taking her to the damn prom.

8

KELLAN

"Hi, Kellan!" Timmy calls out to me, running out the back door covered in what looks like flour. He wraps his little arms around my thigh.

"Hey, big guy." I ruffle his hair. Sand sprinkles on the ground along with the white stuff. "Were you playing in the sandbox or a bag of flour?" He giggles and steps back to look up at me.

"Where's Dara?"

"In da kickton."

I chuckle. "You have to take your finger out of your mouth when you speak."

He takes the slimy thing out and wipes it on my jeans, then giggles again.

"So where's Dara?"

"In the kitchen." *That's better.*

"In the kitchen," Dara yells too.

"Hmm." I cross my arms and cock an eyebrow. "I can't remember where the kitchen is. Can you show me?" His face lights up and he grabs my hand, pulling me along with him into the house.

Dara runs a small daycare out of the basement of her

48

house. That sounds like a dungeon, I know, but it's not. Her house is built into a hill, so only one side of the basement is in the ground. The rest of the level has large windows to let in the sunlight, making the entire floor airy and bright. It also leads right out to the backyard, where a buddy of mine built a playground any child would love to have. Hell, I know some adults who'd have fun here too.

Timmy's four years old and has attached himself to me ever since I met him. His father took off when he was two, so I usually give him a little extra attention. I know what it's like to have your own father run out on you.

As we get closer to the kitchen, the aroma of freshly baked Christmas cookies makes my stomach growl. He pulls me into the mini kitchen I installed for the daycare, and I let out a hearty laugh. There's flour all over the floor and in Dara's hair. The table is covered in half-eaten sugar cookies, cookie racks, cutters, and decorations of all kinds. Christmas music streams in the background.

"What happened in here? Did something explode?" I stand there with my arms out to the sides.

Dara turns around with cookie dough smeared on her chin and a rolling pin in one hand. "What do you mean? We're baking Christmas cookies. This is how a kitchen should always look. Right, kiddos?" Her natural enthusiasm is adorable. The kids scream in delight. One girl hops up and down, then picks up some flour off the floor and throws it in the air. Most of it lands on her shoulders and hair. I bet her mom's going to love that.

I don't know how Dara does it. She lives for the four kids she watches every day. Enthusiasm and creativity seep from her. She's the only one I'd trust with my kids. If I had any.

"I don't want to get in your way. I came by to replace the broken window. It shouldn't take long."

"Sure. We'll be busy in here. It's almost pick-up time too. Don't leave when you're done. I talked to Tricia this morning." I stiffen, then swallow the lump in my throat. *Shake it off.*

"Okay. Once I get your window fixed, I'm done for the day." Her mouth drops open. "Yes, I know. Being finished before five is a miracle for me."

I stayed as busy as I could during Thanksgiving weekend to block out the accident, walking through the days like it was a figment of my imagination, until Sunday. Grady Malone called and texted me several times. I should've called him back, but I haven't. Instead, I picked up the phone to call Tricia but chickened out. Then, when I couldn't keep it out of my head any longer, I hid in my garage to work on the artsy wooden bench I told Dara I'd make for her.

There were pictures of the pileup on local TV and in the newspaper, but not one of Sandy's car. Charli and Tricia shouldn't see what that looked like. It'd rip their hearts out. The article I found did mention the miracle baby who survived after being pulled out of the car by two heroes. I hope they weren't referring to me because I'm no hero.

The past couple of nights, I've been waking up screaming, drenched like someone dumped a bucket of water on me. The same dream replays itself. It's Charli who's killed in the accident, not Sandy. And Noelle's *my* daughter. But Charli's alive in the car long enough for me to tell her I love her and always have, and she says it back. Then her eyes close forever. Devastation and regret drown me when I wake up. Is that what losing the love of your life feels like? The thought of never seeing Charli again mixed with regret from not telling her how I feel is paralyzing. Even if she doesn't feel the same, at least it'd be out there, and I wouldn't have to wonder what my life would be like if she were mine.

A cookie tray falls to the floor, startling me back into reality. *Stay busy, Kell.*

"Hey, Timmy, wanna help me out? Where's your tool belt?" His smile grows wide. I bought him a kid-sized tool belt when he turned four. You'd think I gave him the world when he saw it. He keeps it here because he likes to help me out when I stop by to fix something.

"I know where it is. I'll go get it."

"Good. Wait for me here when you come back," I say. He skips into the playroom. "I have to go get my stuff too. I'll be right back."

Half an hour later, Timmy and I stand in front of the newly installed window, both of us with our hands on our hips. "Awesome job, Timmy. You're going to be a pro when you get older. You'll know how to fix everything in your house for your mom."

"That would be helpful because I don't have a clue," Timmy's mom says from behind us. He runs to her, and she sweeps him up in her arms.

"Look what we did today, Mommy! I can fix windows now."

"You're such a big boy." She kisses his cheek. "I wonder what Kellan will teach you next time? Maybe how to fix the leak under our bathroom sink?"

Cynthia and I went on a couple of dates a while back. When we kissed, we both agreed it was like kissing a wall. We still joke about it today. I help her out once in a while since she's on her own with Timmy.

I'm not sure I want to get involved with someone who has children. What if things don't work out after one of the kids gets close to me? Then I'd be like my dad and leave them behind. The connection to the woman would have to be like no other, without question or hesitation on my part.

"Okay. Time to get out of here." Cynthia puts Timmy down and pats his butt. "Go put your tool belt back. Thanks, Kell." Timmy waves to me as they leave.

After cleaning up and putting my stuff in the truck, I stroll back into the house to find the kitchen in much better shape and all the kids gone. Dara's like Mary Poppins... or she has elves hiding somewhere.

"Do you need my help?"

"Nope. You know I have a system. I put a bottle of Boont Amber Ale in the refrigerator for you."

"Thanks. Want one too?" I offer, opening the door.

"Nah. Beer and raw cookie dough don't mix well." She rubs her stomach and tilts her head. "I don't think so anyway."

I pop off the cap and take a seat at the table. This feels good. It's nice to sit after standing most of the day.

"I'm almost finished with the bench I promised you for outside. I was antsy on Sunday, so it kept me busy. You're going to love it."

"I'm excited to see it, but you know I don't want to talk about the bench," she says, scrubbing the counter. I cough and wipe off my mouth. She continues. "As I mentioned before, I spoke to Tricia today. We talked for a while. She and Charli seem to be doing well, considering what's happened."

"Did you get the funeral arrangements? You didn't mention anything about me, did you?"

She turns around and leans against the counter. "No, I didn't. I was caught off guard though when she asked me how we heard about Sandy's death. My instinct was to say we live in the same town. I didn't like lying to her."

I look away and take another swig. "You didn't lie."

"Whatever. I omitted key information. I still don't understand why it'd be so bad to tell them."

"I told you already. I don't want them to ask me details about the accident. It would destroy them to know what I saw. I wish I could get the images out of my own head. Would you want to know if it were me instead of Sandy? How I suffered?" She shakes her head. "I didn't think so."

The guilt is still eating at me like acid on steel. I hate that

I told Dara. It'd kill me to see Tricia or Charli's face if I confessed that to them. I know I'm an asshole.

"Did you see that one article in the paper?" I ask. "I was surprised that names of the victims weren't listed. It mentioned a miracle baby who lost her parents. And that 'heroes' saved her." I grimace as I say the word.

"Well, she is a miracle, and you are a hero." Dara swats the air. "And you know I don't read the paper. I'm sure it's on social media somewhere. You know, some sick fuck probably posted videos. Have you thought about that? Someone could've posted a video. If they did, I hope it was removed. Of course, Facebook and Twitter censor all the wrong things." She pulls a towel through her hand. "What I can't wrap myself around is that you were there. What a freaky coincidence. Sometimes you have to ask yourself why."

I slouch over the table. "I'll be asking that for the rest of my life. Did I tell you the only reason I was there is because I missed my exit?"

"Shit, that makes it even more bizarre. You were meant to be there." She grabs the cookie cutters from the table, tosses them into the sink, and turns on the water. "If Tricia saw the article, she didn't mention it. Maybe she's smart enough not to look on the web or read the newspaper." Steam rises from the sink as it fills with soapy water. "So anyway, the wake is Thursday afternoon, and the funeral is Friday morning. There's only one viewing. I told her we'd be there for that."

"We're going together, right?"

"Of course. Ariana will take over for me while we go to the viewing. I already called her. And it just so happens that two of the kids won't be there that day. It'll be easy for her."

"What else did Tricia say?" I ask casually, tracing a star in the dusting of flour on the table.

"A lot. Get this." She finally sits her butt down. "Sandy and her wife left everything to Charli. When I say everything, I mean everything. Including Noelle."

Charli has a child now. I close my eyes and swig my beer.

"How is Charli taking it? Did she say if she's going to adopt Noelle? Or whatever the process is?"

"She's accepting responsibility, but they don't know if she'll keep Sandy's house. Tricia and Charli are staying there for now, and apparently, it's in a horrible condition. Charli doesn't live here, so Noelle will be going back with her eventually. At least that's what Tricia said. They're taking it day by day. Anything could change. I wonder how Noelle will fit into Charli's lifestyle. I'm curious how her fiancé took the news. Not that it's any of our business, I guess. We haven't had contact with Charli in a long time."

Fiancé. They've been engaged for at least two years—not that I'm counting—but they still haven't gotten married. If she were mine, I wouldn't wait a day to marry her. I met him briefly at Mickey's funeral; he seemed like a decent guy. He stayed by her side the entire time, at least until I went up to Charli to pay my respects. As soon as she hugged me, he was on her like a hawk, as if I might take her away from him. I spoke to Charli for maybe a minute, and he started pulling her away. I guess I'll have to deal with that again.

But something tells me this time will be a lot different. In more ways than one.

9

CHARLI

I'm yanked from a dead sleep when Noelle cries across the hall. I throw my legs over the edge of the bed and stumble into her room. I pick her up and cuddle her close. "*Shh shh,*" I whisper against her forehead. "I've got you. Let's go get you some milk... but let me change your diaper first. Or is that why you're awake?"

Mom broke down laughing when I tried to change Noelle's diaper or get her dressed the first time. I still feel inadequate, but I'm improving. Almost anyone else could do it better, I'm sure. I'm used to being good at my job and in charge of my surroundings. What a one-eighty this situation has been. But I've never given up on anything before, and I'll be damned if I start now.

Jordan and Lizzy arrived today so they could attend the wake. I told them not to come, but they insisted. I have no energy to fight Jordan right now. Lizzy's easy, so I don't mind her being here. I was hoping that when they walked into the house and smelled it, Jordan would decide to stay at a hotel. He's sleeping on the couch in the living room instead.

We don't sleep in the same bedroom back home, so why should I make an exception here? Lizzy's in the spare bedroom. I told Mom to go home and get a good night's rest. I don't want her to see me with Jordan if I can help it. She'll pick up on the animosity between us immediately. Then the same questions and lectures would follow. I still haven't told her what's going on. When the right time presents itself, I will.

With Noelle in my arms, I walk down the hall to the kitchen. The problem with ranch style houses is that it's hard to be quiet with all the rooms on one floor. That's another thing I would do, add a second level. I grab a bottle from the fridge, then close the door. I jump and the bottle almost slips from my hands when I see Lizzy standing there. Her hair's disheveled, and her lips and cheeks are an irritated red. Maybe she's allergic to the air in here. I don't have the energy to ask.

"Sorry. I didn't mean to scare you. I heard Noelle. Is everything okay?" she whispers.

Grumbles come from the direction of the living room. I roll my eyes. Jordan should have brought ear plugs. Actually, he shouldn't have come at all.

"Yeah. Time for a bottle. Sorry we woke you. You can go back to sleep." All this talking is going to wake up Noelle even more. We won't get any good sleep after this.

"Okay. Well, let me know if you need anything or want to sleep. I have three nephews that I babysit all the time."

"Thanks," I say, placing the bottle in the warmer and balancing a squirming Noelle on my left hip. "You're the best."

"You know, it suits you."

I turn around, confused about her comment, and switch Noelle to my right hip. "What do you mean?"

"You with a baby in your arms. I've been watching how you take care of her since we got here. It seems to come naturally for you. Your face brightens when you hold her and she cuddles with you. I've been working with you for a long time, girlfriend. I haven't seen you smile like this in ages. And it's crazy how much she looks like you."

"Thanks. Mom says she's an easy baby, but we've only had her for a week. It's too early to know that really. But I guess, once the shock of Sandy's death and becoming an instamom wore off a little, my protective instincts kicked in. I'll do everything I can to give Noelle the life she deserves and the one Sandy and Abigail wanted for her. Even if I lose all my hair and sanity in the process." I chuckle.

Lizzy rests her hand on my arm. "I think you're really brave. Your life has changed completely, and you're still standing."

"For now. I'm bound to fu—screw up at some point." I glance down at Noelle, who's almost asleep again. Maybe I'll get some sleep after all.

"Doesn't every parent mess up? Moms are human like the rest of us. They can't be perfect all the time. So it's okay. I am glad you have your mom for support, though."

"Me too. Can you help me with the milk?" She nods and, following my instructions, drips some on my wrist. "Perfect." She smiles and hands me the bottle.

We say good night and go to our rooms. I sit in the rocking chair and enjoy the swaying motion as Noelle drinks.

I rest my cheek against her warm head. "I promise I'll always put you first, sweetie. We'll make your moms proud when they look down on us. And Grandpa, too, who's hopefully with them now. It's you, me, and Grandma against the world." A big yawn escapes me, and I look down at her. She's fast asleep in my arms with the bottle still in her mouth. I carefully pull it out, wishing we could stay this way, but my arm is numb. Even with the awkward movements to lay her in her crib, she doesn't wake up. I kiss her forehead and go back to my room. My mind won't shut off as I lie in bed. In less than forty-eight hours, everything will be final.

~

"Holy shit! Does that baby ever stop crying?" Jordan puts down his coffee cup and covers his ears.

"Watch your mouth. She's a hungry baby. It's not like she can call for takeout." I manage to respond calmly, even though I'd rather lose my shit. I won't do that when Noelle is next to me. I remove the cap from a jar of pureed bananas. "If you can't handle it, leave. I told you not to come here anyway. You should've stayed at a hotel." I turn toward Noelle and make *choo choo* noises for her to open her mouth. A smile replaces her frown.

After a little trial and error, Mom and I have learned what Noelle likes to eat most of the time. We're still on a learning curve, but we're figuring out her daily rhythm too.

Jordan shudders. "Anything would've been better than that horrible couch you made me sleep on. And that bathroom—it's like a swamp, and the green in this kitchen is nauseating." He's complaining like a spoiled child. All that's missing is for him to stomp his feet. How could I have loved someone so selfish and irritating?

"Yummy, isn't it?" I say playfully to Noelle, trying to mask my annoyance and disappointment. I glance at Jordan quickly and see him roll his eyes. He really does hate kids.

I didn't think I liked them either until I held Noelle in my arms.

"I'm your fiancé, Charli." His voice rises and he swings his arm in the air like it's a declaration. "Your sister died—of course I'd be here for you. How would that look if I weren't here?"

I grimace. I almost believe him, but no… actually I don't. He couldn't care less about my family.

He points at my hand. "And don't think I haven't noticed you're not wearing your engagement ring."

He's lucky there aren't any sharp objects in reaching

distance. But how about this jar of bananas? I give him a side-eye. "No one would notice your absence. But since you are here, I need you to be quiet and suck it up for the next few hours. This isn't about you. Show some respect for me and Mom instead of complaining all the time. Your selfishness is ugly."

He starts to say something, but I hold up my hand. "Save your breath. You can forget about any fake public displays of affection or kissing my mom's butt or pretending like we're the happiest couple on earth. There aren't any cameras here. Make your little appearance at the wake and then leave. And if you don't like a baby crying, what the hell are you going to do when I bring Noelle home to my house?"

"You mean our house."

"Actually, no, it's mine. And you know why. Or have you so quickly forgotten that?"

Silence. *Now stay quiet.*

Jordan and I met at a prominent architectural firm. With his dark brown hair, gorgeous hazel green eyes, sexy body, and sense of humor, I fell hard and fast for him. We put all our money into our own architect and interior design business and had instant success with renovating houses.

When I received money that Dad left me when he died, I bought us a house. Since we weren't married yet, a friend advised me to put only my name on the deed. And to have separate bank accounts. I almost ignored her, but something in my gut said to listen. Jordan didn't seem to care at the time. We planned to change it as soon as we got married.

One day a home specialty network approached me about doing one of those TV renovation shows. The producers admired my work. They didn't mention Jordan at first, but once they found out we were together, they thought it would sell the show better if we signed on as a couple.

We decided to sell our business to do the show, and we split that money in half. The show has been a hit ever since.

But things have changed between us. Success went to Jordan's head and it turned him into a selfish, egotistical bastard. I'm not too happy about the changes in me either.

He pushes away from the table, his chair scraping along the floor. "You should pitch renovating this house to the execs. It'd get a lot of attention because of the sad story connected to it." He stands up and stretches his arms over his head. *Sure, change the subject.* It's his favorite thing to do when I talk about our living arrangements.

Actually, I have thought about it, but I can't do that to Sandy. I'll either do it myself or I'll sell it. Jordan doesn't deserve to get his greedy hands on this house. Dollar signs replaced his eyes when he mentioned that it has a lot of potential. He refuses to admit we have no future.

"That's not happening, so drop it," I say firmly. "If anyone renovates this house, it'll be me. *Alone.*"

He leans against the kitchen doorway, picking some lint off his shirt. Looking up, he flicks it off his fingers, then points to me. "Are you going to take a shower?"

Excuse me? "I already did. What's your point?" I sigh heavily. Am I being too harsh when I say I despise him? It's sad, right?

"Oh, you don't have any makeup on, and your hair's just in a ponytail. I thought you might want to look a little more presentable. Those bags under your eyes are pretty dark. Maybe sit with some cucumber slices on them before we leave. And you really couldn't find the time to get your nails done?"

Asshole! I can't wait to be free of this piece of shit.

"What, you want me to look like I do on the show? Is that what you call presentable now? Funny, when we met, this is how I looked all the time. Minus the bags." I point at my face and flash my pearly whites. "A dusting of makeup with some lip gloss, clothes that covered seventy-five percent of my skin, and a toolbelt resting on my hips. You didn't complain then. I think I remember you saying something like it was sexy as fu—"

"But that isn't you anymore. You've changed."

"No! *You've* changed into a selfish pri—monster. I don't even know who you are anymore. I let the producers change my looks for the TV show. I didn't do it for you, and I sure as hell didn't do it for me. I like the old me. It's a breath of fresh air. I don't give a shi—"

I glance at Noelle. *Oops, a million times.* "Look, I don't care what you think about me anymore. And let's not forget that I'm mourning the death of my sister and now have a child to look after. It's not my goal to look like a prostitute who jumped out of a Hollywood movie at Sandy's wake." I stir the bananas vigorously. "Please go find something to do while I take care of Noelle or I'll make you change her dirty diaper."

He disappears like there's a flame under his ass. I chuckle to myself because I don't think I've ever seen him leave a room so fast. Whatever. He's playing a game he won't win. We're a joke. Our contract as a couple is up soon. Then we can go our separate ways. I would only sign on for another show if it were with a different network, under my stipulations, and without him.

Now that I have Noelle, things are going to have to change and fast. I have no idea what's going to happen next. My agent and producers have been very sympathetic, and they're giving me the time I need. Lizzy will take over for me in the episodes we still need to film until things settle. She's done it before when I've been sick.

The last funeral I was at was my dad's. And like Sandy's accident, Dad's death was completely unexpected. Mom found him lying in the driveway next to his car. You're never prepared for someone you love to leave this earth. You think they'll be there forever and there will be an abundance of tomorrows... until there aren't.

I thank God every day that I was able to spend the weekend with him before he died. We take time for granted, even when we think we aren't. When will I learn?

Sandy and Abigail wanted to be buried in the same plot at White Gates Cemetery. They didn't want a church service, only a wake and then burial. It's been morbid, reading all the legal documents they'd had prepared in recent months. I guess they were being responsible parents, but from where I'm standing, it's almost as if they knew they were going to die. With those requests, we decided to have their wakes and funerals at the same time in the same room. Due to the severity of their injuries—something I'm forcing myself not to think about but still wonder—closed caskets were necessary.

Katherine has helped us plan everything. She's been a life-saver, explaining all the legal and insurance documents and what the next steps are, who we have to call or send an email to. She also brought up suing the truck driver or the company responsible for the accident. Right now, Mom and I aren't interested. It won't bring them back, and we don't need the money. Noelle will be well taken care of because of Sandy and Abigail's preparations.

Mom and I walked into the viewing room before anyone else was there. When I saw their closed caskets, my heart pounded in my throat, and I couldn't breathe. My whole body shook and my legs felt too weak to stand. I couldn't stop the sobs. Mom ran over and held me, and we cried together. It wasn't enough, but it took off the edge so we could get through the next hours.

I know I haven't let myself grieve or digest the situation properly. Honestly, I'm a little worried that I'll have a break-down or something. I also feel bad because I haven't had the chance to be there for Mom emotionally. She's burying her oldest daughter. Not too long ago, it was her husband, her soulmate. Now it's just me and her left.

I asked for this to happen.

Mom and I stand in the front as people line up to pay their condolences. I'm embarrassed by my cold, sweaty hands. Jordan tried to stand next to me, but when I didn't introduce him as my fiancé, he stomped off like a child again. *Give me fucking strength.*

Katherine introduces Sandy's friends and colleagues, reminding us that she had a life without us. Every one of these people got to spend the last few years with her, but we didn't. Sometimes I wonder if bitterness is replacing my grief. It doesn't matter because the tears keep flowing.

Several men Dad used to work with show up. People who've known our family for years, who've been to barbecues and parties at our house. I feel a pang of disappointment when I notice Kellan isn't with them. I'm sure Mom's thinking about Dad a lot, making her even sadder. I know I am.

Time goes incredibly slow, but it's almost over and there are fewer people here now that I have to socialize with. My head is pounding like a gong, making me dizzy. My tears seem to have dried up. I'd do anything to sit down and drink a glass of water.

Noelle's crying grabs my attention. Lizzy offered to watch her during the wake but when I glance over at them, Noelle's squirming in her arms. I excuse myself and walk toward them.

"Let me take her, Lizzy. It's quieter now," I say. I wrap Noelle in my arms and kiss her chubby cheek. She's so damn lovable. "Thanks for helping. You weren't lying when you said you knew how to do this. But you and Jordan can leave whenever you want. I know you have a couple hours' drive ahead of you."

"No problem. I'm your assistant, aren't I?" she jokes.

"Jordan went to the bathroom." *To stare at himself in the mirror.* "We're going to leave once he comes back."

I crack a smile. "I don't think babysitting babies *or* adults is part of your job description. I'm sorry you have to deal with Jordan and that you need to take over for me in the last few episodes."

"Ah, he's no different than being on the set. I've dealt with worse." Lizzy juts her chin out in a kind of signal. I assume Jordan's coming up behind me and turn around, bracing myself for what he's going to say.

Everything around me disappears. My tongue sticks to the roof of my mouth, and my heart pounds in my ears. A funny twisting thing tickles my stomach, and I'm entranced by the man standing in front of me.

Kellan Kierney. And, holy shit, he looks absolutely gorgeous!

10

KELLAN

Charli. I know it's her because of her golden hair pulled up, revealing the sexy curve of her neck. And those long, toned legs I could never forget. She turns around as if in slow motion and her eyes flicker with surprise when she sees me. *Fuck.* She's more beautiful than ever. Her tired eyes are still bright, and her pillowy lips are a kissable glossy pink. The little dimple on her left cheek reveals itself when a soft smile appears on her face.

How did I live three whole years without seeing her? Watching her on TV wasn't the same because she didn't look or act like the Charli that's in front of me now. Will the sight of her always take my breath away and make my pulse race?

Dara bumps into my back. "Watch where you're going," she whispers. "What's the holdup?" She moves to the side to stand next to me. From the corner of my eye I can see her head bobbing between me and the people in front of us. "Oh. I see." She nudges me forward.

Noelle is in Charli's arms, smiling away as she plays with her shirt collar. My heart expands in my chest. The similarities are uncanny when they're next to each other. There's no mistaking that people would think Noelle's her daughter. A revelation hits me, rocking me to my core.

My future is standing right in front of me.

"Sorry. I'm back, beautiful," her fiancé says, wrapping his arm around her waist possessively. He glances at me, then squints his eyes. What the fuck is with this guy? His gelled-back hair, expensive suit, and polished black shoes don't intimidate me. Didn't three years ago, and won't today.

Charli rolls her eyes and shakes herself out of his arm conspicuously. He scowls. It takes everything in me not to laugh. She straightens the bottom of Noelle's pink dress, and I notice it. The engagement ring is gone.

"Hi, Kellan. Dara. It's been a long time. Last time was at my dad's funeral, right? That's pretty sad and morbid." Charli moves slightly away from the others. Her fiancé inches forward, but the woman next to him holds him back like he's on a leash.

Apparently, my tongue is paralyzed. I can't speak. Dara huffs under her breath and steps ahead of me. "They say weddings and funerals bring people together."

"I'd rather it be a wedding," Charli mumbles.

But not yours unless it's ours.

"Me too. I'm so sorry, Charli," Dara sympathizes. "My heart breaks for you and Tricia. It's so sad. Especially for this cutie right here." She caresses Noelle's hand and makes funny noises. "Aren't you the prettiest baby?" Noelle shies away from her.

"This is Sandy's daughter, Noelle." Charli waves the little girl's hand at us. Dara continues to babble to her, making her giggle this time.

"Tricia told me you'll be taking care of her," Dara says.

"Yes. Nothing like becoming a single mother overnight. It's been a huge adjustment."

"I can imagine," Dara empathizes. "I wish you a lot of

luck and patience. I'm sure it's hard right now, but it'll get easier."

"I hope so." Charli's eyes find mine. "You're one of the last people who saw Sandy, right?"

My stomach clenches. *She knows.*

Sadness dulls her eyes. "Her friend told me Sandy ran into you a little while ago, talked about working on her house. Is that true?"

Oh. I sag with relief. "Yes. I ran into them at a grocery store a couple weeks ago. That's when I found out they were in Margo Grove. D'you remember, I grew up there. Still live there, actually. It was nice to see her. I met her wife and Noelle too." I glance at Noelle and then back at Charli.

"Dara, Kellan. It's wonderful to see you." Tricia comes up from the side. She's smiling, but it's not reaching her bloodshot eyes. "Thanks for coming." Dara gives her a hug. "Kellan, you've been a stranger. You look as handsome as ever. It's not often that I see you in a suit."

This is my funeral suit.

"A lot of your employees and old coworkers came today. It was such a surprise. It meant a lot to Charli and me." She embraces me, then extends her arms to Charli. "Let me take Noelle from you." Once she has Noelle, she sits in one of the chairs. Dara joins her, and they begin to chat.

Charli steps a little closer. "So how've you been? According to Mom, ColMa is still going strong. Dad would be so proud."

I stuff my hands in my pockets. "Thanks. It's the least I could've done for Mickey. I wouldn't be where I am today if it weren't for him. He was like a father to me." She smiles, but it's as if that's all the energy she can muster up.

"Charli, can I speak to you for a minute?" Her fiancé's back. She clenches her jaw. The other woman tells him to be quiet. Charli ignores him. An awkward silence ensues, and he steps back.

"I'm really sorry about Sandy and her wife. They were too young." I'm not good with words, but what can I say that others haven't already said anyway?

"Thanks." She wraps her arms around her waist. "That's what I keep saying. And asking why this had to happen? Their lives as a family just started. Was Abigail nice?"

An image of her crushed in the car flashes in front of me. I look away for a second and rub my mouth.

Charli's eyes shimmer with tears. She blinks a few times, then dabs under her eyes. And before I know what I'm doing, I pull her into my arms. She stiffens, then wraps her arms around my back and melts into me, resting her head on my shoulder. This is the first time I've held her in my arms like this, our bodies touching, fitting together so perfectly. It's different from when I hugged her at Mick's funeral.

Warm electricity swirls, putting up an invisible force field around us. I want to be the one to take away all her pain and always by her side. Why did I waste so much time avoiding her? I refuse to believe it's too late for us?

My hand strokes her silky hair, and her lavender scent lights up every cell in my body. "Yes. Very nice. I only spoke to them for a few minutes," I say softly. I glance at Dara and Tricia. Both are watching us with wide eyes. They're as surprised as I am, I guess.

Charli pulls away and wipes at the shoulder of my black suit. "Good. I'm so glad. They were on their way to Mom's for Thanksgiving when the accident happened." She brushes a loose lock of hair off her face. "Mom and I are living on fumes. Every day is different. Sometimes I think I'll survive, and the next takes every ounce of energy out of me. I keep thinking this is all a dream and I need to wake up."

I can relate. I feel the same way after what I saw that day.

"So, any wife or kids of your own?"

Huh? This is the last question I'd expect her to ask me. I'm pretty sure Tricia would've told her if I'd gotten married. She looks for my left hand, but it's in my pocket.

"No." I shake my head. "I guess I haven't found the right one yet. Not like you did." She nods, but her face is blank.

Oh, I found the right one, and it's you. Charli's the reason I'm still single. When I saw her at her father's funeral, it became clear as day, she owned my heart. And she still does. Maybe it's because of the conversation I had with Mick the day he died. When I admitted that I cared about Charli, that's when my relationship with Chelsea broke down. I couldn't tell Charli I loved her, but I couldn't pretend I was in love with another woman anymore either. It wouldn't have been fair to Chelsea or any other woman. I've hardly dated since.

"Charli?" The boyfriend—or whatever the hell he is—is back.

"Jordan, I'll talk to you in a minute," she says firmly, like he's on her last nerve. He backs off. She focuses on me again. "I'm sorry. You were saying."

"Just said I haven't found the right one."

"Or she hasn't found you yet," she adds with a twinkle in her eyes.

"Sweetie, why don't you introduce me to your friend." The idiot interrupts us again, sidling up to her like a snake. I guess he doesn't remember me from our brief meeting at Mickey's funeral. *Hmm.* Or maybe he does. He grabs her hand to hold it, but she pulls away. I'd love to know what's going on with them. Her face transforms when he's near. Is that disgust I'm detecting? *If I could be so lucky.*

"Jordan, this is Kellan. We've known each other for years. I believe you met him at my dad's funeral." She makes it sound like we were close friends, but we've barely spoken outside the job. Well, me anyway. She tried to. But I'll play along.

"You were eleven when I met you. Do you remember the Gable's mansion? The housewarming barbecue?"

Her hands land on her cheeks. "Oh my gosh. That was so long ago. How could I have forgotten? A girl plowed into my nose, breaking it, and you pulled me out of the water. Wow. Blast from the past."

"I didn't know you broke your nose," Jordan interrupts.

"I told you," she responds, looking at him like he has three heads. This conversation is beyond awkward. Her eyes drift to mine. "I can't believe you'd remember how old I was."

You'd be amazed at what I remember about you. Her cheeks turn a rosy pink as if she could hear my thoughts.

"I was eighteen. That's when your dad offered me a job. I thought it'd be a summer thing, and look where I am today."

"That's right. Jordan, he was my dad's partner. I'm sure I told you."

"No, I don't recall. Lucky you," Jordan remarks snidely to me. He's so full of shit. Why wouldn't he know that? The atmosphere around us becomes even more tense.

"He was like a son to Dad," Charli mentions with a smirk. She's throwing digs on purpose. The plot thickens.

"Probably like you," I say to Jordan, "seeing that you're in the same business and you're the lucky guy to be engaged to his daughter. Mickey asked me to keep guys like you away from her when she was younger."

Charli's eyes bulge. He chuckles uncomfortably, breaking eye contact. Did I hit the wrong chord? I'm not one to participate in sparring matches, especially not in a funeral home, but this guy screams *asshole*. What the hell does she see in him?

Maybe she really isn't the Charli I used to know.

But did I ever really know her?

No. And that's entirely my fault.

∾

Dara yanks my suit sleeve as we walk out to her car. "What the hell was that about in there? We were in a funeral home, for fuck's sake. Not a bar."

I continue walking. "I couldn't help it. That guy's an asshole."

"I couldn't tell whose chest was blown up more, his or yours. You're thirty-seven years old, not eighteen. So embarrassing," she says, shaking her head.

"You don't have to remind me. I'm not proud of the way I acted. Believe me, I was yelling at myself the entire time. But he doesn't deserve her."

"Oh, and who does? You? *Pfft.* The one who wouldn't give her the time of day since you met her?"

"Unlock the damn car," I demand, clenching my jaw. It beeps and the doors click. I slip off my jacket and toss it in the back seat, then climb in and slam the door. She reaches to start the car, then stops to stare at me. "What?" I mutter. She sits there in silence for a minute, then starts laughing maniacally.

"Holy shit. I'm so stupid. How have I not seen it before? You never hated Charli." She guffaws. I focus hard on the fresh bird shit on the window. "You've liked her all along. You're one of those guys who picks on the girls they like." She swats my arm.

"I didn't pick on her. I ignored her."

"Same thing. It's just as painful." She taps the steering wheel, then twists in her seat, a giant smile on her face. "So you admit it. You've loved her all this time."

Yes. Head over heels in love with her. Bird shit is very interesting. I think I see the *Mona Lisa.* "Don't put words in my mouth."

"Okay, maybe 'love' is a little extreme. But why haven't you acted on it? And why haven't you told me? I'm your best friend, for the love of Pete," she groans, punching me this time.

"Seriously?" I turn toward her. "Oh—let me see. Maybe because I worked for her dad and then became his partner. Or maybe because she's seven years younger than me. Or maybe because her dad told me to keep the guys away from her when she was at a jobsite? That included me. And she doesn't live here, and she's engaged. It wasn't meant to be."

"Who cares about the age difference now. Seven years? Big deal! But did Mickey specifically say that? That *you* should stay away from her?"

"Too many questions," I growl. "And no. It doesn't matter anyway. That was years ago. She's engaged to that douchebag. She has her life wherever it is she lives and her own TV show. Plus, she's Noelle's new mom. I'm a blip in her past and would only be a bad distraction if she gave me the time of day."

"If you say so. But she sure lit up when she saw you. And then the hugging and melting in your arms. I think Tricia and I were waiting for lightning to strike. And don't think I didn't see how cold she was to her fiancé. What's his name? Dickhead?"

A loud laugh bursts from me.

"Something's up with them. It sounded like Charli wanted to provoke him in there. She wasn't wearing an engagement ring either." So she noticed too.

"That doesn't mean anything," I mumble.

"Hmm. Give it time. I have a feeling even more change is coming, and Christmas is right around the corner. I'm always right when it comes to these things. Well, almost. Just not when it comes to my love life. Now let's go to Joe's Diner. I need one of their club sandwiches so I can analyze this situation further."

Not good. Dara loves to meddle.

11

CHARLI

Kellan and Dara say goodbye to us and disappear through the exit. I stand here grinning and replay our conversation in my mind. Years of heavy tension between us disappeared as soon as I saw him in front of me.

His smile was affectionate and kind, and the velvety sound of his voice took my breath away. When he pulled me into his arms, I couldn't have asked for a better place to be. I felt safe, wrapped in the woodsy scent of his cologne. During that short moment, I forgot where and who I was.

A hand wraps around my elbow and tugs. "Can we talk outside before I go?" Jordan requests curtly.

I yank my arm out of his grip. "No. Mom and I still have people to say goodbye to and we need to prepare for tomorrow. You and Lizzy can leave now. I'll call you in a couple days when things settle down."

"If you don't come outside with me, I will make even more of a scene than you just did with that guy, *Kellan*."

I cross my arms. "Seriously? You're delusional. If anyone made a scene, it was you. And you're doing it again right now."

"Charli, take Jordan outside," Mom says with a tightness

73

in her voice that shocks me. Her face is flushed, and her eyes are fixed on him. "Make sure he leaves and doesn't come back." Jordan's mouth drops open. "Don't worry about Noelle; Katherine has her. Please get rid of him."

Wow. This is a side of Mom I don't think I've seen before. I love it.

"Let's go," Lizzy says, urging Jordan toward the exit, following in my tracks.

I storm out the door and walk to the side of the building so no one can see us. I wait for Lizzy to reach Jordan's truck, then I snap. "What is your damn problem?"

"I don't like that guy, Kellan. He looks at you like—" He stumbles on his words.

"Like what? I'd love to hear this one." I cross my arms, tapping my foot on the ground.

"Like he wants you. It was obvious. Even at your dad's funeral. Anyone would have picked up on it. Even Sandy in her casket could see it." *Slap!* I couldn't stop myself. He rubs his face, and I shake my hand from the sting. His eyes squint in anger, but then his face drops in regret. He steps toward me and I move back, lifting my hands.

"Don't touch me ever again and stay the hell away from me."

"Charli, I'm sorry. I shouldn't have said that."

"*Leave. Now.* The problem with you is that you can't stand that someone else might be interested in me. That you'll lose me. Well, hello, Jordan. *Ding, ding, ding.*" I shake an imaginary bell. "You already did—a long time ago. Now get the hell out of here. Don't call me. When and if I'm ready to talk, *I* will call *you.*" I turn on my heels and march back to the entrance. Before I go back inside, I stop for a moment to gather myself. Unfortunately, I don't know what the put-together me looks like anymore.

I can't think about what Jordan said about Kellan. It's so ridiculous. We used to hate each other. Well, he seemed to have hated me. But we're older and more mature now. He hugged me when I needed it, and it felt good to let go for a few seconds. I haven't felt a man against me in a long time. That's all it was.

I push through the doors, where I find Katherine and Mom talking to the funeral director. Mom's gently rocking Noelle in the stroller. Without interrupting, I slip in next to them, pretending like nothing happened. I'd rather hear what's next than think about what just transpired.

Later, once Noelle is in bed and I have my pj's on, I pull a bottle of white wine out of the refrigerator. I shuffle through the drawers to find a corkscrew.

"Do you really need to drink?" Mom asks, filling a glass with water. "You're already running on empty."

And for that comment, I take out another wine glass for her. "Drink some with me. Then I'll answer a few of the questions your eyes have been asking me all day." She cocks her head. "Deal?"

She sighs, giving in. "Only a little bit."

I fill our glasses, and we go into the living room and get settled on the couch. It's not the prettiest, but it's really comfortable. She sits quietly until I finally feel obligated to say something. I swig half my wine first, then curl my legs under me.

"So what do you want to know?"

"I have a lot of questions. Too many for tonight. First, tell me what's going on with Jordan. I have an idea, but I want to hear it from you. You can give me the short story for now since it's late and we have another long day tomorrow."

"Short story. Hmm. We aren't together anymore. Haven't been for a while." *Sip.* Damn, this sauvignon blanc tastes amazing. Right now, any alcohol would taste good.

"Isn't he still living with you?"

"Yep." I cackle. "Separate bedrooms."

"Did he cheat on you?"

"No," I scoff. "Well, I don't know. Maybe. I really don't care, though. It'd probably help me if he did. Per the small print in our contract, we have to be a couple until December thirty-first. Let me tell you how much I regret not having a lawyer read over that thing before I signed it. I was so stupid. Now I feel trapped."

She nods her head a couple of times. "Does he understand that it's over?"

"No. But it's not because he loves me. His true love is money now. He's afraid his career will be over if I quit or walk away from the network. Which I will be doing."

"I'm glad you didn't get married then. I wish you were more open with me. You know you can come to me about anything."

"I know, Mom. But I jumped into this situation with him blindly. We were so excited that we didn't think about the big picture. And believe me, I wake up every morning thankful that I'm not married. Period."

"How long have you been putting up this sham?"

"Four, maybe——" We both remain quiet when we hear a light cry from Noelle. Seconds go by and silence resumes. *Sip.*

"We've had problems most of this year, but I'd say it really went down about five months ago. I'm done with him and the show. He was only here today to make an appearance, and all he did was cause stress. Then he claimed Kellan is interested in me. *Pfft. As if.* Lizzy helped by being a buffer. I felt sorry for her. Maybe I should send her a gift to say thank you."

Her eyes spring open with hope. "Does that mean you're not going back? Will you stay here with Noelle?"

I rub my dry eyes with the palms of my hands. "I don't know, Mom. I still have to work. They're giving me until Christmas, but after that I have to go back. Hopefully by then I have an idea of what I'm going to do." I place my empty glass back on the table, wishing I could have another sip or two.

"Okay," Mom says. "Let me ask it a different way. Do you *want* to go back? If you stayed here, I'd be able to help you. Maybe you could renovate this house instead of selling it."

My head is about to explode. "I don't know," I stress. "That's the best answer I can give you. Let's wait until the funeral is over tomorrow. Then I can move on to the next thing I have to do. Noelle should be my priority over everything else. Can you live with that answer for now?"

She scoots over and puts her arm around my shoulder. I curl into her side. "Of course, honey. I'm not trying to pressure you. This is me, being a worried mama."

"I'm worried too."

"Listen. I'll clean up," she offers, tapping my knee. "Go to bed. Since you sent me home yesterday, I slept like a rock last night. It's your turn. I'll take care of Noelle if she wakes up tonight."

"Thanks. I really need it." We stand at the same time. She picks up the empty wine glasses, then gives me a one-armed hug.

"Remember," she says, "we'll get through this together."

With a forced smile, I nod and kiss her temple. "Love you." Then I turn and drag my feet down the hallway.

"Oh… one more thing. We still need to talk about what happened with Kellan this afternoon."

My eyebrows shoot up. "Mom!"

"Don't worry. Not now. But we will."

I nod, then walk into my room, closing the door behind me. I fall face down on the bed. *Kellan.* I'll admit it to myself —something did happen between us. All the years behind us didn't matter, and it was like a new Kellan appeared. His perpetual scowl and squinty eyes weren't there, making him less intimidating. His stunning blue eyes were brighter than usual, and he was more relaxed. He gets sexier with age and looks beyond beautiful in a suit.

What wouldn't I do to have him holding me right now? I

guess I can dream about him because he won't be at the funeral tomorrow. Who knows if I'll see him again. Just thinking that pulls a string in my heart, making me even sadder.

But he lives in Margo Grove too.

Coincidences happen.

12

CHARLI

8 Years Ago

Can it be any hotter today? As soon as I finished graduate school for the summer, a heat wave blew in. I wasn't going to come home during summer break, but my internship at an architectural firm fell through. It's been a while since I've seen Mom and Dad anyway, so it's probably for the better. I've been busting my ass at school, sitting behind a desk. Working for Dad the next couple of months will do me some good.

Today, I'm helping hang sheetrock in this gorgeous villa that we're renovating. Some workers called out this morning, so I'm filling in. Frankly, I know for a fact they were at McCormick's last night. I know, because I was there with some old friends and saw how hammered they were getting.

"Yo… Charli," Chuck calls, waving a nail gun in the air. "Wanna play?" I drop my head back and laugh. I haven't played this game in years.

"I'm a little rusty, but I'll give it a go. Give me a minute." I guzzle my water, then pack up my empty lunch containers and put them in the shade.

"Hurry up. We only have about fifteen minutes left before we have to get back to work." The guys start stacking bags of cement and another carries the compressor over to Chuck. Time to shoot some cans off the walls with the nail gun. We shouldn't do it, we know—someone could get hurt and Dad would kill us, but it's our lunch break. Time for a little fun. I won't tell anyone, even if I am the boss's daughter. Thankfully no one treats me like I am.

I grab my tool belt, fasten it around my waist, and redo my ponytail. I check my boot laces, then wander over to them. Chuck lines up seven empty soda and Red Bull cans on top of the stacked bags.

"Who's ready to lose?" I tease. "I'm sure as hell not." Behind us, the crunching of gravel announces someone is pulling up. I glance over my shoulder quickly but only see the outline of a truck because of the dust cloud it kicked up.

"Hey, Kell," Chuck shouts when he turns to see who's arrived. "Come on over!" Some of the guys turn around, and a few mumble concern because the site manager has arrived. I don't turn because my stomach is swirling with—I don't know, anxiety? Excitement? I might lose my lunch. How long has it been since I saw him last? A year? Several months, anyway. Will he look at me like I'm an insect or finally treat me as an adult? *Suck it up and look at him.*

When I turn, my lungs freeze and no words come to mind. His gaze drifts to mine, and he stops so abruptly that his boots slide along the gravel and knock him off center. In that instant, every muscle in his arms, chest, and stomach flex through the tight white T-shirt he's wearing. *Talk about eye candy.* His tool belt hangs low on his waist, emphasizing how built he is. I forgot how striking he was.

This raw attraction to him catches me off guard. My gaze connects with his again, and I could swear by the heat in his sky-blue eyes, he's looking at me the same way. With attraction... Lust lights my body on fire. *Get a grip, Charli.*

"Come on, Kell. You against the boss's daughter," Chuck urges playfully with the nail gun in his hand.

I cringe, then slap the back of Chuck's head. "My name's Charli. Remember, jackass? And you shouldn't be waving that gun around. Someone's going to get hurt." The guys erupt in laughter. Did I hear a chuckle from Kellan too? I'm usually treated like one of the guys when I work here. It's not going to stop just because Kellan's arrived.

My heart pounds as he gets closer, but instead of standing next to me, he stops on the other side of Chuck. I reach out my hand for the gun.

"Best out of seven," Chuck says, then gives me some space. "Safety glasses on, everyone, and stand back a little."

I inspect the sixteen-gauge gun and open the magazine to check for enough nails. Then I make sure it's connected to the compressor properly. I glance at the group, but not at Kellan. "Just wanted to make sure none of you screwed with the gun so I'd lose. I have a rep to protect." I wink at them, then put on my glasses.

"Hell, I've seen you use one of those before. My bet's on you, not the moody guy next to me." Chuck elbows Kellan. The other guys agree and laugh along like he's not even here. I'm not sure I can win after that moment passed between us. I'll be lucky if I hit one can.

"Okay. I'm ready." I point the gun at the first can and say loud enough, "I hope you're ready to lose." My lips quirk as the swoosh of air releases and the shot knocks over a can. Chuck whistles. The second one goes down, but I miss the third and the fifth. I knock the last two down, and cheers erupt as if I've already won.

"Hey guys, give the man a chance." I remove my glasses and wipe my forehead with the back of my arm.

Chuck steps back and moves over, leaving me standing next to Kellan. He removes his glasses and hangs them on his shirt collar. When I pass him the gun, his large, calloused hand covers mine, and he doesn't pull away. His beautiful eyes caress my face, stopping to focus on my lips. Then he licks his lower lip, mesmerizing me, making me wish his tongue was on me. My body begins to hum, and my mouth is dry like I've been sucking on cotton balls all day. Where's this undeniable electrical pull coming from? Why now?

"What the hell are you two doing? A stare down? Charli, give him the gun. Are you afraid to lose?" I blink, then pull my hand away. He doesn't have a firm grip on the gun. It starts to fall, and we both grab for it. He manages to catch it before it hits the ground. Maybe it's not safe for me to have a nail gun when he's around.

I rub the back of my sizzling neck and turn forward. "Sorry," I mumble, slipping my glasses back on to create a barrier between us. *Yeah, like that'll make a difference!*

Chuck lines up the cans again. Kellan's still standing next to me, close enough that I can feel the heat coming off him. Close enough that I can smell him—a mixture of freshly cut lumber and sweat. That's something I find highly attractive in a man: one who doesn't mind sweating and getting his hands dirty. Without meaning to, my elbow brushes against his side and I feel a slight electric shock. He doesn't even flinch, but as I lean away, the right side of his mouth ticks up like he's grinning. He lowers his arms and cracks his neck.

"Come on! Break's almost over," Chuck prods and claps loudly. "Safety glasses back on."

Kellan puts on his and aims with steady, tight arms. Instead of watching the targets, I observe his gorgeous face from the side and memorize every line. I don't know if I'll ever get this close to him again. A drop of sweat trickles down his cheek. From the thin layer of stubble that's kissing his jawline, to the angular curve of his cheeks and the slight arch of his nose, to how he's biting his lower lip in concentration, he's a perfect specimen. To top it off, there's a sprinkle of gray that mixes in with his light brown hair. Why does gray hair look sexy on a man? And he's not even thirty yet. I turn away when I see his eyes flick toward me, catching me staring. My cheeks start to sizzle.

Only one more to win. With a deep inhale then exhale, he pulls the trigger. He misses. Chuck roars along with the others. Kellan hands Chuck the gun, removes his glasses, and turns to leave without a word.

I watch him walk away, but I can't resist calling his name. He stops, then turns around. I'm expecting his typical stone face, but instead, a beautiful smile transforms it, making my knees weak. *Wow!*

I snap out of my trance and smile back. We don't say anything, but sometimes you don't need to. He turns around and walks into the villa, and I don't see him again for the rest of the summer.

13

CHARLI

Last night, my agent, Kay, sent me a draft contract for the renovation of Sandy's house. I'm furious as I slam my hand on the kitchen table. Jordan has really crossed the line this time. Man, he works fast. But Kay was surprised too. She knew I'd be livid—I've made it quite clear to her what kind of contract I want.

Now I'm about ten minutes away from my home in Barton. Mom's babysitting Noelle for the day. I didn't tell Jordan I was coming. I've been stewing in my car for the last two hours, so I know I won't be calm if I see him. My main focus right now is to confront him and pick up some of my personal and business things.

As I drive through the streets leading to my house, I try to remember how I used to love it here. How I felt at peace with Jordan in our new place. It breaks my heart now because that love has turned into the complete opposite.

Realization kicks me in the ass. I can't even say this is my home either.

I slow down in front of the house. Jordan's shiny black Ford Ranger is in the driveway and a cherry red Porsche is parked in front. I know that car.

Why on earth would Penelope Wrick, one of the executive producers of *Fast-Track Renovations*, be at my house at ten o'clock on a Sunday morning? I squeeze the steering wheel like it's Jordan's throat. He's had the nerve to invite her over to talk about the contract. I saw him taking pictures of Sandy's house when he was there. But why wouldn't they do it at the studio during the week? And why wasn't I notified about this meeting?

Instead of parking near the house to alert them that I'm here, I park a couple of houses down. Then I walk back and quietly unlock the front door. I push it open slowly, hoping it won't squeak like it does sometimes. I let out my breath when it doesn't.

Once in, I close the door and take off my shoes. Habit, but they won't hear me either. I walk down the long hallway and peek into the open living room–kitchen area. Empty but a complete mess. Dirty dishes are stacked in the sink. Empty wine glasses and bottles are on the counter. Garbage is overflowing. Not important right now. *Hmm.* I search further. I don't see anyone outside. I turn around to head to my office, but stop dead in my tracks when I hear moaning coming from upstairs. A feminine moan. *Fucking hell.*

The hair on my arms stands up, and my pulse spikes. Adrenaline pumps through me so fast it practically carries me up the stairs to about six feet away from the cracked-open bedroom door. *My bedroom.*

Plan. I need a plan. A photo. I grab my phone that's hanging from a lanyard around my neck and open the camera. This could be my out.

I can do this.

One more deep breath.

One foot after the other, I approach the door and push it open lightly. I want to puke at the disgusting sight in front of me, but then confidence takes over. *Click. Click.*

I lean against the doorframe and start clapping. "Wow!

Penelope, you must be really special. Jordan hates doggy style. I guess he doesn't want to see your ugly face."

Both jerk their heads in my direction. *Click. Click.* Penelope screams and tries to cover herself with the sheet, but Jordan is kneeling on it. She rolls off the bed and hits the floor like a dead horse. *Thud.* Hiding will get her nowhere. Jordan scrambles for the sheet, and I walk out of the room. *Busted.*

Jordan naked is something I don't ever want to see again in this lifetime. I don't know if I should be happy or pissed. Maybe relieved? The adrenaline rush fuels an odd excitement. Yeah, this is my way out.

"Charli! Wait!"

"Fuck off, Jordan," I yell over my shoulder as I run downstairs.

I struggle to get my shoes on so I can get the hell out of here, but then I remember that this is my house. I don't have to leave. It takes a few minutes, but then I hear Jordan stomping down the stairs. He finds me in my office, unplugging my laptops and monitor. I glance over my shoulder. At least he has pants on now.

"Charli, let me—" He's got his hands clasped in front of him, and he's begging. Just for shits and giggles, I should snap a shot of this too.

I slam a desk drawer shut. "Nope. Not a word until Penelope gets down here. It'll be in her best interest to stay. I suggest you make sure she doesn't try to escape."

He pinches his lips together and storms out of the room.

Why should any of this surprise me? He's trying to save his ass and his job. Who knows how long it's been going on or how many different women he's fucked around with.

But this isn't the room to deal with them in. I head for the kitchen, wanting a more open space where I can breathe and think. Time passes to the point I wonder if they snuck out. But heated whispers come from the foyer.

"I'm in the kitchen." I stand up straight with my shoulders back. Time to show them who has the power now.

Jordan walks in with a bright red Penelope following behind. She matches the color of her car and, I swear, she looks like she took a shower. *The fucking nerve!*

Before either of them can speak, I place my phone on the counter next to my engagement ring. The lanyard on my phone is wrapped tightly around my hand, in case one of them tries to grab it. It wouldn't matter if they did because I've already sent the photos to my personal email account. The screen is filled with one of those lovely pictures now. *Gag!*

Penelope glances at it and closes her eyes. *Please, let me see tears.* Maybe they'll come once I mention her husband. But she's a heartless bitch, being the boss's daughter and all. She walks all over everyone because she thinks she can. I wouldn't even have imagined acting like that in Dad's company.

"You are not allowed to speak until I'm done." They don't react, but I know they understand. I pull the phone away and hang it around my neck again, making sure the picture is in full view from their angle. "Where should I start?"

From the beginning. Time to let out all my resentment and anger. I walk around the island so there's no barrier between us. They both back up. *Nervous?*

"Jordan, do you see the engagement ring on the counter?" I point to it. "I should keep it since I bought this house and most of everything in it." His eyes flash. "Oh, sorry. Except for your video games and all the mirrors you stare at yourself in.

"But don't worry. I want nothing to do with that ring or any memory that goes with it. I'll admit it—I was in love with you when we signed on to do this show. *As a couple.* We were supposed to be the dream pair of the renovation shows, even though they focused more on my skills." I bat my eyelashes at him. "I couldn't have asked for a better job. I was sad that my dad didn't live long enough to see what I'd made of myself.

But you know what? I'm relieved now, because I'm beyond embarrassed to say I'm a part of this show. What a fucking joke. I actually thought we'd be able to use our skills to the fullest. *As a couple.* Like our contract said."

I turn away from them and walk back around the island. He reeks of sex, and her heavy musk perfume is going to make me break out in hives. Where's a gas mask when I need one? I prop my arms on the countertop and continue.

"Don't get me wrong, things started off really well. I was proud of our projects in the beginning. Then you proposed to me on TV in front of a million viewers. Yeah, it helped me get through the pain of losing my dad. But I think you did it all for show."

"That's not—"

I hold up my hand. "Save it, Jordan."

My phone pings. I look at it just to be a bitch. Then I chuckle because it's a picture of Noelle with carrot all over her face. I show it to them. "Isn't she cute?" Jordan sighs heavily. I drop the phone, and my smile disappears.

"Where was I?" I purse my lips to the side. "Oh, right. Then things started to change. Jordan, you saw dollar signs because of all the extra money we were bringing in from sponsors and commercials. You loved the attention and lost interest in me. Then, the *producers*"—I give Penelope the evil eye—"decided my professional skills weren't necessary anymore and they changed the type of houses we fixed up. Everyone knew I wanted to be fully involved with everything, including getting my hands dirty. Instead, now I have to prance around in god-awful stilettos, looking at color swatches while other people do everything. And don't even get me started on the ridiculous clothes and the makeup you expect me to wear. Then you go and have Jordan walking around with no shirt on, to show off his muscles. Did the network pay off OSHA?"

"You saw how the ratings went up," Penelope interjects.

"Didn't I say to keep your mouth shut?" Her eyes shoot daggers at me, but I don't give a shit.

"Where are you going with this?" Jordan throws in. "So what? You found me in bed with her. I had to find it somewhere since you never put out." Penelope's head whips in his direction.

I provoke her. "Sucks to be used, doesn't it?" I want to point out that she's probably twenty years older than he is, but I don't. She crosses her arms and points her chin in the air. I turn back to Jordan.

"Jordan, usually when people break up and at least one person can't stand the other anymore, sex is no longer involved. Are you really so stupid to not understand that? I know your ego can't handle the blow, but too bad.

"Our contract is up at the end of this month. According to that lovely document, we're supposed to be a happy couple until then. I'll follow through with that because no one will see me. But we're done. Starting January first at twelve a.m., I'm no longer a part of the show or working for this network. Of course, it wouldn't look nice if the power couple broke up because you couldn't keep your dick in your pants with the executives."

Penelope scratches her blotchy neck. *Omigod, are those hickeys?* My throat closes just thinking about it.

"Jordan, you went behind my back to try to use my sister's house for the next project. How fucking dare you?" He averts his gaze, looking down at the ground.

I turn my attention to Penelope. "That house is not for sale and it's not up for any discussion. I am done. Done! I will never do another show or appearance for this network. Nothing. If you ask even once, I will post that damn picture on every social media page and have a special one framed for your sweet husband and father. Your husband's too good for you.

"Back to you, Jordan. This house is in my name." I nearly

break one of those stupid acrylic fingernails, stabbing the counter with it. "You said you'd put your money into investments for us to build a strong financial future and to pay some of the monthly bills. I sure hope you did. Now it's *your* financial future. I don't need you or your money.

"I want you out of this house by the end of the month. I'm going back to Margo Grove, and I won't be back until you're gone. And believe me, I will check that you are out."

His eyes bulge and his mouth drops open. "That's less than three weeks. That's not long enough."

"Really? I think it's pretty generous, considering. Don't you? Maybe you can sleep between Penelope and her husband. You can take whatever furniture you want because I don't want anything to remind me of you or our past. However, my office is off limits. And if you don't leave—let me reiterate—the picture is blasted."

I wrack my brain for anything else to say. Nope, that should do it. Silence paralyzes the house.

"All right then. I'm going to pack up some stuff, and I don't want you here while I do it. You've got five minutes to get out of here because I'm nice like that." I flash them a fake smirk.

"Charli, let's talk in private after Penelope leaves."

"We are done here," I say with finality. "I've said my part, and I don't care one bit about anything you might have to say. Especially after this and, and after how you behaved at Sandy's wake last week. Get out."

His posture droops, then he snatches the ring off the counter and walks away defeated. Penelope follows, leaving her musk behind. I open the sliding glass door to let in some fresh air.

While I'm waiting for them to leave, I load the dishwasher and wipe down the counters. Then I respond to Mom about that adorable picture. My heart warms as I look at the photos of Noelle on my phone. My sister created a beautiful girl.

Excitement is still pumping through my body, making my heart palpitate. I'm not trapped in this mess anymore. I'm not tied to Barton either. I can do whatever I want now. I'm free! A happy dance is warranted, but I'm not alone.

Ideas swirl in my head as I pace back and forth in the kitchen. There are too many, so I pull a pad of paper and a pen out of a drawer and start writing like a madwoman. I stop when I hear whispering again, and then the front door slams shut. Holding my breath, I wait a few more seconds. With the pad and pen in my hand, I run to the front door and lock it. Kind of stupid since he has a key, but it feels good anyway. Both cars take off down the street.

What should I do so I can leave as soon as possible? I dash upstairs and load a large suitcase with clothes and stuff from the bathroom. Once that's done, I go get my car and park it in the driveway. I put the suitcase in the trunk, then grab the empty boxes I brought with me and take them inside. In less than an hour, the boxes are full of my personal and professional files, laptops, monitor, and everything else I can think of that I might need to work with at Sandy's house. And I head home.

"Hey, Mom," I say excitedly when she answers the phone. "I'm at the gas station not too far from Margo Grove." I took a different exit off the highway to avoid where Sandy's accident was.

"Already? That was fast. You sound quite peppy. I can hear the smile in your voice." *Me too.*

"I'm jumping out of my skin with excitement. I'll tell you about it when I get home. Would you mind watching Noelle a little longer? I have a stop to make before I get there."

"Sure. It's such a beautiful day, I thought I'd take Noelle

for a walk in a little while anyway, and maybe do some yoga while she's playing."

"Super. Thanks. Another thing, can you please text me Kellan's home address?" Mom might be a little older, but she's pretty tech savvy. She doesn't use an old-fashioned address book. She stores everything in her phone.

"Kellan's?" Her curiosity drifts through the phone.

"Yes, Kellan's. It's Sunday, so I don't think he'll be at the office. And send me his number too, just in case I don't see him. Can you do it as soon as we're off the phone, please?"

I'm someone who needs instant results when I have an idea. Impatience is one of my worst flaws.

"O–Okay. I can't wait to hear whatever it is you're so excited about. We could use some good news around here."

Staying in Sandy's house is a big reminder that she's gone. It doesn't help that the place is so depressing. It's hard to see the bright side when we're in that house all day. But if things go my way, it won't be like that for much longer.

"I haven't felt this excited in a long time. I'll call later. Wish me luck." I hang up before she can respond. After a few seconds, my phone lights up with his address. I type it into my navigation system. And then panic sinks in.

What if Kellan treats me like he used to? *Ah, don't let him be a kill joy.* I have a business proposition for him. I don't need him to be warm and fuzzy, but please don't let him ignore me again. Today is my day. No one is going to ruin it.

14

KELLAN

This color had better come out right. Dara asked for blue or more like the color of Charli's eyes. I drop my head. *Do not think about her.* That's easier said than done. Since the viewing, it seems she's all I *can* think about. Concentrating on work has been nearly impossible, to the point some of my team have asked me if something's wrong. And I've been staring at this damn metallic powder for I don't know how long. I hate it that the last two times I've seen Charli have been at funerals. Mick's death was a turning point in my life, making me change a lot of things. Now it seems to be the case for Charli. Again, poor timing. Will there ever be a right one? *Stop thinking.*

I open the container of turquoise metallic powder and go to pour it in the epoxy but stop at the last second when a silver BMW pulls into my driveway. I don't recognize the car. The door opens and—I must have inhaled too many fumes because I can't believe it. Charli stands next to her car, shading her eyes from the glaring sun.

I grab a rag off the workbench and wipe my hands, then head out to the driveway. Even from far away, her gorgeous smile radiates pure happiness. A complete contrast to the last time I saw her.

She waves when she sees me, then jogs my way. I tuck the rag in my back pocket.

"Hi! I'm so sorry I stopped by unannounced. I really wanted to see—I mean, talk to you, and it couldn't wait." Excitement oozes out of her. So which is it? Did she want to see me or talk to me? For some reason, wanting to see me carries more weight.

I almost don't know how to react because I've usually walked away or avoided her. I don't ever want to do that again, but how do I change without being obvious? Does it matter if it is? She'll probably be the one to walk away from me once I shower her with the attention she deserves.

"I'm not going to let you ignore me this time," she says playfully.

"Who says I want to ignore you?" *See… that wasn't so hard.*

"Well, then, I guess today's my lucky day." *And mine.* She bounces on her heels; her eyes are bright and cheery.

"So what's got you so excited, and what does it have to do with me?"

"Sandy's house." She swings her arms back and forth. "I want to renovate it, and I'd like you to help me. Like Sandy wanted. It all became clear to me today. This is what I want, no, *need* to do. For Sandy and Abigail. And most definitely for Noelle." She's talking so fast it's hard to keep up.

I place my hands gently on her shoulders and say, "Charli, slow down. Take a breath." She laughs lightly and tries to stand still.

"Sorry. I'm freaking out a little bit," she blurts, shaking out her hands. "Oh, but not in a bad way," she hurries to assure me. Now I chuckle and pull my hands away, shoving them in my pockets.

"So you want to renovate Sandy's—"

"House. And I want to ask if you'll help me. I'm overflowing with ideas and can't wait to start. And before you say no, can you come over to the house and listen to some of the ideas I have. Have you ever been in it?" She waves her hand. "What am I thinking? Of course you haven't. Have you?"

I laugh. How much coffee has she had today? "No, I haven't been inside. I've only seen it from the road. It definitely needs some work." I scratch my scruffy chin.

She grins. "Wait until you see inside. Old, dirty carpets everywhere, even in the bathrooms. Typical seventies-style house with green, yellow, and brown everything. The kitchen is atrocious. Basement is dark and grungy. Well, the whole house is. And it smells. Some of the radiators don't work, so the house is cold and damp. But it could be awesome with a lot of TLC. So what do you say? Want to see it?"

"Um, sure. What day would work for you?" I pull out my phone to open my calendar.

"How about now?" she suggests with pleading eyes.

"Right now?" I don't think she's kidding. I look back over at the bench.

"There's no time like the present." She raises her eyebrows in encouragement. "Mom and Noelle will be there."

How can I say no when she's so enthusiastic? It's a chance to spend time with her. Dara's bench can wait another week. And maybe I can find out what's going on with her. Does this mean she's staying in Margo Grove? What about Jordan?

"Um. Okay. Let me clean up what I was doing first. It should only take a few minutes."

"Oh, I interrupted you. I'm sorry! Was it something important?" She peeks over my shoulder toward the garage. "Can I see? Or am I being too nosy?"

What the hell is going on? We haven't spoken like this since the day we met. Easy and friendly. Well, we did a little bit at the wake. Today is different. Not that I *want* to stop talking to her. Ever. Shutting her out isn't an option anymore.

"Um. Sure. Follow me." She walks with me into the garage. "Welcome to my little workshop and garage."

"It's far from little." She twirls slowly, looking around, then inspects the shelves with her hands behind her back. Standing next to the bench, I watch in amazement. This feels... normal and easygoing. I hadn't given us a chance to be relaxed around each other because I didn't trust myself.

"I'm working on this bench for Dara. She saw one like it somewhere and took a picture. She asked me to make her one and I was up for the challenge. It's a work in progress." I open my phone to show her the picture and lift it up. "This is what it's supposed to look like when it's done."

She leans in to inspect it. "Wow, it looks like water is running through the wood." Her finger traces the screen.

"Exactly." I pull the phone away, then point to a wide and deep groove that runs along the middle of the otherwise flat piece of wood. "A mixture of metallic powder and epoxy gets poured in there. I was about to prepare the mixture when you arrived. This is the color I chose." I pick up the container and hand it to her.

She lifts it toward the light and it sparkles. "It's beautiful."

"Just like your eyes. It's the first thing I thought of when I saw it." *Damn! Did I take a truth serum or something?*

Her face softens, and she hands the container back to me. Our fingers brush as I take it from her. I try to ignore the flash of warmth in my gut just from that simple touch.

"That's sweet," she says. "I'd love to see it when it's finished."

I place it on a shelf and twist it until the label is facing forward, then line it up next to the other powders I've bought. "Who knows when that'll be. I only work on it on Sundays."

"Does that mean you'd rather work on it now than go with me to Sandy's?"

"And ruin your good mood? I'd never forgive myself." *Literally.*

The corner of her mouth perks up. Even if I managed to put that wall back up between us, it wouldn't matter. Her smile would knock it back down in a second anyway. Somehow her power over me is beyond my control now. Is it because of my fear of losing her before I can tell her how I feel? Or because I don't want to fight my feelings for her anymore? *Both.*

"Ruining my mood would be hard to do right now. I'm still high on adrenalin." Should I ask why she's so happy or wait until she feels comfortable enough to tell me? I don't think her excitement is only about the house. Something else must have happened.

"Okay, then let me change my dirty clothes. Want to come in or should I meet you there?" We walk outside and I close the door behind us.

"I'd love to see the inside of your house. It's beautiful from out here. It looks like an old barn. Is it?"

I nod. "Yep. So is the garage. If I remember, they were built in the fifties. The foundations were still in good condition, so I converted them."

"Was it red like the color it is now?"

"It was similar. I wanted the exterior to look as close to the original as possible. I can show you before and after pictures sometime. Mickey helped me out when he had time."

"Hmm. I think I remember Dad mentioning it. I was in my own world after I went off to college and didn't live at home anymore." Her voice trails off and it sounds like her mood is changing. Not if I can help it.

"Come on, let me show you inside. Or should I be nervous about what you'll think? You *are* Mickey's daughter. That's a lot of pressure."

She cocks an eyebrow. "Right. You can lay off the flattery if that's what it is. I'm sure I'll love it. I've admired your work over the years."

Oh, you have, have you? My heart rate kicks up a notch.

"Sorry if it's a mess. I wasn't expecting company," I say over my shoulder.

"If it looks anything like your perfectly organized work-shop and this pristine front lawn, I'm sure it's fine. Do you use scissors to trim the edges?"

I drop my head back and chuckle.

"From the little time I was in there," she continues, "I saw how your workshop was divided into sections. Electronic tools in one corner, spotless, lined up by type and size. Hand tools hanging on the wall in another corner, also arranged by type and size. I saw how you placed the powder container so it was exactly lined up with the others. And don't think I didn't notice the contraption you built on the ceiling for easy access to your electronic nail gun. Very impressive."

I haven't looked at a nail gun the same since our competi-tion years ago. I wonder if she remembers? That's the last time I let my barriers down around her and let my emotions get the best of me.

"You saw all of that in the few minutes you were in there?"

She twists at her waist with her arms propped on her hips. "Yep. Dad loved that about you. How organized you were because he wasn't. And details are my specialty. It comes with our job, doesn't it?"

I grin and open the front door. "You're right. Come in."

15

CHARLI

"This house is amazing," I gush, standing by the door in awe. In front of me is a large open area with a cathedral ceiling and sturdy oak beams. The entire main wall to the left is exposed red brick. Straight ahead is a spacious living room separated from the kitchen by a rustic bar with barstools. Two large skylights let in the perfect amount of sunlight to balance the darker contrast of the brick against the white walls. "It should be in a magazine. Why don't you have pictures of this on the company website?"

"Thanks. That's a compliment coming from you, Ms. *Fast-Track Renovation* herself."

I roll my eyes. "Please don't remind me. You said you didn't want to dampen my good mood, so let me give you some advice. Don't mention that show again." The last thing I want to do is pull him into my personal bullshit.

His hands lift in peace. "Sorry. Now you make me even more curious. But that's a good idea—I should put pictures on the website. Don't know why we didn't." He waves me forward. "Come on. Let me give you the grand tour."

We make our way through the living room and into the kitchen. Everything is perfectly neat and the kitchen is spotless. No dirty dishes in the sink. A complete contrast to my kitchen in Barton. Sandy would love it. But even with the cozy atmosphere, it's as if nobody lives here. Almost like it's a showroom. An extra-large bag of Reese's Pieces and a couple of bananas sitting next to the refrigerator give it a little life.

"The rustic accents are perfect on these cream cabinets and wood butcher-block countertops." I caress the smooth surface, and my fingertips tingle from the cool finish.

"Here's the dining area. I've put exterior bifold doors in some of the houses I've built and really admired them, so I installed them here. Makes it easy to go out to the deck, brings in more light, and helps cool off the place during the summer." He opens the doors and a welcomed breeze blows in. I close my eyes and inhale the fresh air. It's so peaceful here.

"Let's go this way." He leads me back through the living room and then to the left down a long hallway. I'm distracted by his perfect ass in the black jeans he's sporting. And don't get me started on those broad shoulders and solid traps on display in his form-fitting black T-shirt. *Business, Charli.* I look away when my cheeks start to burn. My steamy thoughts are probably a side effect from my lack of sex. I've lost track. Pitiful.

I get my head on straight and comment, "The barn must have been huge." *I know what's probably huge.* I chuckle to myself. He glances over his shoulder, and I straighten my spine. *Get it together, Charli!*

With an encompassing sweep of his arm, he says, "This part was for cows. That's why this whole section is long and narrow." I scan the bathroom and his office quickly. Again, squeaky clean and very orderly.

"The stairs ahead lead to the second-floor main bedroom and bathroom. It wasn't part of the original structure. I wanted a separate sleeping area." He doesn't offer to show it to me, and I don't ask to see it. It feels too intimate for some reason.

"I'm really impressed. Dad must have loved working on it with you. It's different than what his usual jobs were." What stands out is that this house is not necessarily for a family. It's more a bachelor pad. Does he want to be on his own for the rest of his life?

"I think he did. It had its challenges, and you know how Mickey loved challenges. He said it was a way to learn something new and spark your creativity at the same time."

I chuckle. "Yeah. That sounds like Dad, all right." A strange silence comes over us, as if we're hurting by talking about Dad. I'd do anything to have him here.

"Let me go up and get some fresh clothes. Make yourself comfortable."

"Okay. Take your time." He trots up the stairs and disappears behind a door. I'll admit it, I'm curious what it looks like up there. I tap my forehead. *Stop thinking about him taking off his clothes.* I remember him in his tight T-shirts when I saw him at the jobsites. It was a long time ago, but the memories feel like they were yesterday. They still make my temperature rise.

He's probably just as fit today, too, from the way his clothes were clinging to his body. But that's not why I'm here. I'm here for business, not to drool over someone I've known forever but don't actually know at all.

I wander over to the open doors to the backyard, letting the little details of his house soak in. There's a slightly feminine touch mixed in with all the rustic décor. Candles and a few plants are spread throughout. Soft pastel blue pillows and blanket accent the cream sofa and armchair. For a broody man, I'd have expected darker colors. Who helped him decorate? A girlfriend? A weighted sensation pushes on my chest. Am I jealous?

Come to think of it, he did bring a woman with him to Dad's funeral. I talked to Kellan briefly and hugged him for about a second, but I didn't speak to her. There were so many people at Dad's wake and funeral, I don't remember most of it. Jordan was all over me and wouldn't leave my side. At the time I liked it.

Shaking my head to forget about the past, I stare out into the distance. Is he lonely living here by himself? Shit, maybe he does have a girlfriend—or maybe a few!—and isn't alone at all. He said he hadn't found the right one for him, but that doesn't mean he's single.

These strange, random thoughts don't make sense to me. Why are we talking and interacting as if we just met today? Or like we don't have a history of him avoiding me like the plague most of the time. I know people can change, but I can't help questioning it. Why now? For me, maybe it's because he's managed to wake my body from its long winter sleep. I ruffle my hair out of frustration. Maybe any hot guy would do that to me right now.

"You okay?" I jump at his sudden presence behind me. "Sorry. Didn't mean to scare you."

"This place is so relaxing. Almost like a vacation home." I turn around and am rendered speechless. His short hair is damp like he took a quick shower. The cobalt Henley he's wearing makes his eyes a dreamy blue that I could get lost in if I'm not careful.

"That's why I love it. Work is stressful enough. I wanted a place to come home to that would help me unwind. One of my favorite things to do at the end of the day is sit out on the deck with a beer, surrounded by silence."

I don't know if I felt like that with my house in Barton. Maybe in the beginning. The garden is fenced off to the neighbors, but I can still see into their houses through certain windows. There's constant noise, whether it be a lawn mower, dogs barking, or kids playing in the street. But that's only on the weekends. I'm hardly home before seven during the week.

Here, it's only you, surrounded by nature. There's probably no light pollution either, letting the stars shine brightly. Sandy's house is quiet too, though not as quiet as here. I can see why she and Abigail wanted to raise Noelle there. If the house is renovated in the right way, it'd be perfect for any family with little kids. Excitement sparks in my chest again.

"What's that smile for?" he asks. It must be contagious because his face lights up with one too. Man, he's gorgeous. *Control yourself!*

"I remembered why I'm here. Ready to go see Sandy's house? Mom must be wondering where I am."

"Sure. Let's go. I'll follow you in my truck."

16

KELLAN

I liked it too much. She wasn't in my house for more than an hour, but it felt like she belonged there. Her lavender perfume drifting through the air brought my house to life. I growl with frustration. I've wasted so much time, so many damn years. Why would I deserve her now?

Reality kicks in as we pull up in front of Sandy's house and park in the driveway. There's no chance for us. She belongs to Jordan and Noelle. As a family. But then why isn't Jordan helping her if he has so much experience and they're engaged? And what is it about their relationship that doesn't feel right to me?

Focus on the house!

I climb out and stand next to the truck, inspecting the house from a distance. The lot is roughly one-and-a-half to two acres. Plenty of space for an addition. The front lawn is overgrown and wild. The grass has burnt patches in several spots. Bushes directly in front and a large tree to the left are overbearing, blocking sunlight from entering the house. The old wooden porch might be salvageable. The garage door has seen better days. The roof looks original.

I've driven by this house several times over the years but

haven't paid much attention to it. It was empty for a while. It's an eyesore when you compare it to the modernized versions of it on either side. The neighbors were probably hopeful the new owners would renovate it. And now look what happened.

I amble over to where Charli's standing. Her big cautious eyes find mine, and I smile to show my approval of the house. Her stiff posture relaxes. And that's when I know I have to say yes to whatever she wants because it's the only possible way to spend time with her.

The accident pops back into my mind. I know I should tell Charli I was there, but—No, I can't think about the past.

She bumps me with her elbow. "So? Here it is. Wait till you see inside!" She rubs her hands together excitedly. She's adorable.

"Have you met any of the neighbors yet?"

"Yes. It seems Sandy and Abigail made a great impression. They were only here for a couple of months, but it felt like the whole town came to say how sorry they were. Mom and I were really blown away. Our fridge was full for a week. Some of them showed up at the viewing too. And Noelle seems to have stolen many hearts."

"Well, those Brannon eyes have a way of doing that. They suck you in and you never want to let go. I should know," I mumble, then hope I didn't say it loud enough for Charli to hear. But the light in her eyes and the quirky grin on her face tell me she did.

The front door swings open, pulling our attention away from us. Tricia walks out with Noelle. Charli runs up to them, pulls Noelle into her arms, and cuddles with her. She blows raspberries on her neck, making her wiggle in delight. I try to block the visions of Noelle trapped in that damn car.

"You like it when I do that, don't you?" Charli coos. Tricia chuckles, watching them adoringly. Proud grandma. At least something good came out of the accident. "Want to say hi to Kellan?" Charli raises Noelle's little arm and waves it at me. I step closer and shake her little hand. She wraps her tiny fingers around my forefinger and grins. Drool dribbles down her chin. We lock eyes, and I think she remembers me. I look away and step back.

"Hi, Kellan. This is a nice surprise." Tricia embraces me. In a lot of ways, she's been more a mother to me than my own. After Dad left, Mom became distant and wasn't attentive or affectionate with Dara and me anymore. Her heart was broken, so I understood to an extent why she closed herself off. Tricia's warmth made up for it later on. She lets go and I step back. "So why did Charli bring you here? She called asking for your address, but she didn't tell me why. Let me guess, it's something about this house."

"What else would it be for?" Charli responds quickly. Wow, that stung. But really, what else could she possibly need from me?

17

CHARLI

"I warned you it was an eyesore and that it smells." Mom and I stand in the foyer while Kellan wanders into the living room. He's in work mode now. The mode I'm used to.

"It is pretty narrow in here. Not much space for a lot of furniture. The windows need to be replaced." He walks over to the fireplace, then bends down. "The chimney needs to be checked. I'm curious about the condition of the floors under all this carpet."

"By the time we're done, there won't be any carpet in here. If you think this is small, you should see the kitchen. One major thing I want to do is open this wall." I knock on it. "It needs to go."

"It's probably a weight-bearing wall," he adds. "Something to look into."

"Let me show you the kitchen." He follows me and I step to the side by the kitchen sink.

"Yeah, this is cramped. You could build out, expanding the open kitchen–living room area. Your plot is big enough that zoning shouldn't be a problem."

I nod. "I thought the same thing. It's on my list of things to check out. Come and look at the rest of the house."

Mom takes fussy Noelle from me and follows us as we walk through. He doesn't say much, which makes me crazy. I remain quiet so I don't disturb him. After a few minutes, Mom disappears.

When we're finished with our walk-through, we find her busy in the kitchen. Noelle's sitting in her highchair, slapping the tray. "If you two are done, why don't we sit down at the kitchen table," Mom suggests, "and have some coffee. While you were looking around, I made a fresh pot. This little cutie is hungry, and I want Charli to explain her sudden burst of energy and excitement."

I glance at Kellan and he nods. He still hasn't said anything. So annoying. We move into the kitchen. I'm surprised when Kellan takes the seat next to Noelle at the small round table and moves closer to her. He looks so big sitting there. I grab a jar of applesauce out of the cabinet and a pink baby spoon from the drawer. Kellan picks up a rattle from her tray and shakes it in front of her. She reaches for it, but he pulls it away before she can touch it and rattles it again. They do this back and forth while she squeals loudly. I should record the sound for whenever I need a pick-me-up. He chuckles along with her. Mom and I join in too. He could make any woman's ovaries do the tango.

"I think you have a new fan," I say. "You're welcome to come here anytime if you promise to make her laugh like that again." He lets her capture the toy this time, and she waves it in front of him. I slip into the chair on the other side of her.

Mom places coffee mugs and spoons in front of us, then brings over the coffeepot, milk, and sugar. "Here you go. Help yourself," she says. Kellan fills his mug and offers to fill ours. We both nod.

Mom wastes no time and jumps right in. "So start explaining yourself, Charli."

I open the jar and stir the applesauce. Noelle becomes fixated on the food instead of Kellan. Perfect timing.

"Kellan, before I showed up at your place, I was at my house in Barton picking up some things to bring back here. Something unexpected happened that was both a shock and relief at the same time." Mom and Kellan glance at each other, then at me. "Without getting into details, the outcome is that I'm done with the show." I feed Noelle another spoonful.

"What?" Mom exclaims. She reaches out to grab my arm, almost knocking her coffee cup over. "Does that mean you're staying here?"

"Yes. *For now*," I emphasize. "If a different network approaches me with an awesome offer, I might be tempted to stay in Barton or go wherever they'd base the show."

"Does that mean Jordan will be coming here to help you?" Kellan asks with a twang in his voice, sitting straight in his chair with stiff shoulders. I glance at Mom quickly, hoping she won't say anything. She sips her coffee.

"No," I respond. "This is my house and my project." Kellan's expression softens, and he relaxes into his chair. "Anyway, once I realized I was free from certain obligations, something special burst in me and it became clear what I needed to do. Mom and I have discussed selling the house, but I don't want to do that anymore. At least not yet. I want to renovate it like Sandy and Abigail dreamed, only better. They had pictures and ideas written down in their files, and I've had ideas wreaking havoc in my head since I walked in. I haven't felt this inspired in years." I beam, hardly containing myself. As if Noelle feels my excitement, she squeals and wiggles in her seat.

"You sure do love that applesauce, little lady," Mom declares, pride reflecting in her eyes. "You like to get messy too." We chuckle as I wipe Noelle's face with her bib.

"That's where you come in, Kell." I reach over and grab his hand that's resting on the table. His confused eyes glance at our joined hands, but he doesn't pull away. Man, he's hard to read.

"Because I like to eat? Or because I like to get dirty like Noelle?" A sly curve hits his mouth. His playfulness is a welcome surprise.

"Ha ha. What I meant is, I'd love to work with you and your team. And maybe with a couple connections I have. I wouldn't trust anyone else with this project. I don't know how busy you are right now, but I'd like to start as soon as possible. Get things lined up."

He pulls his hand away and grimaces. "Charli, I can't commit to anything until you have some firm goals. You know the drill. I'd love to work with you on this, but it takes time, a lot of planning, permits, and manpower."

"I know, I know. That's where my experience from the show comes in. I'll be the architect and interior designer. Between the two of us, we have tons of connections. My main reason for going back to Barton this morning was to pick up my laptops and work-related materials. Now I'll have my software to create a plan and sketch up my ideas. Sandy had blueprints and other documentation showing what's been done to the house in the past. It isn't much. I want to gut the place completely and start over."

"If you want it done fast, you can't live here with Noelle," Mom says pensively. "I don't have the space for you. Where would you live? Noelle needs stability—she shouldn't be shuffled from one place to another."

"I know. I know. I'll have to find a place nearby that I can rent. Hopefully, the solution will present itself."

"You'll have to think about daycare if you'll be working all the time," she adds, still concerned. "I can help out, but I need to get back into my routine too."

"Again, I know. There's a lot to think about and even more to do. Believe me, it won't be Noelle keeping me up at night; it'll be this."

Kellan stands up and puts his empty coffee cup in the sink, then leans against the counter with his arms crossed. *Sexy as sin.* He looks good in this ugly kitchen. He'd look good anywhere.

"Let me ask around," he says. "I know a lot of people in town. I'm not sure they'll rent on a short-term basis, though. Plus Christmas is only a couple of weeks away."

I press my hand to my forehead and moan. "With everything going on, I keep forgetting it's Christmas. Mom, we'll have to check if Sandy has any decorations, maybe in some of those boxes in the basement. This'll be Noelle's first Christmas, and she turns seven months on the twenty-fourth. We have to make it special."

She places her hand on my shoulder. "We will. Let's focus on the house right now."

I nod, suddenly feeling overloaded, then look back at Kellan. "Anything you can do would be helpful. It can't hurt to ask around. A small house or apartment close by would be perfect. Then I could come home if there's an emergency or something. I'll search the internet tonight."

"I'm on it." He winks at me, then pushes off the counter. "If you have time, can we walk around the house again and go out back? Then you can tell me what some of your ideas are in more detail."

I glance at Mom. She waves us off. "Go ahead. We'll talk later. I already know your thoughts. Take your time." She wets a clean dish towel and walks over to Noelle to wash off her face and hands. "I'll distract this little munchkin. I don't know for how long. She missed you, Charli."

"I promise, I'll be all yours tonight," I say, caressing Noelle's soft cheek. "Tonight's bath night. Your favorite."

I stand up and turn to say something to Kellan, but I stop. The soft grin gracing his lips could melt anybody's heart. I'm going to find out what's going through his head even if it kills me. It's time to solve this mystery.

A little while later, we walk slowly down the driveway. I've talked his ear off for the last half hour. Now he nods and says, "I agree with you. It has a lot of potential. Adding a second level will be a lot more complicated, expensive, and time consuming. You'll need an engineer."

"I already have somebody in mind. I've worked with her several times and we get along well. She knows I'm a stickler with timelines."

"Well, I look forward to seeing what you whip up with your fancy software." He grins at me, and I shove him playfully.

"Hey, that software saves a lot of time. You have all your fancy machines and tools—I have my software and the ideas in my head." I tap my temple.

We get quiet as we reach his truck. "This is nice," I say just above a whisper with my hands clasped in front of me.

"What is?" He rests his back against the truck and crosses his arms and legs casually, clueless to how sexy he looks. Tingling begins in my chest, as if strings are trying to connect my heart to his. Maybe his heart will allow it someday.

I'm suddenly nervous and start babbling like Noelle. "You… me… talking." I laugh. "We've never interacted like this before and it feels so easy. I like it."

He looks at me and there's warmth in his eyes. And then his phone rings. I hate phones with a passion. He glances at it and huffs.

"Sorry, Charli. I need to take this. It's Dara. I've been waiting for her call." He answers it, still looking at me warmly. "Dara, give me a second."

I take a few steps back with a big smile on my face that I can't control. "It's okay. I'll call you soon. I have your number. Hopefully in a couple days. Stop by if you want to see the house again." *Or me.* "Thanks for coming." I wave and turn around, hoping that he's watching me walk away. I feel like a teenager again, but I don't remember feeling this giddy about any man. Not even Jordan.

After a few steps, I can't fight the urge to look back at him. I turn around and electricity sparks through the air, lighting me up. He's watching me intently and hasn't moved from his spot. His phone hangs at his side. I walk backward until my butt finds the door. As I step inside, he pushes away from the truck and turns to leave. I close the door and collapse against it.

"Oh, boy." Mom's grinning at me like she often does when she thinks she's onto something. "I don't know what I want to know more about—that smile on your face or what happened in Barton this morning. I have a feeling they're two completely different things."

"Okay, okay. How much time do you have?"

"I'm in no rush."

"Good, because I'm a freakin' mess."

18

KELLAN

"Why do I keep finding you and your damn truck in my driveway?" Dara steps to the side to let me in the door, letting the scent of freshly baked something waft out into the fresh air. "Or were you waiting for our Chinese delivery to arrive? How brotherly of you. Thanks for paying."

Once we're in the kitchen, I place the bags on the table and eye the pan of brownies cooling on a rack. I chuckle to myself because she's a baking machine. She's like a hummingbird, where she can eat whatever the hell she wants. Since she has a rotating door for visitors, cake or cookies are always on reserve.

I walk over to the sink to wash my hands diligently. If I don't, I'll hear it from Dara. She's like a drill sergeant with the kids at the daycare and adults when it comes to handwashing.

"Jinxy, Jinxy. Time to eat," she calls out, shaking the bag of cat food. Within seconds, fat Jinx trots in, dragging his belly across the floor like a duster. How does that cat even move?

"You feed him too much. He doesn't have your metabolism."

She chuckles. "He's only spent two of his lives; he still has seven left. He's gotta live a little." He rubs up against her, purring.

"You're seriously mental when it comes to him." Jinx growls at me, then dives into the cardboard bits that are pouring out of the bag.

Placing a beer and plate on my normal spot at the table, she asks, "So what are you overthinking today, and where were you when I called? I thought I heard a woman's voice." Her eyes widen as I reach for a fork. "Holy shit, were you on a date and didn't tell me?"

The fork slips from my hand and clangs to the floor, scaring the shit out of Jinx. She picks it up, pets him to calm him down, throws the fork into the sink, then grabs a clean one from the drawer. I reach for it, but she doesn't let it go. She's waiting for an answer.

"A date? You're crazy! And why do you think I have something on my mind?" *Hmm. Do I want a spring roll or not?* I drop one on my plate. Dara grabs the fried-rice container and scoops out a nice serving. We sit down across the table from each other.

"Again, you were sitting in your truck for longer than what is considered normal. But you're not normal." She giggles to herself while separating her wooden chopsticks. I'm glad she thinks she's funny. "So, tell me. What's up today? Maybe I can help. Pass me the sweet and sour sauce, please." I toss her a pack and it slides off the table. "Jeez." She bends over to pick it up.

"Charli," I mutter.

"Huh?" She sits up quickly in her chair. "Did I hear you correctly?"

"Charli. I was at her house, or should I call it Sandy's house, when you called."

She slaps her hand on the table. Jinx spazzes out again and runs into the living room. Poor guy. "Get the fuck outta here! I like this story already. I knew there'd be more." I roll my eyes. She's way too excited.

"She showed up at my house today, full of sunshine, asking me to help her renovate the house."

"Please tell me you weren't a dick. You said you would, right?"

I sputter my beer, then wipe my mouth. "Do you want to know what happened or not?"

She shoves a spring roll in her mouth. That should keep her quiet for a few seconds anyway. I continue. "Charli showed up glowing, almost jumping out of her skin. I could've watched her all day." I grin, remembering. "She was talking so fast, I thought she was going to pass out. I ended up showing her my house. It felt really good to have her there. Like, *right*, you know? Then we went to see Sandy's house, and she held my hand in front of Tricia."

"You're kidding!"

"No. And I didn't stop her. It's like I have no strength to resist her anymore. And I don't know why."

Dara reaches over and squeezes my hand. "Yes, you do, Kell. We both do. But back up a minute. If she wants you to help her renovate that house, does that mean she'll be around for a while?"

"Yep. Not permanently, though. She said she'd be interested if she got another offer for a show. That was an elbow in the ribs. She still has a house a couple hours away. I don't know if she owns or rents it."

"Does that mean her fiancé Dillon will be here too?"

"Jordan."

She snaps her fingers, giggling. "Why can't I remember his damn name? Oh, who cares?"

"That's another thing," I say, waggling the fork between my fingers. "Something happened today when she went to her house in Barton. She told us she's done with the show and made it very clear he won't be involved. And she still wasn't wearing a ring. But… I don't know. If she's engaged, I need to keep it professional."

"There was so much animosity between them, I'm surprised the funeral home didn't start to shake. They have to be through, but then, why doesn't she flat out say it? Of course, if they *are* over, you can go in and save the day. Be patient." She eyes me devilishly.

"I've been patient since she was eighteen," I groan. Her grin turns upside down. "She wouldn't talk about what happened. Her main focus was the house. But if they are over, her heart doesn't seem to be broken. Happiness radiated off her. Or maybe relief."

"Intriguing. There must be a good story there," she mutters, twirling a chopstick.

"Long story short, she wants to start right away with the renovations. She doesn't want to live at the house when it's in upheaval. That means she needs to find another place to live with Noelle." *Let's see if she thinks of the same house I did.* I load my plate with beef and broccoli.

"Why not Mom's place? It's fully furnished with three bedrooms. It's not fancy, but I'm sure it's in better condition than her house, at least from the way the outside looks."

"It's paradise compared to that place," I say with my mouth full. While we eat, I describe what it's like inside.

"Why would anyone want carpet in their bathroom or even the kitchen?" She shudders. "I can smell the moldiness just thinking about it. Mom's not coming to visit this winter, and no one has booked the house for vacation. We could use the money."

"Would you have space in your daycare for Noelle? I think Tricia would take her a couple of days, so it wouldn't be all week. Charli wants to be hands-on and I'm sure she'll be on-site every day."

"Of course. The kids would be thrilled to have a baby in the house. Did she ask you about the daycare?"

"No. I don't even know if she knows you run one. I offered to ask around about a house, but I already knew I would offer Mom's place if you agreed. I didn't want to mention it until I talked to you first."

"Oh, did you now?" She nods her head. "You're being awfully nice."

"Shut up." I search around for something to throw at her and I only come up with food. She'd kill me.

"You know, we haven't talked about Noelle. Charli is basically her mother now. You usually avoid dating women with children, so I'm wondering what you're thinking about that. And don't forget—both their lives have been completely turned upside down. You are thirty-seven. Are you ready to settle down and have a family?"

"I can't believe I'm going to admit this to my sister." I groan. "Every time I see them together, my heart beats a little faster. I can see a future with them both. I want it all." I scrub my hands over my face. "One day, I want to go home and find them waiting for me as a family. Noelle standing next to Charli, holding her hand, and Charli's other hand resting on a baby bump. *Our baby*. Is that too far out of reach?"

Dara's looking at me with a warm expression, her head cocked to the side. "Why is it so hard to say that to me? Because you're a man? It means you're human and have a heart. If you've been in love with her all these years, then of course you're going to feel this way. And it's *okay* that you do." She puts her chopsticks on her plate and grins at me. "You should invite her to my Christmas party next weekend. Let her mingle with people from Margo Grove. Try to be around her in a social setting... when you're together, not work related. Let her see the awesome, amazing person you are. Life doesn't have to be about work all the time. If she's single again, go for it. What do you have to lose? Don't let somebody else scoop her up."

"What if she finds out somehow that I was at the accident?"

She grunts. "There wouldn't be a 'what if' if you'd tell her yourself. The longer you wait, the angrier or more disappointed she'll be. And it's not just her. It's Tricia too."

I nod and throw my napkin on my empty plate. "I know." Time to change the subject. "Let's open our fortune cookies."

She tosses me one. "I bet mine's better."

"Then trade."

"No way!" Laughing, we pull them out of their wrappers.

"Let's do it at the same time, like we used to," I suggest.

We break them open like it's a competition. She raises her fist with the little white paper in it. "Me first." She reads it and drops her head back. "You will be hungry again in one hour."

"That pretty much sums you up. You can eat some brownies."

"That's utter bullshit." She tosses it on her plate. "Your turn."

I unfold it and read it aloud. "You will soon gain something you've always wanted."

"I told you! I can't wait to see how this all ends up."

Me too.

19

CHARLI

"You, young lady, need a bath. You're a little stinker." I told Mom we could talk more after Noelle goes to sleep. A six-month-old is a real distraction when you're trying to have a serious conversation. Especially one that will take more than five minutes.

Mom sleeps at the house less and less, but tonight she agreed to stay so we could talk. I told her after the funeral that I needed to learn to be on my own with Noelle. She's now my responsibility. Forevermore part of my life. And I'm okay with that. More than okay.

I balance Noelle on my hip and test the water to make sure it's not too hot. "It's perfect. You ready?" She squeals. I'm amazed at how much she loves baths. She splashes the water as soon as she touches it, getting me wet along with her. I should take her to swimming lessons. Mom comes around the corner with her phone and snaps some pictures.

After a fun bath, Noelle falls asleep quickly. I tuck her in her crib, then Mom and I retire to the living room. I place a bottle of white wine and glasses next to the baby monitor on the table. I was going to stay up late to work on plans for the house, but I'm bone tired. I haven't had time to set up my laptop and monitor in the guest bedroom. I have barely enough energy to chat with Mom.

She sits near me in a cross-legged position like one of her yoga poses. I hope I'm as flexible as she is when I'm her age. Even when she stays here, she gets up early and does her yoga routine. I prop my legs on the table and, with that refreshing wine in hand, let my head drop back on the couch.

"Charli, talk to me," Mom says, tapping my thigh. "What happened today in Barton? No short versions. Give me the details so I'm not wondering what's going on every time you're sad or quiet. Sandy wasn't the only quiet one these last few years."

My head shoots up and my blood boils. "That's not fair. I'm nothing like her."

"That's true, but you haven't been honest with me either. It's easy to keep things to yourself when you're at a distance. We used to be close, and you used to tell me everything... well, almost everything." She sips her wine, then places it on a coaster.

"I was—I *am* embarrassed," I confess, my voice louder than it should be. I cover my mouth and sit up straight.

"Why?"

"Because I wasn't as successful as everyone thought. The show was popular because Jordan and I were a couple. Then they wouldn't let me utilize my professional skills; I couldn't work on the site. I basically had to look pretty and pretend that Jordan and I were the masterminds behind everything. Oh, and be madly in love. If that's what we were, then love is overrated." I shake my head.

"It killed me that Dad died before he could see the first house we finished. Now I'm so thankful he didn't. I wanted to make him proud after all the support he gave me. It's because of him that I was excellent at my job."

"You still are. Never doubt that. Now that you're free of

your contract, you can find something new or go back into your own business."

I nod several times, biting on a fingernail. I finally removed the acrylics after Kellan left. My nails are so damaged and they look horrible. I take a deep breath and blow it out.

"When I got home this morning, I found Jordan screwing one of the producers."

She gasps. I can't look at her. "That little shit."

A tiny grin escapes me. I love this side of Mom. Somebody hurts her kids, and she is ready for battle.

"I'm so sorry, Charli."

"I'm not," bursts out of me. "It's the best thing that could've happened. That one stupid move from him gave me a way out. Let me just say, the photos I took are what got me out of my contract. Or they will, anyway."

Mom shakes her head. "I still don't get it. I thought you were happy with Jordan. You had the fairytale romance. He proposed to you on TV."

"We were happy until the show became popular. After that, money and his ego were all that mattered. As long as the money's coming in, he'll do whatever the producers want. He's basically a sell-out. So not only did I have to look like a prostitute to make the producers happy, I had to fake loving him too. But that's all done."

"Thank heaven. It's nice to see you as your natural self. You know, without all the makeup and your interesting wardrobe." She hides a smile by taking a sip of wine.

"Every single piece of clothing I had to wear on that show should be set on fire." She lets out a laugh in agreement. "And I wish I could do it personally."

"I assumed that's what you wanted at the time," she says, shrugging her shoulders.

"Mom, please. Did I ever dress like that in the past?"

"No."

I rest my elbow on the back of the couch and prop my head up on my hand. "I like dressing up for a special occasion but not every day. I miss being hands-on at the construction site. You know me—I was the happiest whenever I could help Dad. I wanted to learn everything to enhance my career as an architect. I know the ropes better than anyone I've worked with. Even Jordan."

She unfolds her legs, moves closer to me, and holds my left hand. "Charli, you're only thirty years old. You have so much life ahead of you. You can still do that."

"Yeah, but things are more complicated now. I'm a mother." I throw my hands up. "I have a beautiful six-month-old baby girl. She has to be my priority."

"I understand, but you need to be happy too. The happier you are, the happier Noelle will be. You can sacrifice things, but don't sacrifice yourself or Noelle."

"I know. Everything became clear to me today. I'm meant to renovate this house. It's the least I could do for her. For her giving me Noelle." *Is that my guilt talking?* "I can't explain the urge inside me. I would start tomorrow if I could. And that's why I pulled Kellan into this."

A little smirk tugs at her lips. *Here we go.* The real inquisition is about to start. I'd much rather talk about Kellan than Jordan, but I'll need a second glass of wine for this. I refill our glasses, mine more than hers.

"Don't look at me like that." I point at her smiling face, but can't hide my own.

"You know I have a soft spot for Kellan. He loved your dad and would've done anything for him. Including avoid his youngest daughter." She looks at me from the corner of her eye while straightening her shirt.

"What do you mean, avoid me? Anyway, he did more than *avoid*. He looked so annoyed whenever I was around. There were times when Dad asked him to show me how to do something and he acted like he'd rather jump off a cliff."

"Charli." She sighs. "You are incredibly smart but so clueless too."

"Can you spit out whatever you're trying to say? My brain isn't in the mood for code talk."

"Fine. Let me say one last thing, and then I'll let you go to sleep. He didn't avoid you because he didn't like you. Trust me, it was the opposite. Call it a mother's intuition. Anyone who saw how he looked at you when you weren't looking thought the same thing. I can't say I approved of his tactics, but I think there was a reason behind them. Your dad noticed too, but he didn't get involved." She kisses my forehead, grabs our glasses, and disappears into the kitchen.

I fall onto my side and prop my head on a cushion. Is it possible that he's wanted me all this time? There were those couple of moments that we shared in the past... times when I almost couldn't breathe. There's a constant buzz of electricity in the air when we're together, but I assumed it was tension. Sexual tension? It surely was on my part.

I let my eyes close slowly and find myself smiling as I drift off to sleep.

20

KELLAN

3 Years Ago

"Over here, Kellan." Mickey waves to me from a table in the corner of the diner. He asked me to meet him here this morning. This is unusual. It's been years since we've had breakfast together.

"Hey, Mick. How's it going?" We shake hands, then I sit down across from him.

"Not bad for a Monday. Busy weekend at the Brannon house."

"Oh, yeah? What happened? Big party?" I ask, reading over the menu even though I already know I want a ham and cheese omelet.

"Let's order first." He waves down a waitress. She takes our order and brings our coffees to the table.

He takes a drink, then sets his cup down. "I didn't ask you to meet me here to talk about work," he says. I eye him warily.

"Okay. Is something wrong?" I ask, rubbing my thighs.

"Maybe." His eyes bore into mine.

"What? Just tell me. You're making me nervous."

He clasps his hands on the table. "Right before Charli and Jordan were supposed to drive back home last night, he pulled me aside. He asked me for permission to marry Charli." My stomach lurches. He lifts a finger in my direction. "My point exactly."

Huh? "What do you mean? I didn't say anything."

He arches an amused eyebrow. "You didn't have to. It's commendable that he asked me, but there's something missing in their relationship. I can't quite pinpoint it. She tells me how much she loves him, but I don't know if she's trying to convince me or herself. When you have your own kids, you want to see them marry their soulmate. I want Charli to have a relationship as strong as Tricia and I have. Sandy too."

"So what was your response?"

"Before I could answer, Sandy interrupted us. Then Charli came in the room, ready to leave. He left without an answer."

This is coming from left field. I haven't even met this Jordan guy. I've only heard about him through Mick and Tricia. What little I do know though, I don't like him. But that's jealousy speaking—which I have no right to feel because I'm in a relationship myself. And that makes me a dick. I don't like where this conversation is going.

"I'll be honest, Kellan. I've imagined Charli being with you. Or someone like you."

I lean back in my chair and look away for a second, my jaw set. "Mick, I really don't know what to say. Why are you telling me this?"

"Because I think you've had feelings for Charli for years."

My stomach turns, and I'm second-guessing the omelet. And damn if he isn't watching.

He nods his head and quirks his lips. "The way your face just dropped confirms it, doesn't it?"

I scan the diner to see if I know anybody, like I'm doing

something wrong. In a way, I am. "Mick, I'm with someone. Chelsea lives with me."

He lifts his hands in peace. "I know. I know. Please hear me out, and then we'll never talk about this again if you don't want to. Okay?"

I nod, sweat pouring down my back.

"You can tell me to shut the fuck up and that'll be the end of it. But I want you to be honest with me. You can trust me with anything. We've known each other for a long time. It won't leave this table."

I nod again because my tongue is tied.

"If you'd met Charli somewhere else and you weren't my partner, would you have been interested in her?"

Am I really going to say this out loud? If I do, my biggest secret and fantasy will be out in the open, and I won't be able to take it back. And this is Charli's father. He deserves my honesty. I close my eyes.

"Yes." *I love her.* I won't let myself say that out loud.

He nods, a satisfied look on his face. "Thank you for being so loyal, but I hate that it's taken possible happiness from you and from Charli. I see how you look at her when you think no one's watching. And she does it too. It's the way I've looked at Tricia since the minute I met her. She was only twenty-one at the time. We have a ten-year age difference, you know."

"I know." He's told me several times.

"Did you hesitate because of that too?"

"Yes." My quick answer makes me feel like I'm being interrogated by the police.

"I waited until Tricia was twenty-four before I gave in to my heart and asked her out. I couldn't wait any longer. I'm lucky I didn't lose her in between. She thought it was ridiculous that I worried about our age difference."

"But I met Charli when she was a lot younger than twenty-one."

"I know. I respect the hell out of you for that because she

was indeed too young. I can't say I agreed with how you've brushed her off since then, but I know why you did it. The Brannon women are hard to resist." He shakes his head. "Man… Tricia's eyes."

I chuckle. It's funny to see his heart on his sleeve. Then my insides twist again. Do I think about Chelsea this way? *No.*

"Wait. Does Tricia know about this? About what we're talking about?"

"I didn't tell her Jordan asked me. I plan on doing that after work tonight. I wanted to talk to you first. But a while back, she hinted or wondered about your feelings for Charli. We didn't want to get involved. She'd probably kill me if she knew I was here with you."

This stuns me because I didn't think he withheld anything from her.

"Mick, so what do you want? Are you asking me to break Jordan and Charli up or something? That's when I'll definitely tell you to shut the fuck up."

He roars in laughter, causing customers to look our way. "No. I wish the circumstances were different, and I wish I'd said something sooner. Or I wish you would've talked to me about it. But I guess it's too late."

Those words cut me like a knife. *Too late.*

"I didn't want to risk something going wrong. You've given me so much, and I couldn't live with myself if I ruined our friendship. Or lost your trust. But Charli and I are in two different worlds… It wasn't meant to be." The knife slides in deeper, slicing through my heart.

His shoulders sag and he sighs. "I would've given you my blessing. There's no one I would've trusted more with Charli. You're a good man, Kellan. I'm proud of who you've become. Chelsea better make you happy. But if circumstances change, don't hesitate for a second. Promise me you'll go after what you want."

I thought I was happy, but this puts a wrench in everything. All the feelings I've had for Charli have been hidden in the back of my heart. I wasn't expecting them to be released out into the open. But he's waiting for an answer.

"I promise," I say, then I let silence fill the air as I digest what I just agreed to. "Thanks, Mick. This means a lot. I've always wanted to make you proud. I hope you know how much I appreciate you giving me that chance when I was eighteen. You've changed my life. I love you like a father."

"And I love you like a son. Now I'm really going to shut the fuck up because our food's coming. So what's on your schedule for today?" And like a flip of a switch, we move on to something else like nothing unusual happened.

I've been going over our conversation all day, though, imagining how amazing life would be if Charli and I could somehow end up together. I was so worried, and here the whole time, I could've had Mick's blessing. The weight on my chest gets heavier as I realize what I'm thinking.

Guilt pours in because I shouldn't be thinking about this. My heart belongs to Chelsea. Right? We're happy, but after what happened this morning... will that change? I take a couple of deep breaths, then come to a decision. Like I said, it's too late. Charli's in love with someone else and is about to get engaged. I'll cherish everything Mick said to me, but I can't act on it. Maybe this is the closure I needed. Maybe now I can stop wondering what could've been. Maybe now I can move on and forget about her.

One more deep breath.

Who am I kidding?

I'm so lost in my thoughts that I don't hear my phone ringing. When I do, I hit the button on the steering wheel, assuming it's Chelsea. "Hey, Chels."

"Kellan? It's Sandy." Her voice cracks, and I panic. Why is Sandy calling me?

"Sandy, what's the matter?" I pull the car off to the side

of the road. Her whimper comes through the speaker loud and clear. "What's going on?"

"Mom found Dad— She found him... she found him lying on the ground next to his truck in the driveway."

I feel the blood drain from my face. "Is he all right? Did he fall?" He was fine at work today. I didn't notice anything strange. At breakfast, nothing was out of the ordinary other than that bizarre conversation.

"No. I'm so sorry, Kellan. He died from a stroke." She breaks down, sobbing. "There's nothing we could've done."

21

KELLAN

Pfft. Sunnyville's CVS is crowded this morning. Christmas music is blaring overhead. Why is it so loud? I'm not in the mood for this. Shaking my head, I whip out the list of things I need, grab a basket, and wander through the aisles, picking things up. Rubbing alcohol, bandages, Advil, shaving cream, toothpaste, deodorant, Snickers, and Reese's Pieces. A man has his priorities.

I head for the checkout and notice the long line to the register. Swearing under my breath, I pull out my phone and scroll through my emails. A baby starts to cry, but I ignore it. Then it gets louder and louder. I hear a soft voice apologizing to someone.

"Oh my gosh, I left my purse in the car. I'm so sorry," she says in a high-pitched panic. *Charli?* The baby's cry becomes louder. *Noelle?*

I peer past the people in line and see a disheveled Charli at the counter with Noelle bawling her eyes out, her cheeks streaked with tears. Charli's face is as red as a forbidden apple, and her eyes shimmer like she's going to burst into tears too. I shove my phone in my pocket and take long strides over to her, right on time to hear the woman next in line mumble into her phone, "Fucking babies." *Bitch.*

"Can I please go get it?" She looks at the guy behind the counter and then at the line behind her. She doesn't notice me.

He huffs and rolls his eyes. "I guess. Hurry up because there's a line." *Dick.*

"That won't be necessary," I intercept. "Add these items too, and I'll take care of it." I hand him my basket, and Charli whips her head in my direction.

"Kellan," she croaks. "You don't have to do that." Noelle cries out again. Charli closes her eyes and presses her lips together.

"Can we move on here? I have to go to work," the rude woman snaps. It takes everything in me not to tell her where to shove her phone. I get a glimpse of the items in her basket. Condoms and pregnancy tests.

I step between her and Charli. "I want to help you. Take Noelle outside, and I'll be there in a second." She nods and pushes the cart out the door.

The guy rings it up, and I pay. Then I grab the bags and turn around to the bitchy woman. "Have some compassion for other people," I say. "You were a baby once too." I glance at the items in her basket and add, "And if you aren't careful, you'll be the next one in here with a screaming baby. Merry Christmas." Someone behind her snickers, and she clutches the basket close and snarls.

I turn away with a satisfied smile on my face, then walk out the door. When it comes to Charli and Noelle, I'll defend them until my last breath. Noelle's crying guides me to where Charli's car is. When I find them, Charli's walking back and forth, bouncing Noelle in her arms, trying to calm her down.

Once I get close enough, I say, "Pop the trunk." She turns around, pulls the keys from her pocket, and clicks the button. I place all the bags inside and close the lid.

"You're a lifesaver. Thank you."

"Are you okay? Is Noelle sick?"

"I don't know," she groans. "This is the first time she's acted up like this. Maybe she's teething, but I think she's too young. I'll have to ask. She has a doctor's appointment next week for a checkup. She's probably hungry. She hasn't eaten since early this morning. Or maybe her diaper's full. I don't know!" Charli shakes her head. "Now I know what those poor moms feel like when their kids act up in the store and everyone gives them dirty looks and makes nasty comments. Just when I think I'm getting a handle on things, this happens. So mortifying. I don't think I've ever shook or sweat so much."

"Try to ignore those people. You're doing great. You've only had Noelle for a couple of weeks, right?" Her face melts in appreciation, and Noelle quiets down a little bit.

"Yes. Thanks again for your help. Let me put Noelle in her car seat so I can pay you back."

"Don't worry about it. You can buy me a drink one day." That came out of nowhere. The side of her mouth perks up, then she bends over to take care of Noelle.

"Good idea," she responds from inside the car.

"Look, I know you need to go, but I was going to stop by your house today."

She pops her head out of the car, her hair in disarray. She looks beautiful anyway. "Really? Why?"

"I might have a house for you to rent."

"Wow, that was super-fast. I'd invite you over now, but I know you have to work and it'll probably be pretty chaotic in my house."

"Unfortunately, yes. I have a meeting in a little while. But I'd much rather spend the day with you girls."

"*Pfft!* Yeah, right. With a screaming baby? I don't think so. You should be running the other way."

Not an option anymore. The need to be near them and to take care of them is too powerful.

"Are you home tonight? I can stop by after work." I could just call her, but I want to see her. I'm probably making it really obvious.

Noelle starts crying again, and Charli shuts the door. She walks quickly to the other side, almost banging into the cart. I push it out of the way. "Don't worry. I'll put it back."

She opens the driver's door. "Listen, why don't you come over for dinner? If Noelle calms down, I want to work on 3D plans. I can show you my progress and offer you that drink. Send me a message if you can make it," she says quickly, looking back at Noelle. "Oh. You don't have my number. I'll send you a message so you have it. Okay. I have to go before one of us has a mental breakdown."

"Get in your car." I smirk, walking up to her. She slides in, and I close the door. Once she turns the car on, she opens the window. Noelle is in a full-blown fit. My heart clenches for both of them. It's hard to be a single mom, no matter how old the child or how many there are. It makes me think of my mom and what she went through, raising Dara and me alone.

"Thanks, again." She waves, then pulls out of the space and drives off. I don't move right away.

So many damn years wasted, avoiding her. My reasons don't seem so noble anymore. But I can't focus on the past. It is what it is. The last few days have proven how easy it is to be around her. She's laid back, strong, smart, and beautiful. No, she's more than beautiful. Her bright smile blankets your skin with sunshine, leaving you warm even on a chilly day. A sweet angelic face like hers could melt the coldest of hearts.

She smiled at me like that many times, and I brushed it off. I was showing respect for her dad by dismissing her. I shake my head. The magnetic pull is still there, even after all these years. It's time to do something about it.

When I arrive at the office, Jay pounds me with project

timelines, delays, and estimate approvals before I can fill my coffee cup. I'm so far behind because I've been distracted. Pleasantly distracted.

He follows me to my desk, still talking. I lift my hand to stop him. "Thanks for the updates. I know there's a lot going on. But there's another project that's been brought to my attention." I pull my chair closer to the desk.

"Really? Is that why you're smiling so much? Your moods have been all over the place the last few days." That's an interesting way to describe them.

"Yeah, well. You know how Mick's daughter died." He nods. "Turns out his other daughter, Charli, inherited her house in Margo Grove. She wants to renovate it."

"Charli's the one from that show, right? My wife loves it." Jay started working for me after Mick died. He doesn't know the whole history I have with the Brannons. "Would it be for her show?"

"No. Not at all. She's asked me—well, the company—to work with her on it. This is something personal to me, so I want to do whatever we can."

"Do you have any details yet?"

"A few. Only her ideas at this point. I'll be working with Charli to get things moving. She's eager to start right away. She'll be the architect; she's working on the plans already. It won't be a quick fix. The two main things she wants to do are add another level and an extension on the back of the house."

"We're already strapped as it is, Kell. How big is the house?"

"About a thousand square feet. Depending on what she decides, it could double."

He rubs his crinkled forehead, obviously concerned. "We'll have to hire more contractors."

"I know. We'll do what we have to, to make this house as perfect as possible. I have no problem getting my hands dirty with this one. I want to be involved in every single step. Nothing gets past me or Charli."

"Understood. That's what I'm here for. Once you have the details, I'll get the ball rolling."

"Thanks."

I watch him leave my office, then sit back in my chair and stretch. I glance at the picture of Mickey on the wall. He's standing in the middle of the crew at the company's fifteen-year anniversary party. Everyone was devastated when he died. He touched so many lives. I wasn't even sure I had it in me to keep the company running without him. Going into the office every day, knowing he'd never be there again... It was one of the hardest things I've ever had to do.

Tricia helped me get out of my head. She convinced me I could do anything because Mick had believed and trusted in me to be his partner. I don't know how many times I picked up the phone to ask him a question or to get his advice on a project. There are still moments when I wonder how he'd handle a situation.

It's true what I said to Jay. I will make sure this house turns out exactly the way Charli wants it. Even if it takes longer than planned. Maybe I can entice her to stay here and not move back to Barton.

I start sifting through the stack of files Jay left me. My phone chirps and vibrates, and I have to search for it through the mess on my desk. My chest warms when I see a message from Charli.

Charli: Hi! Now you have my number. Noelle fell asleep in the car and then ate like a champ when we got home. She's a happy camper now. Phew. Dinner tonight? 6:30?

That's a little early for me, but I'll figure out a way to get there on time. Usually I'm very diligent when it comes to work. But for her, I'll risk it. Time to take advantage of the people who work for me instead of being my usual control freak self.

> **Me:** Are you sure you want me to have your number? I might start spamming you.

I wait to see if she's online. Bubbles appear, and I grin.

> **Charli**: Mom seems to approve of you, so I'll take my chances. Please don't turn into the old Kellan. You're more fun. 6:30?

> **Me**: The old Kellan left a couple of weeks ago and hasn't been back. He might pop up when he's working, but you can kick his ass out the door if he bothers you.

> **Charli**: Good to know. I think he made a short appearance last night at my house. So, 6:30?

> **Me**: I confess. He did.

> **Me**: Glad to hear Noelle is better. See you at 6:30.

> **Charli**: Looking forward to it.

> **Me**: Me too. I'll bring some beer or wine and some milk for Noelle.

> **Charli**: Lol. Be careful, she might steal your heart.

I want to say she already has. They both have. It's been a while since I've been excited about something that's not work related. I remind myself that this isn't a date. But I'll do anything to spend time with her... even if it's platonic.

But if I have it my way, it'll be a lot more. Soon.

Shit! I'm nervous as fuck. Since when? Only Charli has the power to do that. Is it weird that I went to Target to buy a toy for Noelle? And that I wrapped it? Is she going to think I'm kissing her ass or becoming a sap? Well, I'm about to find out. I press the doorbell.

Several seconds pass with no response. I press it again.

"I'm coming," Charli calls. Then the door swings open. "Hi. I'm sorry!" She's winded with rosy cheeks. I can't imagine why her TV show thought she looked better with all that makeup they had her wear. Her natural look is so much more attractive.

"No problem. It gave me a few seconds to relax."

"I was in the middle of changing Noelle's diaper. Never a quiet moment around here."

Well, that went over her head.

Rattle. Ding dong. Zap. Zing. Noelle's giggles come from somewhere in the house. Charli laughs. "She's in a good mood. Come in, please." She steps to the side, and I squeeze through.

I inhale deeply. "It smells great in here."

"Thanks. Better than the musty smell. I've been airing out the house as much as possible since the weather has been so nice. Lasagna's on the menu. I hope that's okay."

I lift the bag with the wine in it. "I brought bottles of white and red. I wasn't sure which you preferred."

"Any wine's my best friend lately. Thank you."

I show her the bag with Noelle's toy. "I brought a little present for Noelle too."

Her eyes widen. "No, you didn't. That was so not necessary but *incredibly* sweet." I pull it out of the bag, and she gushes more. "It's even wrapped! Let's go watch her open it."

I follow her into the living room, placing the wine on the coffee table. "So that's where all the noise is coming from." Noelle's in some kind of activity seat next to the couch.

"She loves bouncing around in that thing. There were a bunch of toys and things like this already here when we brought her home after the accident. It keeps her in one place. I'm a bit nervous for when she starts crawling. She's going to be all over the house. I guess I have some time before that. At least that's what they tell me." She lifts Noelle out of the seat. "Let's sit on the couch."

She settles the baby with her back against the cushions, then Charli and I sit on either side of her so she won't fall off. I hold the gift out in front of her. Her hands reach out instantly. I rip off a little piece of the paper so she sees what to do. It takes a while. Eventually, Charli opens it and hands it to Noelle, who lifts it up and shakes it.

Charli reads the label. "It's a *Sassy Shower Bath Ball*." She turns over the packaging to read the description. "Wow. This is perfect. Noelle loves the water, so she'll love this. I can't wait to try it out. Thank you." She rubs my knee. "You're so thoughtful." I place my hand on top of hers and gently squeeze it, enjoying every second.

"She's a part of you now, so I couldn't come here empty-handed. I heard you say she loves to take baths."

She leans her head to the side and makes that same face I've seen a few times now. Like her chest is expanding or she's melting because of something nice that I did or said. The only reason I can identify this look is because I get the same feeling when I see her happy, when she laughs, or when she looks at Noelle when she does something sweet.

Finally, she pulls her hand away and stands up. "Okay, let's take her seat to the hall so she can watch us in the kitchen. It's too narrow in there for this big contraption. Would you bring her?"

"Sure." I twist on the sofa and pull Noelle to me, then stand up. She's light as a feather. She claps her hands and flashes me a big toothless smile. I take a few steps, then stop when I see Charli. She's bent over the baby seat and her chest is on full display. Her black V-neck shirt hangs open and her red bra frames the perfect cleavage. My imagination takes off in the wrong direction at the wrong time. With full willpower, I aim my focus on Noelle's runny nose and think of a cold shower. *Speaking of.*

"Charli, I hate to ask this, but would you mind if I took a quick shower? I didn't have time to go home before I came here. I was outside most of the afternoon." She stands up and from the corner of my eye, I see her readjust her shirt.

"As long as you don't mind carpeted bathroom floors that smell like mildew and tiles that are falling off the wall." She smirks when I look at her. "But y'know…" Her flirty gaze drifts up and down my body, making heat thrum through my veins. "You look pretty good to me."

I laugh. "You're only saying that because I brought wine and you want me to help with this house." I waggle my eyebrows. "You don't have to butter me up."

"Think what you want, but we both know it's not true."

Her eyes hold mine. This is a side of her I didn't expect. I'm not complaining, but I can't say I'm not confused.

I break eye contact. "I have clean clothes in my truck. Let me go get them." I bend over, and together we stuff Noelle's pudgy legs through the holes in the bouncy seat. Noelle squirms a little and holds out her hands to me as if she wants me to pick her up again. Charli props her hands on her hips.

"Look at her… one little present, and she's hooked on you already."

"And here I thought it was my personality." I laugh, holding my hand over my heart.

"Nah, she knows what she wants when she sees it. Like all the Brannon women do."

Damn! She's not getting away with that. "So do I." My gaze holds hers this time, then her cheeks turn a pretty pink.

Funny… I flirt with her, and she gets nervous. She looks away, twisting her necklace back and forth. Then glances at her watch. It hasn't been often that I've seen her bashful or flustered. Not since her prom night, at least.

From the time she was young, Charli has radiated confidence and knew what she wanted. Her dream was to become an architect and an interior designer, and she accomplished that by graduating at the top of her classes. She'll probably teach me a thing or two when we work together.

She gives me a shove toward the door. "Get your butt in gear. The lasagna should be ready in about twenty minutes."

22

CHARLI

I wait for the front door to click shut before I exhale. Holy hell, does that man ignite something in me. I didn't intend to flirt so directly, but the thought of him in my shower... perfectly naked... where I shower... the water kissing every beautiful muscle on his body... Then my imagination goes further, both of us showering together. Him standing behind me, lathering up my body with soap, my head resting back on his shoulder, his hands caressing my swollen, sensitive breasts, feeling him hard against me.

It's really hot in here all of a sudden. I shake out my shirt to cool myself off.

His truck door slams shut, and I rush over to Noelle, hoping he doesn't see me all flustered. The door opens, and he walks in with a small bag in his hands.

"So come with me. You'll need to use the bathroom in my bedroom because the shower doesn't work properly in the guest bathroom. Let me get you a towel too," I say as he follows me to my room. I stop short once we walk through the door. "Wait! I need to check if the bathroom is clean. Give me a second."

"It's okay. I don't mind."

"Well, I do. Just give me a second." After seeing his house so spotless, I rush into the bathroom and look around. My birth control pack lies on the sink. A purple bra hangs from a towel hook, and a box of tampons and some panty liners are on the back of the toilet. I scoop it all up and toss the whole mess into the cabinet under the sink. Then I grab a clean towel and do another quick once-over. This bathroom is so hideous, it's like someone burned scrambled eggs and threw them against the wall. I sigh. There's nothing else I can do to make it nicer.

"Noelle is crying. Should I go to her?" he asks from the bedroom door. Isn't he sweet? Jordan wouldn't go near her. He complained about every noise that came out of her body.

"Nope. The bathroom's all yours. Here's a towel. It's a bit chilly in there because the heat is wacky. I only have feminine body wash. I hope you don't mind."

"Not at all. I like the way you smell," he says with a velvety voice. Butterflies fight over him in my stomach. If I attack him before the night is over, it's all his fault.

Noelle whines again, and I look at my watch. "Only ten minutes left before the lasagna's done."

"I'm on it. See you in a few minutes."

I smile but don't move. What if he isn't flirting, and I think he is? That would be so embarrassing. But I was flirting too. Is this the right time and place when Noelle's here? Would that be considered wrong? Shouldn't I have thought of that before I invited him over? My intent was all business, but once he got here looking like heaven sent him... that became a secondary thought. But romance should be at the bottom of my priority list. *Damn it, Charli! You're both adults.*

He clears his throat. "Is there something else?"

"What?" I shake my head. "Um. No. Why?"

"You can stay in the bedroom if you're worried I'll steal something, but we're running out of time before the food is ready." Laugh lines form around his eyes.

"Oh. Sorry. Yell if you need anything." I close the bedroom door and smack my forehead with my palm several times. *What the hell was that about?* "I might need something harder than wine tonight," I mumble as I walk over to Noelle. She quiets down when she sees me.

I kneel close to her. "Want to watch me make a fool of myself tonight?"

"Bababa."

"Does that mean yes? I should make you some popcorn—you're gonna have a front row seat." I kiss her forehead, then walk into the kitchen.

I peek into the oven and am relieved that dinner isn't burned. A few more minutes yet. What else needs to be done? Oh! The wine. Where did he put those bottles he brought? I snatch them off the coffee table in the living room. The white is warm, so I place it in the refrigerator and take out one of mine. I grab some wine glasses and place them on the set table along with both bottles.

He's not done yet, so I turn off the oven and let the lasagna rest inside. "What do you want to eat tonight?" I ask Noelle, opening a cabinet where the baby food is stashed. "How about some top-of-the-line pureed organic spaghetti Bolognese? Pasta just like we're having. But no wine, young lady." *Zing. Ding.* I take out a jar and twist off the cap, catching a whiff of it. *Gag.* Why do we feed them this shit? I place the jar in the baby food warmer on the counter.

"I guess that's a yes," Kellan says from behind me. I jump, then turn around. "Sorry. I seem to do that to you. Sneak up behind you after I've taken a shower."

"It's okay. I'm getting used to it. Take a seat. I hope you don't mind sitting on one side of the highchair like you did the other day. Other day? That was yesterday! Ignore me. I'm losing my da—mind." No, I'm distracted by the tight white T-shirt that shows off his solid biceps and those low-hanging jeans that outline his trim abs.

He turns around and lifts Noelle out of the seat. He rests her little butt on his bent arm and holds onto her hand. There's something so sexy about a large man holding a baby. Her cute body is so tiny next to his broad shoulders and muscular chest.

"Do you want to sit next to me? I smell like lavender just like your mom." *Mom.* It's still weird to hear that.

She nods her head like she understands him. I'm melting for so many reasons right now.

"You can put her in the highchair if you want. Dinner's ready." I watch as he walks over to the table. Instead of putting her in the chair, he sits down and holds her on his lap, facing me. He bounces her lightly, and she starts laughing. "I'm glad I didn't feed her yet. She'd spit that right up. I've learned by experience."

"Lucky me." He laughs. "I hung my wet towel over the shower rod to dry."

"Thanks. Hopefully it won't pull the rod off the wall. I'm waiting for something to break every time I'm in there."

"Oh, don't worry. We'll make this house look beautiful." *We will?* "Won't we?" he says in Noelle's ear. She giggles. I'd have the same reaction, if not more, if he were whispering in my ear.

"How do you know? You haven't seen my plans yet."

"You make all the houses you touch beautiful. I have no doubt this place will be amazing when it's done. So much so that I don't think you'll want to sell it." I'm not so sure about that. "Your dad bragged about your work all the time. I think he showed me every house you designed, in and out. And I'll confess, I watched a lot of your shows."

"Really? You watched my show? You don't seem like the type."

"I'm usually not, but I will if there's someone I want to see."

I never could read his face before, but now it shows every shade and every thought. I love it.

Resting my elbows on the countertop, I say, "See? This is the Kellan I like. Flirty, funny, open, positive, friendly eyes, eyebrows not stuck together…"

"Okay, okay. I get the point." His lips tug up at the corners.

"Did Dad really do that? Show you the houses I designed?"

"Yes. He was really proud of you and knew you'd go far. He spoke about you all the time in front of the crew." Hearing this almost makes me cry. I miss him so much, but I don't want to put a damper on this night.

The sensor light on the warmer turns off, alerting me the food is ready. I take the jar out and bring it to the table. "Okay, white wine or red?" I ask Kellan. Noelle lets out a squeal when she sees me stirring her food.

He stands up, puts her in the highchair, and straps her in. "Where's your corkscrew?" he asks, walking over to the drawers. "I'll take care of the wine; you take care of the lasagna. Sound good?"

"Perfect." I must be dreaming.

I open the drawer it's in, and the handle falls off. I burst out laughing. "Do you see what I mean? Falling apart." I toss the handle on the counter. He takes the corkscrew and walks to the table. Gingerly, I open the oven door, worried it will fall off too.

"That looks delicious. I'm starving. It was a hectic day so I hardly ate," he compliments when I place the dish on the table. "Red or white?"

"White for me, but feel free to open both." I watch him unscrew the corks and realize he's left-handed. I'm surprised I haven't noticed that before. *That's because your eyes are glued to his ass all the time.* "You'd better eat before you drink that wine," I joke. "I don't want you getting drunk on me. Even though it'd be interesting to see. You've always been too serious. It's nice to see you so relaxed. I saw it from afar when you were around your work buddies and Dad, but never with me. Why is that?"

He doesn't answer, just tweaks an eyebrow. Noelle smacks her hands on the chair tray so loud that we both twitch.

"Whoa! Somebody's hungry."

Interrupted again!

Kellan holds out my glass. "Here you go."

I take the wine. "Thanks."

He lifts his glass of red. "To new beginnings, in more ways than one."

"To new beginnings," I echo. We clink our glasses and sip. *Nice, loaded statement. Care to explain it?*

"Come on, let's sit down so we can finally eat."

Kellan serves us big portions while I feed Noelle. There is no stress with him here. We're like a well-oiled machine, but we haven't done this before.

I pull a napkin from the holder and wipe my mouth. "How is it you're so good with kids? Do you have some that I'm not aware of?"

"Not hardly," he says dryly. "Blame Dara. She's always loved kids, made a fortune from babysitting, and now she runs a small daycare out of her house. She insisted that I learn how to take care of kids so my future wife would love me even more." *I'll have to thank Dara someday.* "I remember, we agreed —no, she forced me to watch our friends' two kids for the weekend. One was about Noelle's age at the time. I learned how to change diapers, feed them, play with them... I was exhausted by the end of that weekend. My clothes were so disgusting, I was tempted to toss them."

I laugh at the expression on his face.

"A lot of my friends have kids," he continues. "Plus, with Dara having a daycare, I'm around her kids a lot because I'm her handyman. I've become pretty close with one little boy." He tells me about Timmy while I finish feeding Noelle.

"He's lucky to have you as a friend. That's sweet that you bought him a tool belt. You can bet Noelle will be getting one as soon as she's old enough."

"I went on a couple dates with Timmy's mom a while back. It didn't work out. It's hard to date a woman with kids because... Well, if we don't work out, I don't want to be seen as a father figure and then end up leaving. I know what it's like when your dad runs out on the family. I'd have to have a really strong connection with the woman to date her."

"Thanks for the warning," I snarl, looking away from him. Does he not realize how that sounded? Is it his way of saying that nothing will happen between us because I have a child now? Was I imagining the electricity in the air, the flirting, and heated stares between us? Why do I suddenly feel like someone punched me in the gut and the lasagna is about to come back up? Well, screw that. Noelle and I are a package deal. If a guy doesn't like it, screw him. And that includes Kellan.

He reaches over and captures my hand. "Charli, that—"

Noelle squirms in her chair and bangs her sippy cup on the tray, pulling me back to earth. Kellan laughs and I pull my hand away.

"You've got quite the arm," he jokes with her. She bangs it again, smiling so big I can hardly see her eyes. It warms my heart anyway.

"How's the lasagna?" I ask, suddenly feeling mellow.

"Delicious. Speaking of daycare and all that, do you want to know about the house that's up for rent?"

"Oh my gosh. I totally forgot. I'm enjoying your company so much." *Was enjoying.* "So tell me."

I just need to forget about him naked in the shower and all those other fantasies. It's not happening. I rest my chin on my propped up folded hands.

"When my mom moved to Florida years ago, she didn't sell the house. It was paid off, so we convinced her to renovate it and use it as a vacation rental or for whenever she came for a visit. It's fully furnished, and no one's renting it right now. You're welcome to go see it if you want."

That grabs my attention and perks me back up. "Wow. That'd be amazing. After all the years our families knew each other, I was never at your house. I forget sometimes that you grew up here."

"Look at it and then make a decision."

"You see the condition of this place. The only reason I'm staying here is because Noelle is familiar with it and I know it won't be like this for much longer. It's made me appreciate what I have much more."

He nods. "Also, Dara has a spot free for another child if you're interested. Then you'd be all set with someone to watch Noelle and a temporary place to live. After I left here last night, I went straight to Dara's house to talk to her about it."

"And she's okay with it?"

"Of course. She was excited about having a baby in the group. The other kids will be thrilled. And don't worry, Dara is awesome at her job."

"Wow. I can't believe you would do this for us."

"It's the least I could do. Your family has given me so much. I wouldn't be where I am today without Mickey and Tricia. This gives me a chance to give it back."

So that's all this is. Payback. What a fucking letdown. Well, since it's business, I have to take it.

"When can I see the house and talk to Dara?"

"We could show you tomorrow night if you want. Bring Tricia along."

"Wow, this is all happening so fast. I really need to get my butt in gear with this house. I only worked for about an hour today," I admit, massaging my temples.

"You can show me what you have after Noelle goes to sleep. Or should I leave before then?" He lifts his glass.

"You can sta—" In slow motion, I watch as Noelle flails her right arm, tossing her sippy cup. It hits the stem of Kellan's wine glass just as he's taking a sip, spilling the red wine down his clean white shirt. *Oh, shit!* I shoot up off the chair and grab some paper towels. "I'm so sorry." I stop short because he's laughing and babbling to Noelle about what happened. He's so calm.

"What happened here? Did you want to tell me something?" he says to her, pulling his wine-stained shirt away from his chest. She flashes him a sauce-stained smile as if she's saying sorry. My heart squeezes so hard I can barely breathe. Can I picture us as a family one day? *Yes.* Are Noelle and I excluded from his no-dating-single-moms rule? Why would we be?

I turn around because tears are prickling. I'm so stupid, and something else that I can't pinpoint is pulling on my heart.

His chair moves and I look back at him. "I guess this is a work shirt now," he jokes.

My eyes zone in on the wine spot right on the bulge of his jeans. I'm jealous of the wine. Holy heatwave. *Think of something else, like stepping on a nail with your bare foot.* "Oh no. It's on your jeans too. Are they new?"

"The T-shirt is, but don't worry about it. I have a million just like it. And the jeans are old." He waves it off like it's no big deal. "Do you mind if I take off my shirt and put some salt on it?"

"No, not at all. I have a box in a cabinet somewhere." I'm a blabbering idiot. My heart is pounding for no damn reason as I shuffle through the cabinet, knocking shit over. *Get a grip.* "Found some," I say, turning around with my hand up in the air, shaking the box of salt in front of Kellan's half-naked body. Then the box slips from my grip and lands on the floor, shooting salt everywhere. I'm pretty sure my chin just hit the ground and my tongue is hanging out like a dog's, dragging through the salt. I kneel down but my eyes trace from his deep V, up his defined six-pack, to his tight pecs, shiny with a hint of wine, then to his Adam's apple that's bobbing away. My appraising eyes land on his knowing ones, and I'm speechless. And I'm screwed because all I want to do is touch him and lick the wine off his chest and he knows it. But I can't do that.

"Do you have a dustpan?" he asks with a devilish grin, sucking my embarrassment out of the air.

And in that moment of silence, a strange but familiar noise comes from Noelle. Her face is bright red, and she's pushing. Really? Now she decides to add salt to the wound and poops her brains out. Any ounce of sexual tension left is out the window now. Especially when the smell makes its way over to us.

"Okay… this is an awkward change in events. Sorry about that." I pinch my nose, and Kellan chuckles.

"Charli, go take care of Noelle. I'll clean up the kitchen. I live on my own; I know what to do."

"What about your shirt?" I ask, picking up Noelle, trying hard not to breathe.

"I'll put whatever salt I can salvage off the floor on it and I'll wear the dirty one home. I might smell."

"Nothing is worse than this little stinkpot in my arms. Say bye-bye."

He leans over and kisses her forehead, then steps away waving his hand in front of his nose.

"Told ya," I simper, and leave the kitchen. Once I have Noelle on the changing table, I realize she needs a bath. She's a mess. I clean her up as best I can, then wrap her in a towel and carry her to the guest bathroom. At least the bathtub works in there. While the water is running, I put Noelle in her towel on the floor with a couple toys. Then I listen to Kellan moving around the kitchen.

I look at myself in the bathroom mirror. My hair looks like a bird's nest. Frizzy curls frame my face. And shit… is that baby food on my chin? And look at those dark circles under my eyes. Ugh, I need a facial. When? I have no time.

When the tub is filled enough, I lift Noelle and prop her on my hip for a second. Suddenly, something warm and wet works its way through my jeans. I pull her off my hip and watch as she pees in the air. My brain is too slow, and I stand there while she continues to go to the bathroom on the carpet. Like it isn't dirty enough.

"All done," Kellan announces, stepping into the bathroom. "I heard the water running. Here's the ball I bought Noelle."

"Don't come in," I snap. I rush to the toilet and hold Noelle over it for her to finish her business. Can I be any more embarrassed tonight?

"What can I do? Let me help you."

"No. No." I shake my head, taking a very long, calming breath. "Sorry. This is too much for me right now. Can we call it a night?"

"I can watch Noelle so you can get changed."

Once Noelle's in her bath seat, I turn to the sink to wash my hands. His eyes lock with mine in the mirror. A tingle works its way down my spine. "I know you're trying to help but *please* do me this favor. I'm not trying to be a bit—" I bite my tongue. "Please go home. I'm in over my head right now and exhausted from this hellacious day," I mumble, turning off the water. His face drops, and he pushes off the doorframe.

"Charli," he sighs, taking another step into the bathroom.

I turn to face him with my hands raised. "Don't come any closer! There's pee all over me and the carpet. Thank you for tonight, but my brain needs to shut off for a while."

He nods, not happy with my answer, then hands me the toy. I take it from him and give it to Noelle. "Okay," he says.

"I'll talk to Dara tomorrow morning about looking at the house. I'll give you a call or send a message. The lasagna's cooling off on the counter. Don't forget to put it in the refrigerator. I cleaned up the salt and wine too."

"Thanks for your help today. Sorry it ended like this. You're smart to stay away from single moms."

He glances at Noelle happily shaking the ball, then flashes me a forced smile. He waves, and seconds later, I hear the front door close. I lean against the doorframe and let the tears flow.

I'm so confused and utterly exhausted.

23

KELLAN

In a split-second last night, Charli's mood changed from playful to cold. I mean, I guess I understand. The wine glass, the dirty diaper, the bathroom accident—it was a lot. But she didn't have to shut me out. We were getting along great, and next thing I knew, she was cold as ice and practically pushing me out the door.

I called her this morning instead of sending a text about when to meet at the house tonight. That conversation wasn't much better. She was nice but still not herself and ended the call quickly. The tables have turned. I had put a wall between us, and now she's doing it. At least I think that's what's happening.

"Would you stop pacing the living room!" Dara demands, searching through Netflix. "You're making me antsy. Come and watch the *Christmas Chronicles* while we wait. I love this show. Kurt Russell is one sexy Santa."

I roll my eyes. "I'll pass."

She twists on the couch to face me. "Hey, did you invite Charli to my Christmas party? More people are coming than I thought."

"How many?"

She bites her lip, not answering right away. Finally, she says, "Over thirty? I've asked a couple of friends to make some dishes for me. I have to start cooking tomorrow."

"I don't know why you do this to yourself every year. It gets bigger and bigger. I can pick up the alcohol or whatever you need."

"You know how much I love to throw parties. My friends look forward to my Christmas party every year. The weather should be nice and not too cold. People can hang out outside on the deck. Maybe you can help with setting up tables."

"Sure. Whatever you want. I have to work until twelve on Saturday; after that, I'm all yours."

I look out the window and my stomach flutters. "They're here." She turns off the TV and stands up. I let her answer the door.

"Hi, Charli, and you too, you little cutie. Are you already in your jammies?" Dara greets them, shaking Noelle's little foot. Then she embraces Tricia warmly. "Come in."

"Hi, Kellan," Tricia greets me. "This house is adorable. It's like a little cottage. It'd be wonderful if this works out." She steps to the side as if she's willing me to talk to Charli. Dara motions to Tricia and they walk into the dining room.

"How was your day?" I inch toward Charli, feeling like a complete idiot. The cold, weird vibe is still there, and I fucking hate it.

"Not bad. Productive. Mom came over this afternoon so I could work," she explains, bouncing Noelle on her hip. "Thank God Sandy obtained the blueprints. It makes things a lot easier for me. I have the first floor mapped out, including the extension of the kitchen. There are a couple of things I'm not satisfied with, but I'll figure it out. The more I play, the better the house looks."

Noelle extends both arms, but Charli angles her away from me. "Don't bother Kellan." Noelle wiggles in protest.

"She doesn't bother me. Let me hold her while you look around the house."

Reluctantly, she hands her over. "Thanks."

I tickle Noelle and hold her high in the air. She chuckles with her hand in her mouth, her pacifier dangling from her pajama top.

"Be careful. She had dinner not too long ago. Don't say I didn't warn you," Charli snickers. At least I got a chuckle out of her.

"Where do you want to start? Kitchen?"

"I'll be honest, just standing here, I'm already tempted to say yes. It's so much better than Sandy's. Too bad it's dark outside already. But I'm sure it's much brighter in this house with all the white walls and big windows. I feel like I'm in a jungle at Sandy's during the day. I think Noelle would like it better too."

"So, you see the stairs in front of you. There are three bedrooms on the second floor. One bathroom in the hall and one en suite. We can look at that after. To the left is the dining room and kitchen." I motion for her to go ahead of me. Dara and Tricia are still in the kitchen, whispering about something.

"Don't you love it already, Charli?" Tricia beams.

"My house or daycare is a three, maybe four-minute drive away. And you saw that Sandy's house is only about ten minutes from here. You can't beat that. Right?" Dara should have gone into realty with her selling skills.

"The space in the kitchen alone would be nice. Noelle wouldn't have to play in the hallway while I cook," Charli comments.

Noelle grabs her pacifier and tries to put it in my mouth. I shake my head like a goofball. Then she tries it again. When I shake my head again, she mimics me by shaking hers too. We giggle together like we're old pals. Suddenly I feel eyes on me. I glance at the women. Tricia gazes at her granddaughter warmly with a grin on her face. Dara bursts out laughing. And then there's Charli, who doesn't have a face at all. It's still, lacking emotion. She walks up to us and takes Noelle from my arms.

"Let's move on. Noelle needs to go to bed soon." She walks out of the kitchen, toward the living room. Noelle whines and twists to look over Charli's shoulder toward me.

What the fuck? Tricia and Dara watch her leave and then look at me with questioning eyes. I shake my head and shrug my shoulders.

Dara urges us to follow Charli into the living room. She takes the lead after this, and I add to the conversation when needed. By the time we're finished looking at the house, Noelle is in a full-blown fit like she was at the CVS. Tricia takes her from Charli. "Is that all? If yes, I'll go to the car with her."

"I'll be there in a minute, Mom."

"Maybe hurry because she might fall asleep before we get home. Thanks, both of you. See you soon." She blows kisses to Dara and me. Once she's out the door, Charli stands in front of us.

"Thanks for the tour. I'd like to sleep on it one night and then tell you tomorrow. Who should I call?"

"Kellan," Dara says too eagerly. "Even if you don't want to rent the house, you can stop by the daycare to check it out. Oh, wait. I have an idea. I'm having a Christmas party on Saturday. Why don't you come? Be around some adults, get to know the people in town, lots of yummy food and alcohol. A little Christmas spirit does the body good."

It's hard to say no to Dara when it comes to her love for Christmas. Charli's face lights up and then her smile disappears again.

"I'll let you know. It's very tempting, but I have to see if Mom can babysit. I can't drop everything for a party anymore, among other things. This is my new life." I could've sworn I heard a twang in that comment. Whatever it was, it was aimed straight at me even though she looked at Dara when she said it. "Thanks for the invite and for taking time to show us the house. Have a good night." Again, she looks only at Dara, then leaves like I wasn't even there.

Fuck, that hurt. Now I know what it must've felt like every time I blew her off.

Payback's a bitch.

24

CHARLI

"What was that in there?" Mom presses after Noelle has calmed down. "Why were you so cold toward Kellan? I thought you two were getting along. Didn't you have him over for dinner last night? Did something happen?"

What's with the questions? I squeeze the steering wheel like I'm wringing someone's neck. Whose, I have no idea. But I sure wouldn't mind punching something right now. I blow out a frustrated breath. "I don't want to talk about him right now."

"Charlize!"

Jeez, Mom. What am I, fifteen again? I squeeze the wheel even harder.

"Mother!" I mimic. "Your suggestion that he has feelings for me is a load of crap. Yes, I'm attracted to him more than I should be, but he made it clear last night he wouldn't get involved with me."

"Oh, dear." She sighs. "What did he say?"

"He said he doesn't get involved with single moms. Talk about a smack in the face. Then Noelle pooped her brains out, peed all over me and the bathroom carpet. It was all too much. So what did I do? I closed myself off. Now it's my turn to put up a wall."

I don't say much more during the short ride back, and she doesn't ask.

Mom puts Noelle to bed while I start some laundry in the basement. I'm almost done when she joins me. "Before I go home, I'm going to ask you one thing."

I sigh and look at her, stopping to lean my arm on the machine door. When will the questions end?

"I'm tired, Mom. I really don't have time for this."

"Did he actually say he wouldn't get involved with you? Or was it a general statement?"

"No, he didn't say it directly but why wouldn't it include me? *I am one of those single moms.* I don't have the luxury of running off to go on a date or fall in love. And I'm not going to let just any man be around Noelle. So now, I'm going to keep our relationship platonic and strictly business." I pour detergent into the machine, turn it on, and go back upstairs. She follows me all the way to the kitchen.

"Look at me, Charli." I drop my head and take a deep breath. "Please? Then I'll go home, and you won't hear it from me again. It'll be up to you what you do with it."

With my eyes squeezed shut, I turn around.

"Open your eyes."

"Fine." I open them, and she places her hands on my arms. Her eyes fix on mine, giving me the motherly stare I'm used to.

"Kellan has had feelings for you for as long as I can remember. Yes, he could've handled it a lot better than he did. And maybe now too." My stomach somersaults like a gymnast going for an Olympic gold medal. "I don't know why he didn't act on it. Maybe because he worked for Mickey. He's extremely loyal. I've probably said that already."

I think back to Sandy's wake. Kellan mentioned that Dad

told him to keep guys away from me. Was that true? What if it is—it's still not an excuse.

"He still didn't have to be such an asshole all the time. I've had my fill of assholes."

"Language," she huffs.

"Don't start. Let me be me when Noelle isn't nearby. Maybe his attitude has changed because now he doesn't want me because I have a child. Or maybe he still thinks I'm engaged. If I'm off limits, it doesn't matter how he acts." I cringe as I hear my own words. Nothing makes sense.

Mom shakes her head. "Listen to yourself, Charli. Why didn't you confront him instead of stewing on it? You're adults. And you make it sound like you have a disease because you have Noelle now. That's not being very nice to her. You can't blame her for this situation. Look at how he adores that baby. And how you adore her too. It's pretty obvious you aren't engaged anymore, but you should tell him yourself. And why you haven't told anyone is another issue."

I pull away from her and set some clean bottles on the counter to fix them for tomorrow. This is my life now. I'm not just babysitting someone for a long time. This is permanent. I'm not alone anymore. It's me and Noelle. We're a team, a unit, a *family*. She has no right to question that.

"I love Noelle, Mom. That's not even an issue. And sure, he adores her. But if Kellan has feelings for *me*, he's going to have to convince me of that. Surely that's the least I deserve after how he's treated me for so long." I turn my back to her to work on the bottles again. "And why would I want to get involved with someone anyway, when my life is a complete mess? I can only handle so much stress. And I want to forget about Jordan."

"Dara said she's having a Christmas party on Saturday. Did she mention it to you?"

Here we go. "Yes."

"I can babysit if you want to go. You should socialize a

bit. Get to know people from around here. Especially if you're going to stay."

"Until the house is finished."

"Yes. Th–that's what I meant," she stammers.

"I'll let you know my decision tomorrow. About the party and renting the house."

She rubs my shoulder. "Okay."

"Mom." I turn toward her quickly and hug her tight. "You know I'd be lost without you. I'm sorry for being so pissy. My chest feels so heavy, like I can't breathe. Everything is just... overwhelming, and the pressure on me is building. On Sunday, I felt like I could conquer the world, and now I feel like this, this *fragile woman* who has no idea what to do about anything. I hate these ups and downs. I'm so out of my element."

She rubs my back soothingly. "You'll get through it. I'll help. You're a strong, determined woman, and you've worked your butt off for what you wanted your whole life. But you're dealing with new things now. Don't give up. Give yourself some leeway. I promise it'll get easier. Other fires will pop up as you go, but you'll learn how to put those out too. And I'll always be here for you and Noelle." She leans away from me. "Go to the party. If not for you, do it for your old mom."

I let out a light laugh. "You're not old. You do the firefly pose better than your thirty-year-old yoga teacher."

She shrugs. "Yoga has gotten me through a lot since your dad died. Why do you think I still do it, and even more now after Sandy? Maybe you should try it with me."

"I did, and I made a big mental note to avoid it at all costs," I tease. "I'd rather shoot my nail gun or swing a sledgehammer at something."

She gives me a hug. "You're smiling again, so my job is done here for the day. I'll see myself out."

I kiss her cheek and lean against the doorframe as she

walks away. When she reaches the front door, I call out, "I'll say yes to the house. And the party."

She turns around with a sly smirk. "I know."

And then I'm alone, and the dark, dreary house closes around me, reinforcing why I need to say yes. I hope I don't regret it.

~

I'm on my third cup of coffee, and I still haven't called Kellan. I stare at the phone, then look at the overflowing basket of clean clothes sitting next to me. I don't want to do either one. I crinkle my nose. *Call Kellan.* It's eight thirty. He should be up, maybe even at work already.

Instead of going straight to bed last night, I worked until midnight. Noelle didn't wake up until almost six, blessing me with more sleep than usual. I feel replenished and ready to kick some major ass.

I unlock my phone and search for Kellan's number, then press call. So much for kicking ass. I'm nervous as hell to hear his voice. Then his soothing tone travels through the phone, and my closed-off heart betrays me again.

"Charli, I was just thinking of you," he murmurs. His soft voice almost sounds like he's still in bed. I picture him lying on his side, shirtless, with a crisp white sheet draped below his belly button, revealing a lickable V line. "Charli?"

"I'm—I'm here. Sorry. Sleep—Sleep well?" I cringe in my chair and pretend to choke myself with one hand.

"Not especially."

"Oh. Sorry to hear that. I hope I didn't wake you." I trace my finger around the edge of the coffee cup. Why do I have a feeling it's because of me?

"Nah. I'm about to make another coffee. Since I couldn't sleep, I've been at the office for a while already. I can get more done in an hour when I'm alone than when my team's here anyway. I'm a bit behind."

Is that because of me? Of course not. He had a life before I showed up. *Get over yourself.*

"I won't keep you long then. I want—"

"You sound happier today, so my sleepless night was for nothing." His voice is a quiet monotone. I can't tell if he's annoyed or trying to make a dry joke. "So did you make a decision?"

"Yes. I'd love to rent your house. As soon as possible. I don't know how much longer I can stay in this place when I see what kind of house Noelle and I could be living in. I'm convinced there's a monster living in the basement." His light laugh tickles my ears, making me smile. "It really is perfect for my situation, and the rent's very generous."

"I'm glad to hear it. Your body language and mood last night told me otherwise."

I'm not going to defend myself or apologize. My reasons were valid. *Are* valid.

"How fast can you write up a contract?"

He hesitates. "I guess by the end of the day. Fast enough?"

"Oh, wow!" I jump up from my chair. "Yes. I thought it'd take a few days."

"If you promise to stay in this mood, I'll make it a priority." Finally, there's some amusement in his voice.

"I promise." I flutter my eyelashes. Not that he can see me. *Where's your wall, Charli? Screw the wall!*

"Good. Can you give me your email address? I'll need some information from you."

"Sure. It's c-h-a—"

"You know what? Forget it. I'm not worried about a contract. I know you and your family. There's no one I trust more, besides Dara. Just tell me when you want to move in. We can exchange bank information then. Once we've finalized the projected timelines for the renovation, we can come back to a contract. Since it's furnished and the kitchen has all that you'd need, you shouldn't have to move too much."

"I'd like to take some of Noelle's bedroom furniture with us. Obviously, she needs her crib and the changing table. Oh, and maybe the rocking chair." I rake my hand through my wild hair. "That should be the only bulky stuff. I can take my time transferring other things over, stuff like clothes and food from the cabinets. And whatever else comes to mind."

"If you want, I could have you moved in by tomorrow. I'd like to clean the house beforehand, though. It's been sitting empty for a while."

"You really don't have to do that."

"I'd do anything for you, Charli," he says firmly, like he's making a promise. I close my eyes, imagining his lips caressing the skin under my ear when he says that. How can a man's voice break down walls, and how will I be able to stay away from him? The anger I felt yesterday is gone. I don't know if it disappeared overnight or when he answered the phone.

I have to tell him I'm not engaged. Mom says it's obvious. But what difference would it make if he doesn't get involved with single moms? *He's had feelings for you...* It doesn't look good if people think I'm engaged and I'm openly flirting with Kellan. Total mind fuck.

"Anything, huh?" I tease. "We'll see about that." I can't help the giant smile on my face.

25

KELLAN

Dara and I pull opposite corners of the white sheet and hook them around the edges of the queen-sized mattress.

"Charli called me today," Dara mentions casually.

"And?" I hate making beds with a passion.

"She's coming to the Christmas party." She peeks at me from the corner of her eye.

"That's cool."

She throws a pillow at me. "Give me a break. Don't pretend that your insides aren't getting all gooey. And stop trying to act like Charli's going to be like any other renter we've had in this house. What's with the sullen mood all of a sudden?"

I slip a white pillowcase over the pillow. Dara finishes straightening the bedspread, and I toss the pillow to the head of the bed. "I have to tread lightly. Something's bothering her or making her pull away from me. She still hasn't said anything about Jordan. She sounded better today, but—"

"Stop with the buts. If she's the one, it'll happen. You're both adults. But neither of you are acting like one," she jabs, walking around the bed toward the door. "Flat out ask her if she's still with Jordan. But the chance of that has to be a hundred percent *no*. You two'll be together a lot over the next few months. Let things move forward naturally. You've waited how many years to open your heart to her, and now you're doing it during one of the hardest times of her life. Be patient and help her when she needs it. She needs a friend and someone she can count on. Make sure it's you and not some other idiot."

"Are you calling me an idiot?" I joke.

"If the shoe fits," she says over her shoulder with a cheeky grin as we walk to the next bedroom, which should be Noelle's. It used to be my room. The third one doesn't have enough space for a crib. "She'll be at the Christmas party. Entertain her a bit since she won't know anyone. And if I'm too busy, you can show her the daycare rooms downstairs."

We finish the top floor, then head downstairs and into the living room. Dara's Christmas fetish has shown up here too. "Let's get some of these Christmas decorations up," she says, "because I really need to go. I told you I need to start cooking for the party. You're lucky—I had a little tree and some extra lights at home. I hope we aren't overstepping by decorating without her consent."

"I think she'll love it." I open the box and pull out the tree while Dara sets the tree stand in the corner where we agreed to put it. "We wouldn't be putting up a tree if Noelle could crawl or walk. That would be a disaster in the making. Actually, the whole house would have to be babyproofed."

"Why don't you finish the tree," she suggests, "and I'll put up the garland on the fireplace. Then I'll move onto the stairwell. I have a couple of things for the bathrooms and the dining room too. I already put the candle lights in the windows upstairs. It's too bad I can't be here to see their reaction when they arrive." Her voice gets wistful. "I almost wish they'd wait till nighttime. I would've loved to surprise them when it's dark out and only the Christmas lights on in the house."

"That would be fun," I agree. "But I think Charli wants to get Noelle settled early in the day. She's worried she won't sleep well being in a different house."

"Understandable," she replies. Her efforts at untangling the lights are making things worse. I chuckle. My phone rings on the dining room table. I walk over to get it. My stomach flips.

"Who is it?" Dara calls.

"Charli," I respond.

"Ooh la la."

"Hey there. How are you?" I walk back toward the Christmas tree with Charli on speaker.

"Hi, Charli," Dara says loudly into my phone.

"Hi, Dara. Thanks for letting us move in so quickly. I can't wait."

"No problem. We're almost done here. See you soon. I'll try to stop by tomorrow night."

"Okay. See you tomorrow."

I switch off the speaker. "So, how's it going?" I rest my back against the archway between the hall and the living room.

"Pretty good. I'm trying to pack up some stuff. I was looking at Noelle's furniture. The pieces that I want to take are pretty bulky, and I don't think I can move them myself. Would you mind helping me with that? I mean, you've already done so much. Maybe I could borrow your truck for a few hours."

Of course I'm going to help her. "Char—"

"But if you're too busy, I can rent a U-Haul or something for a day."

"Don't even think it. I was going to meet you here in the morning anyway. I'll go to your house instead. Then we can load the truck with as much as you want. That way, there'll be fewer trips back and forth when you have Noelle with you."

"Are you sure? I really hate asking, but I need to simplify

things. And who knew how quickly I'd find a place to rent. I promise I won't bother you again this week unless it's to talk about the renovations."

"I already told the crew I'd be in late tomorrow." Even though I'm constantly reminded about how much shit I need to do when I'm at the office. My temples throb just thinking about it.

"You're awfully nice for a landlord. Do you provide moving services to all your renters?"

"Nope. Only for ones who have the most alluring turquoise eyes and know how to shoot a nail gun like a sniper."

Dara bursts out laughing next to me, and Charli sounds like she's choking on something.

"You remember that day?" she whispers.

"Every little detail. And not because I lost the game."

"Then why?"

"You know exactly why, don't you?" I provoke her.

"Mmhmm."

I pat myself on the back. One win for me. "Sweet dreams, Charli. See you at eight tomorrow morning."

She needs a friend and someone to rely on. I can do that. It won't be easy because the more I'm with her, the more I want to kiss her, touch her. I won't act on it until she tells me she's through with Jordan, but just dreaming and fantasizing about us together isn't enough anymore.

"You didn't give this house justice. It's even more adorable in the daylight. I love the white siding and the evergreen shutters." Charli turns to me, beaming. Noelle claps her hands like she approves too. "Thank you so much. I can't wait to see the inside again with the light streaming through the windows."

I lift my hand, dangling a key chain from my finger.

"Then let's not waste any time. Here's a sparkling new key for you. This is your home as long as you and Noelle need it. You can do the honors." She takes it from my hand. I hold out my arms. "Give me Noelle so you can open the door."

"Okay." She's bubbling with excitement as she hands Noelle over.

"Want to see your temporary home?" I mutter to Noelle. She pinches my ear once. Does one pinch mean yes or is it two?

Charli unlocks the door and opens it slowly. We step into the foyer, and her eyes go wide. She covers her mouth. "You decorated for Christmas? For us?" She tosses her purse on the couch in the living room before she walks over to the Christmas tree. With her delicate fingers, she gently touches one of the Christmas balls. Then she does the same with the garland on the fireplace.

With her back toward me, she stands still with her head hanging forward, bracing herself against the fireplace with one hand. I observe her and it looks like she's rubbing her eyes. "What's wrong?"

"Give me a minute." She takes a deep breath and shakes out her arms, then turns around. Her eyes glisten with tears. *We messed up.*

"Charli, I'm sorry. Dara was worried that you might not like it. I can take everything down if you want," I offer with concern, walking toward her. "I thought... I mean, since it'll be Noelle's first Christmas—"

Without warning, she wraps herself around me and Noelle, then lays her head on my chest. Her lavender scent infuses my senses, making me light-headed. Maybe I'll plant lavender around my house so it'll smell like her every day. Her body wrapped around us, making us one unit, is all I could ask for. I don't want to let them go. This is exactly what being a family would feel like.

"No one has done something like this or made me... me

and Noelle feel so special," she mumbles against my chest. Does she feel my heart hammering? I squeeze her closer to me and kiss her forehead softly. Noelle plays with Charli's fluffy hair. "Thank you so much. Not just for this. For being patient. For everything. It's hard for me to rely so much on people."

"You're welcome. It's a tough time for you and your mom. There's nothing wrong with asking for help."

"I know. But I'm used to being independent. I don't like being this vulnerable. It's something I'll have to get used to, I guess. And I usually don't cry this much."

"Charli, look at me." Her glistening blues find mine. "I'll always be here for you." She melts into my side with her hand on my chest, then she glances at my lips that are so close to hers. I want to kiss her, but I won't. This is not how I envisioned our first one.

Noelle breaks the moment. "*Ouch!*" Charli leans over and tries to remove the baby's firm grip from her hair. "Let go, you little stinker." Once her hand is free, Charli blows loose strands of hair out of her face. "No pulling hair," she says firmly to Noelle, tapping her nose. Her lips twitch trying to stay serious, but I know she's fighting back a smile.

"So, the Christmas tree…" I say to lighten the conversation because I'm on the brink of laughing.

"Right, let's get to it. You need to get to work."

I grab the tree remote. "Look—you can change the color of the lights to your preference. And you can make it look like a disco. All with a touch of two buttons. Now you have a reminder that it's Christmas."

"And that I need to get some Christmas shopping done," she chortles. "Where did you get all the decorations?"

I switch Noelle to my other arm. "Dara. She practically has her own store at her house. Her Christmas obsession has gotten a little out of control. You should've seen the animated Santa she wanted to bring. I said forget it because it would probably scare Noelle. It scared me. Wait until you see how her house is decorated at the party. Inside and out. *National Lampoon's Christmas Vacation* all the way. She should take out insurance just for her holiday collections."

She locks eyes with mine and smirks. "Who said I was going to the party?"

"One of Santa's elves." Noelle squirms in my arms, then Charli takes her from me.

"They gossip, huh?" She laughs, then says, "I was hesitant to say yes because I get a little shy when I don't know anybody. But it'd be nice to meet new people and speak English instead of baby talk." She kisses Noelle on the cheek. "No offense, little girl."

"Please come, even if it's only for a couple hours. You need to see the daycare too."

She cocks an amused eyebrow. "You don't have to do that."

"Do what?" I say, scratching my jaw, knowing full well what she means.

"Convince me. I already said I'd go. I'm looking forward to seeing you dressed up again. I have a thing for guys who get hot and sweaty from manual labor, but you, in a suit, are pretty impressive. I like seeing the different sides of you."

She is definitely not engaged. Game on.

"Well, if you like me sweaty, let's unload my truck."

26

CHARLI

I had to go shopping this week to buy an outfit and shoes for Dara's party. I only packed the essentials when I left the house in Barton, not partywear.

"So how do I look?" I spin around in front of Mom and Noelle. I hang the short black leather jacket off my finger, then toss it over my bare shoulder, pretending to be a model. "I hope I don't freeze my butt off. But that's what the jacket's for."

"Beautiful. That jumpsuit was made for you. I like that the top is red and the bottom is black. It makes your legs look even longer. And your heels aren't over the top. This outfit is *you*, not the crazy ones you had to wear on the show."

"Please don't remind me, but thanks."

She grins and pushes me toward the door. "Okay, no more dilly-dallying. Go have some adult fun. Noelle and I have some exciting plans, and you're not invited." On cue, Noelle yawns. "Granted, she won't be up for very long."

"I know you want to watch *It's a Wonderful Life* with a bowl of popcorn. It's so much cozier here than at Sandy's house. Maybe I'll be home in time to watch the end with you. It's my favorite part." I slip my arms into the jacket and pull it on.

"I surely hope not. Stay out and have fun. Let loose. I'm here and Noelle will be fine. And no drinking and driving." She points her finger at me like I'm a teenager going to a party.

"Okay, okay." Bending over, I kiss Noelle's cheek and then Mom's. "I feel like I'm in high school. You know, I still hate walking into a room full of strangers. How was I able to be in front of a camera every week? You'd think I'd be over it by now." I grab my new purse and keys.

"Don't forget the bottle of champagne," Mom reminds me.

"Oh, right! Thanks. That would've sucked." I scurry to the kitchen to grab it off the counter, then back to the front door. "Okay. I'm going. Wish me luck."

"Watch out for that silly stuff called mistletoe. It's known to make people kiss or something like that," she says, a little chuckle escaping her.

Wishful thinking.

A little while later, I'm standing in front of Dara's house, enjoying the warmth emanating from the lights on her house and bushes. Her electric bill must be astronomical. A smiling Santa Claus, who looks like he's been hitting the mulled wine, stands in the middle of the front lawn next to his sleigh. Reindeer are scattered around like they're eating the grass. A bunch of elves are building a snowman. All are brightly lit.

It might be over the top, but it's beautiful. A car stops in front of the house. Party guests, I guess. Then a camera flashes and I hear kids' voices. I laugh as the car drives away. Mom and Dad used to drive us around to look at decorated houses too.

I approach the front door with the champagne in my right hand, patting down my outfit with the other. Christmas music drifts through a slightly open window near the porch. Through the picture window, I can see a couple of people standing near a large Christmas tree. I ring the doorbell, then step back, begging my nerves to calm down.

Maybe I should've said yes to Kellan when he offered to drive me to the party. I wanted to, but I don't want to rely on him to take me home. Relying on him is getting too easy anyway. That wall I'm trying to build only gets up to my knees before it crashes back down. But no matter how attracted I am to him, I still need to guard myself.

I haven't seen him since the day he helped me move in. In some ways, I'm glad. I need to focus on Sandy's house, get into a rhythm with Noelle, and find some time for myself. When he's around, my brain short-circuits and I'm distracted by his woodsy, clean scent and pure vigor. And when he sweeps those sky-blue eyes over me, I'm ready to combust. I'm not sure I hide it well.

I'm not going to put Noelle in daycare until January. Mom offered to come every day, but I told her to go off with her friends and get back into her old routine. I know she misses her yoga classes and her other activities. Just like me, she's dropped everything since Sandy died. She needs her life back too.

The door swings open. "Charli, you're here! You look gorgeous!" Dara exclaims. "Come in. Oh, you brought champagne. I love you even more." She takes it, and I step through the door.

Of course, a bunch of people turn to see who's arrived. It's like being the new kid in class. My face gets warm. I probably look like I wore too much blush. Dara sets the bottle on a table, then leads me into the living room, introducing me to a bunch of people whose names I've already forgotten. This place is hopping, and I think the electric Santas, snowmen, and Rudolph are trying to socialize too. I chuckle when I see how much mistletoe Dara has hanging around the house.

I glance at my watch and see that I've been here half an hour already. My mouth is dry from talking so much. Kellan hasn't shown himself yet. I know he's here because his truck was parked outside. Where is he?

"Come on. Let's get you a drinkie." *Finally*. Dara wraps her arm around mine and grabs the champagne from the table. She leads me to a corner in the living room near the kitchen where she has a bar set up. A small Christmas tree graces the table, decorated with twinkling white lights and stunning crystal snowflakes. I look at one close up.

"Are these Swarovski?"

"Yes! A friend of mine showed me one she bought, and I became obsessed. A new unique snowflake comes out every year. I love them so much, I buy as many as I can find." She leans in and whispers, "They aren't cheap, but I said, screw it."

"I don't know how much they are, but they're worth it. Look how they sparkle against the white lights."

She grins and points to the large selection of drinks. There's a big punch bowl full of eggnog. I shiver because the last time I drank that, I got sick after. "What would you like?"

"White wine. Something with a kick." I slip out of my jacket and toss it over my arm.

"Look at you, girlfriend! That outfit is so sexy. Wait until Kell—never mind." Whatever she's insinuating Kellan's reaction will be, I hope it's what I surely intended when I bought it. She lifts a bottle out of a large silver bucket of ice. "Check out this wine. I found this gem when I was with some friends in Napa Valley for a little wine-tasting tour. Want to try it? It's dry with a strong zing at the end. Let's see if you can taste which fruit's in it."

"Sure."

She pours what's left into a wine glass and hands it to me. I take a sip and almost laugh at Dara's curious face. "Mmm, delicious. Just what I like." I lick my lips and swallow.

"Right?" she remarks enthusiastically. "And?"

Sip. "Hmm. Grapefruit? That's it. Grapefruit. Right?"

"Correct! I have a couple boxes in the garage. I'll drop off a bottle or two one night."

"Wine delivered right to my house. How can I say no to that?" I joke. "I love this town."

"Please, it helps me get it out of here. My waistline is expanding from too much alcohol intake." She purses her lips. "Or maybe it's my constant baking."

Yeah, I don't think so. Dara is a beanpole. She has been ever since I've known her.

"You're too funny. I don't think you have a problem there."

She laughs. "Kellan and I were born here and grew up in this town. I didn't think I'd come back after I graduated college, but I realized right away how much I missed the small-town feeling. Most of the people I know here are good folks and would bend over backward for their friends and neighbors."

"I experienced that with Sandy's neighbors. Some people aren't open to same-sex marriages, so Mom and I didn't know what to expect. It was amazing how sad they were and how everyone offered to help us. Some even came to the funeral."

"That's the way it is here. I love it."

I grew up in Marimount. It's at least double the size of Margo Grove, maybe more. When I was younger, I found it stifling and couldn't wait to go off to college and conquer the world. Now I wonder if I'm getting comfortable here. Going back to live in Barton isn't very appealing right now. Jordan and I made friends, but it was mostly with other couples. I don't have a lot of single friends like Lizzy.

An older blond woman approaches the table and grabs a glass. "Great party, Dara," she says.

"Hey, Kerry. Thanks! Let me introduce you to Charli. She moved into the cottage a couple of days ago." We shake hands. Dara turns to me. "Kerry lives in Sunnyville. She's a reporter for the *Sunnyville Post*."

"Wait, has anyone told you that you look just like the woman on *Fast-Track Renovations*?" Kerry looks me over. "She wears a lot more makeup than you, though. You're prettier."

"Thank you." *I guess.* I clench my jaw.

"She *is* Charlize!" Dara blurts out before I can say anything else. *Great.* "Funny story, actually. Kellan was Charli's father's partner."

"Nice. Where is your delicious brother?" she mutters, looking through the crowd eagerly.

"He's around somewhere," Dara responds with no interest.

"Is he still single?"

Really? She has to be in her fifties.

"Yes... But I think that might change soon."

Oh? I sip my wine, pretending to be oblivious to this conversation. Is she talking about me or someone else?

"Damn," Kerry says, snapping her fingers. "Whoever snags him is a lucky girl. He's too young for me anyway." *Bingo.* "One can fantasize."

Dara chuckles under her hand. Kerry turns to me, blinking her eyes several times like her mind is spinning with questions.

"Charli," she says, "I absolutely love your show. It makes me want to run out and redecorate my house. Your talent is amazing. Is your sexy fiancé here too?" She scans the room again.

Whoa! This chick needs to get laid. I'll definitely be home in time to watch the end of *It's a Wonderful Life* if more people recognize me or start talking about Jordan. I want to forget about that part of my life tonight.

"No, Jordan's not here," I reply dryly. I almost said we aren't together anymore, but it's none of anybody's business. If I tell anyone, it'll be Kellan, not Dara or a stranger.

"Charli's renovating her sister's house here in Margo

Grove," Dara divulges, pushing the conversation in another direction.

Kerry's face drops. "Shit, that's right. Now I'm putting two and two together. Your sister and her wife died in that horrible car accident on Thanksgiving." *Don't want to talk about it.* "A colleague of mine wrote a piece for the newspaper about that. Gut-wrenching. Did you see it in the paper?" *She keeps talking.* "And what a miracle about their daughter, that some people pulled her out of the car. Such heroes." She places her hand over her heart and taps it, giving a sympathetic smile. "I'm so sorry for your loss."

Save me again, Dara! She's too busy looking around the room for someone or something. Should I start looking around the room for no damn reason too?

"Thanks." *It's a damn Christmas party!* "Before my sister died, she bought a house here to renovate. So I'm going to finish it for her." I'm trying to focus on the house to keep Noelle out of the conversation and maybe change the topic. I don't want to hear any details about the accident. What we got from the police will haunt us for years. We don't need any more. This is what has been good about staying in the house since Thanksgiving. I haven't had to explain myself or answer unwanted questions. Now I feel exposed.

"So, Kerry. What would you like to drink?" Dara interrupts.

"What a beautiful story. I should suggest to my colleague to do a follow-up article. Or I can do it." *That diversion didn't work.*

I shake my head immediately. "No, thanks. That won't be necessary."

She sifts through her purse and pulls out a business card. "If you change your mind, here's my card. It's nice to write articles about something uplifting. The news is so depressing." I take the card and put it in my purse.

"Thanks for the offer. I'll keep it in mind. I'd really like to get through the holidays."

"Oh, sure. I can't wait for the next season of your show." She turns to Dara before I can respond. I sigh in relief. "So which wine should I taste next?"

"Dara, where's your bathroom?" I ask, hoping for an escape.

She points to the right. "Down the hallway and the last door on the right."

"Thanks. I'll be right back. Nice meeting you, Kerry." I place my empty glass on the table and make my escape.

Where the hell is Kellan?

A few minutes later, I look in the mirror, touching up my lip gloss. At least I'm not the only one who thought I wore too much makeup on the show. *Kellan won't be single for long.* I mimic Dara to my reflection. What the hell is that supposed to mean? Has he been seeing someone? Why all these mind games then? Is she here tonight? I hated being with Jordan, but being single sucks too.

Someone knocks on the door. "One minute," I respond, glancing at my watch. One more hour tops, then I'm out of here. Bah humbug.

I wander back to the bar and pour myself some seltzer, then drop a lemon slice in it. Suddenly I smell his signature scent and feel his presence behind me. Heat embraces my back. Excitement bubbles under my skin, and I haven't even seen him yet.

"Hi," Kellan purrs, his voice sinful, his warm breath caressing my shoulder. I slowly turn around, my eyes downcast. I'm almost afraid to see how gorgeous he looks, that he'll see what the nearness of him does to me. I can't help it though—my eyes trace up his body, and my stomach twirls. My cheeks tingle with heat.

He's breathtakingly handsome in his maroon button-down that hangs open with a snug white collared shirt underneath. The sleeves are rolled up to his elbows, revealing his muscular forearms. His hair looks freshly cut and as sexy as ever with the gray showing through. There's a hint of scruff along his angular jawline. All my worries from the conversation with Kerry disappear. Tonight is different. This is not work related, there's no Noelle, and I can do whatever I want.

The electricity popping around us is stronger than ever. If he goes off the market, it will be because of me. No one else can have him. I almost laugh at myself. Where's this possessiveness coming from?

His eyes wander over my face and down my neck, stopping briefly at the swell of my breasts. My heart hammers in my chest. His gaze continues slowly down my belly and my legs. "Charli," he sighs with desire. "You've never looked more beautiful. All eyes are on you tonight."

"I'm only interested in one set of those eyes. Maybe you know him."

"Really?" He looks over his shoulder, then leans in closer. His fresh aftershave swirls around me, blocking out everyone in the room. "What's his name?"

I take a step back. "It's a secret." He follows me like we're doing the tango.

"I know everybody in this room. And I'd have to say, eyes have been turning since you walked through the door in that sexy outfit. Is it new?" He moves closer and I take another step back for fun, running into the wall.

"Yes. I only have jeans and leggings here. I thought I'd treat myself to something nice and more my style."

His eyes flash. "I definitely approve."

"So you saw when I arrived, and you're just now coming to say hello?" I peek at him from under my eyelashes.

"Get a room," Dara mutters as she walks by, light laughter following in her wake. Kellan ignores her, but I grin, although my focus is mainly on him.

"I wanted to watch you from afar like I have in the past.

But this time is different. I allowed myself to enjoy it. It's cute how nervous you were when you arrived. Your cheeks turned the color of your top." His eyes travel to my chest again. The leather jacket was unnecessary. Being so close to him has every inch of my body in flames.

"Hey, Kellan. Long time no see," a brunette interrupts boldly, pushing herself between us. She puts her hand on his chest. I gape at her and he steps back, pushing her hand away.

"Hi, Andrea," he responds dryly.

"I haven't seen you around lately. We need to catch up." His eyes flick to mine for a second. My eyebrows raise. Old girlfriend?

"Andrea, let me introduce you to my friend." She glances at me with territorial eyes, then does a double take.

"Wait, I know you. But how?" *No, no, no! Please don't say it.* She bites her lip and ponders. What is the polite way to tell her that she has red lipstick all over her teeth?

She figures it out. "I know! You're Charlize from *Fast-Track Renovations.* Am I right?"

I swallow the lump in my throat and deflate. Kellan moves around her to my side. He rests his hand on my lower back, and I forget what my name is. *Please get me out of here.*

Andrea shakes her head. "Nah. You can't be her. Why would she be here in this little town? I absolutely love that show. Have you ever seen it?"

"Yes." *Someone, please interrupt us.* Maybe light a Christmas tree on fire or blow an electrical circuit.

"Charlize and Jordan have amazing talent, and the chemistry between them is so steamy. And he is so damn hot." She fans herself. "He's the main reason I watch the show, if you know what I mean." She wiggles her eyebrows drunkenly. "I wonder if he has a twin brother?"

I glance over my shoulder at Kellan. His stormy eyes are locked on Andrea and his lips are pressed together so tightly they're white. Tension is spewing off his chest as it rises and falls rapidly. Andrea's clueless and keeps talking.

"They should have their wedding on the show like when he proposed to her. That would be a fairytale come true. Dontcha think?" My eyes pop wide and I swallow deeply. This is insane.

"Andrea, we need to talk to Dara. We'll see you later." He takes my glass, reaches to hold my hand, then stops.

"Oh, okay. I need to eat anyway. The margaritas I've been drinking are going to my head." She staggers off.

Without a word, Kellan leads me out of the living room to the hallway where the bathroom is. He takes a key out of his pocket and unlocks a door across from the bathroom. Once it's open, he turns on the light and motions for me to go down the stairs. He locks the door behind us and follows me down. At the bottom of the stairs is a short hallway with another door at the end. I stand in the middle, then I see his frustrated gaze. Or is it predatory? Whatever it is, I like it. Maybe too much. My body anticipates his next move.

I walk backward as he steps forward, just like we did upstairs. He follows me to the door until my back's pressed up against it. I let my jacket and purse fall on the ground. He rests his hands on the door beside my head, caging me in. His alluring smell sparks a wildfire in me. My eyes wander his arresting face, and my body trembles with need.

He leans in and traces his nose along my jaw. "Tell me you are no longer engaged."

My heart's going to explode out of my chest. "I'm not. Kiss—" His lips are on mine, ravaging them like he's starving for my taste. I wrap my arms around his back, sinking into his hard body. He licks my lower lip, and I open willingly, moaning when his tongue finally twists with mine for the first time. Nothing before has prepared me for the onslaught of emotions and desire that drum through my soul.

"I've waited so long," he murmurs, peppering kisses along

my chin, then under my ear. "So long to kiss your sweet pink lips."

"How long?" His lips and tongue sear the swell of my chest. Goosebumps race along my skin, making me shudder. My hand cups the back of his neck, encouraging him to keep going. I want his warm lips all over my bare skin. This is out of control, but I don't want to stop.

"Years. Too many years." He moans against my skin. "You taste better than I could've imagined."

I guide his face up to mine and take his mouth with fervor. My hunger increases for him, and I wish we were somewhere else. His hard body rocks against me, making me wet between my thighs. This man who I thought hated me, in reality, wanted me all this time. He's bringing my body to life in ways I didn't know were possible.

Someone unlocks the door at the top of the stairs and opens it. We jerk apart.

"Maybe there's some down—" Dara stops when she sees us, then chuckles. She knows full well what we were doing. "Or maybe not." She closes the door swiftly and locks it again.

He embraces me, and I melt into him, wrapping my arms around his waist. "Now that I've finally tasted you," he growls, "you know I won't be able to stop."

"Don't stop. Ever." I grip the sides of his shirt and tug. "This better not be a one-time thing."

He leans back and rubs his thumb gently across my lower lip. "Nope. These lips are mine now."

"Getting a little possessive already?"

"Would that bother you?" He skims his lips along mine.

I push him away gently so he'll look at me. "Not when it's you, but I have a lot of questions you need to answer first."

He cocks his head to the side with a smirk. "Really? So do I."

"I know." I bend over to pick up my jacket and purse. He

pulls the same key out of his pocket and opens the door he had so nicely pinned me against. "Are you in the mood for some fresh air?"

I curl my finger through a belt loop on his pants. "Oh, I'm in a mood all right, but not for fresh air."

He turns toward me and cups my face with his hands. His dark eyes are full of desire. "You have no idea how much I hate that we're at this party. I want you at my house, in my bed, under me. And I promise you, it will happen. But not tonight."

My heart stops. I love this side of him. Direct, fiery, and possessive. I'm so turned on, I don't know what to do.

He runs a finger along my jawline. "That kiss let out everything I've been trying to hide and tamp down. I won't be able to hold back anymore." He ravishes my lips one more time. "I don't want to only show you what you mean to me. I want you to feel it too."

"You're killing me. Why did you wait so long?"

"Let's go outside. I really don't want to have this conversation in the middle of Dara's playroom. There's a set of swings we can sit on out back. Let me grab some clean blankets. There are fresh ones in the back room. I don't think we want blankets with cheerios stuck to them." He chuckles. "I'll be right back. Look around. This is where Noelle would play if she came here."

I put on my jacket, then walk around the large room looking at the toys, stuffed animals, a piano, a play kitchen, some bookshelves, and a reading nook with beanbag chairs. Noelle would be happy here, I'm sure. A large mural of a lavender field, bright sun, fluffy clouds, and a rainbow is painted on one wall. Maybe it's a sign since I love lavender. The adjacent walls are the same color yellow as the sun in the mural, giving the room a sense of warmth and peace. That alone would make anyone happy to play here. I find myself smiling but then it disappears.

What the hell am I doing?

"I'm back. Let's go," Kellan says with a couple of blankets in tow.

"No. I can't do this." I shake my head. He stops in his tracks.

"What? Why not?"

"We need to be completely open with each other before we can take this any further."

"I agree. That's why I want to go outside so we can talk."

"No, I need to say this to your face where I can see you. Not in the dark." He looks at me quizzically. "Do you want to know why I acted the way I did the other night when you were over for dinner and then when you showed us the house?"

"Yes. That hurt like a bitch."

I wrap my arms around my waist. The air around us shifts from playful to tense.

"You said you don't date single mothers."

"Shit." He tosses the blankets over a chair and rubs his face.

"You do realize that's what I am now. This isn't a temporary thing. If you can't accept that, then we have no chance. No matter how attracted I am to you—because, wow, there's no question about that—I'm not looking for a casual hook-up. We have too much to risk. Especially if we want to work together."

Kellan inches closer to me. "Charli, I'm sorry. That was the stupidest thing I could've ever said to you." His serious eyes capture mine. "The *only* single mother I'd approach in this lifetime is *you*. Without any doubt or question in my mind."

"But why now? What is this sudden interest after all these years?" He's going to talk whether he likes it or not.

"Do you really want to have this conversation now?"

"Yes." I cross my arms. "We've been skating around each

other like we're in high school. I don't want to do it anymore."

"I don't want to do this here. Let's go somewhere else."

"But—"

He grabs my hand, and kisses the top of it. "Don't worry about Dara." How did he know I was going to say that? "She wants us to be together." *Really?*

"Your house?" I suggest. "It's the only place I can think of where I'd feel comfortable and we'd have no interruptions. Maybe we could sit out on your deck. Not in your bedroom. Not now anyway."

He caresses my cheek with the back of his hand. "I'd love that. But are you sure?"

I nod my head.

"Okay. Stay here. I'll go tell Dara, then we can leave through the back gate." He picks up the blankets and returns them to their closet, then dashes upstairs.

I walk around the playroom again. There's a picture on the wall with a photo collage of Dara and the kids. One is from Halloween. I chuckle out loud. Dara is a unicorn with a massive horn sticking out of her head.

Kellan comes back and stands behind me while I keep looking at the photos. He points out one where he's kneeling with two boys who are covered in paint. He chuckles. "I had to paint something for Dara one day. She asked if these two could help me out. The one to the left is Timmy. It was a complete disaster, but they had a lot of fun. I'm not sure Dara will ever ask me to do that again."

I turn around. "What did she say about us leaving?"

He walks over to the door leading out to the back. "She said something like, 'Have fun and use condoms.' And wondered if we wanted some cheesecake."

I guffaw. "Don't get your hopes up, mister." I poke his side. "I forgot how funny Dara is."

"Come on. Let's go." He holds out his hand. I place mine in his like we've done it many times before. I love it.

"I'm all yours."

He pulls me close to him, brushing the hair away from my face. "Is that a promise?"

"Depends on how well you explain yourself. It better be convincing."

He smiles seductively, then pulls me through the door.

27

CHARLI

I park behind his truck and quickly send a text to Mom. Kellan walks up to the side of my car and opens the door for me. He sees me put my phone away.

"Everything okay back home?" he says with concern.

"I'm sure. I sent Mom a message letting her know I'm here. Just like Dara, she'd love to see us together."

"Really? Something else for you to spill. Then I'll make sure you have something good to report back to her."

I get out of my car, and look up at the sky. "Wow, it's so clear tonight. The stars seem so close. And you get to see this every night."

"I'm sure you had a similar view of the stars from Sandy's house."

"It didn't cross my mind. You saw the backyard. The deck looks like it would collapse if more than one person stood on it. The only things I like in the backyard are the large oak trees." I get the chills thinking about that house.

"That's true. But we're going to change that."

"Together," I say, glancing at him. The only thing illuminating us is the car's interior light.

"Yep, together," he murmurs, reaching for my hand. I

take it and close the door. "Let's go in. Once the sensor light goes on, we'll be blinded."

He leads us into the house, and eventually we end up near the kitchen. "What would you like to drink?" he asks, peering into the fridge.

"I'll be honest, only water. I have to drive, and I want us to be sober when we're talking."

"And I hope some hot kissing gets added in there too," he flirts. I pretend to think about it. "Come on, just a little?" he begs, closing the refrigerator with his elbow.

"Maybe a good-night kiss when I leave. If you're lucky." I look around. "I don't see any mistletoe anywhere. Your luck just ran out." Actually, there are no Christmas decorations at all.

Inching closer to me, he cups my cheeks. "I'll do whatever you want if it means you'll spend time with me." I close my eyes to enjoy the moment. He kisses my nose.

I place my hands on his chest. "I wish I'd have seen this side of you sooner. I still can't wrap it around in my head that you're the same broody Kellan. Who'd've known you have a sense of humor, a heart of gold, and can melt my heart with your sinful lips. I keep thinking you must have an evil twin somewhere, and he's going to jump out at any minute."

"Sinful lips, huh?" He wraps one hand around the back of my neck and plants the softest of kisses on mine. "No evil twin. I needed to guard myself. Give me a chance to explain." I nod, and he rumbles approvingly. "All right. Then let's go see the stars. But first, let me get a couple of things."

Minutes later, we're sitting on a sofa outside, surrounded by candles and starlight. Little bowls of pretzels, chips, and Reese's Pieces are spread on the table. Ed Sheeran streams through the bifold doors. A blue blanket from the living room couch keeps my feet warm. Kellan sits on the end of the sofa, his arm resting on the top. His fingers are inches from my shoulder. I sit back and sigh in comfort.

"Back at Dara's, you said you wanted to see my face when we talked. It's still pretty dark even with the candles." A relaxed smile curves his face as his fingers stroke my shoulder.

"I know, but I've changed my mind. This is a lot better than what I was thinking. I'm relaxed here and it's more intimate… romantic. No interruptions yet." I'm constantly on high alert, waiting for my phone to ring. There's no such thing as turning off my phone anymore now that I have Noelle.

"I'm glad. So where should we start? I want us to put everything out on the table because I don't know how long I can wait until I kiss you again."

His direct honesty throws me off kilter. Again I remember the old Kellan and look away. The man next to me is a completely different person. One I'm wildly attracted to and who I want to get to know much better.

He scoots over and puts his hand on my knee. "Look at me, Charli." I hesitate but then give in. "Tell me what you're thinking."

"I'm wondering who you are. How are you the same Kellan who couldn't stand being in the same room as me for more than five minutes? He would've never spoken to me like this."

He presses his lips together, contemplating what to say, I'm sure. Finally, he says, "Ignoring you or being distant was the only way I could stay away from you."

I tilt my head back in surprise. "What do you mean? Why?"

"When I met you with your big turquoise eyes, you were only eleven and I was eighteen. I already knew you'd be the prettiest girl when you got older. And a heartbreaker. Then I started working for your dad, watching you grow up as the years passed by. Working on the sites, learning everything you could. Hanging out with the crews like you were just one of the guys. There was no chance for us. I had reasons, but they don't really matter anymore."

"What reasons? Tell me. I want to know what made your eyebrows permanently stick together and your jaw rock solid every time I was around." I trace my finger over one of his eyebrows, down his cheek, and then along his jawline.

He takes my hand in his. "The age difference was a huge problem for me. When you were a teenager, I was already in my twenties. We were in different stages of life, and I was convinced it'd be frowned on if I ever showed interest in you."

"The prom?" That day is still so clear in my mind. I want to see his reaction.

He groans. "You were so fucking beautiful… You had your hair down like it is now. I remember every single detail of that blue dress, your shoes, even the color of your lipstick." He brushes my hair over my shoulder. "It was the first time I saw you dressed up and really saw you as a woman. I still remember how that dress drew out the blue of your eyes. You took my breath away. You still do. It killed me to watch you with your prom date when you were taking pictures in front of your house. I wanted to take you. That was when I realized how deep my feelings were for you. And… I let you see it."

"I remember what you said. Word for word. You made me feel beautiful and confident, and I couldn't stop thinking how your eyes… reached deep inside me. I saw a softer side to you in those few minutes. Like now. But the next time I saw you, it was like that moment vanished into thin air." I squeeze his cheek. "Evil twin. And it better not happen again."

A light laugh escapes him. "You looked perfect. Stunning, actually. But my heart wasn't ready for it. Plus, I had to walk away out of respect for you and your parents. I worked for your dad, and that job helped me make enough money to go to college and help my mom pay the bills. Mick took me under his wing and taught me everything I know today. I didn't want to disappoint him or overstep somewhere I shouldn't be. So I sacrificed what I wanted."

"If he were still alive, I think he'd be really happy if we got together."

He stands abruptly and pulls up a chair so he can sit directly in front of me. Then he takes my hands in his again. I love it that he's constantly touching me, as if I'm going to run away.

"Your dad would've been happy. I know because... he told me."

"Wh–what?" I stutter. I push up off the sofa and step away. He follows me. "When did you talk to him about me? And why am I only hearing about this now?" A sudden flood of sadness and anger washes over me. "Dad never said a word about that to me."

"Charli, please don't be upset. Please listen for a minute, okay?"

I wrap my arms around myself, wishing my dad were here to explain what happened that day.

"The day Mick died, he asked me to meet him for breakfast. I found it strange because it was so out of the blue. I wasn't prepared for what he was going to say to me. He asked me flat out if I had feelings for you."

I cover my face and pace the deck. "Oh my God. What did you say?"

"Yes."

My breath hitches at his quick response and I stop in my tracks.

"I explained to him exactly what I just said to you."

"Was he mad? Is that why he asked?"

"Surprisingly, no." Kellan looks away for a moment, hesitant. Then he takes a breath and says, "He told me that Jordan had asked permission to marry you the night before."

My stomach plummets, and tears pool in my eyes. "I

didn't know Jordan asked him. He didn't say a word about that. But why did Dad tell you?"

"Are you sure you want to know?" He eyes me cautiously. "I'm not trying to upset you. And maybe I shouldn't have even told you. Nobody knows about that conversation."

"So what did he say to Jordan? I'm assuming, yes."

"From what your dad told me, he didn't get the chance to answer because they were interrupted. Then you went home."

"This is so fucked up. I wonder if Mom knows about all of this," I say, biting on my lip. "She's made comments lately how she thinks you've had feelings for me for a long time."

"He told me he was going to tell her that night. That time with Mick was a gift, not knowing he was going to die that day." His voice cracks, making me want to cry even more.

I take a deep breath. "Go on."

"He knew you were about to get engaged, and I was with Chelsea. I said it wasn't meant to be, even though my heart was screaming the opposite. And then Jordan proposed to you on TV. That was the final twist of the key to my heart. I locked my feelings for you in here." He places my hand on his chest. "And I had to let you go." A lone tear runs down my cheek and he wipes it away with his thumb.

"Mick asked me to promise that if there was ever a chance for us to be together, that I'd grab onto it. I never thought that time would come. And then Sandy died, and things were different. So I'm doing it." He shifts and holds my hand. "I want you, Charli. I always have. Hiding isn't an option anymore."

I shake my head and take a step back. "No, you don't. It's not only me anymore. I'm a package deal with Noelle. Things are different now."

"I know. But I want you both in my life."

"Look. I don't want to get my hopes up, especially after tonight. If I let you in, and then you leave because you realize you don't want a child who isn't yours... or any child at all?" I shake my head. "I can't do that."

He grabs my hands again and pulls me closer. "Forget what I said. When I saw you with Noelle in your arms, I can't explain how my heart clenched. She looked just like you, and it was like I could see my future. That's why I know it's different and this is the real thing.

"I'm sorry. I know I'm throwing everything out there. Give me a chance to show you what you both mean to me. Forgive me for how I've treated you. I didn't want to hurt you, but I thought it was the only way. If you choose me... us... you won't regret it. I promise."

28

KELLAN

We stand there staring at each other. Her eyes search mine, her expression revealing the struggle inside. Finally, as if she's made a decision, she steps closer and cups my face with her cold hands. Her warm lips press against mine, and she slowly slides her tongue across them. Wrapping her up in my arms, I open for her and greedily deepen the kiss. I try to erase all her doubts about my feelings for her and replace them with promises. Reluctantly, I break the kiss before it gets too far out of hand and nibble on her lower lip. "Does this mean I'm forgiven?"

She pulls her head back. "Are you just trying to get another kiss from me?"

"I'd be kissing you all night if I could. But I'd rather not do it out here," I confess with a flirty grin.

It's such a weight off my chest to finally tell her how I feel and what has been going through my head all these years. Every day for the rest of my life, I'll show her how much she means to me.

"Maybe you're forgiven." A grin grows on my face. "On one condition." And it's gone.

"Anything."

She pinches my chin. "It's pure honesty from here on out. No secrets."

My gut twists, and I swallow hard. *The accident.* Would it make us closer if I told her about it? Why did I have to be at the wrong place at the wrong time? But if I hadn't been, maybe we wouldn't be here right now.

"Pure honesty." I peck her lips one more time.

"The moment I knew I was attracted to you at a different level was when we played that stupid nail gun game." She grins and her cheeks turn a soft shade of pink. "You showed up at the site, and you looked so gorgeous. I was twenty-two, and you were the first guy I felt that thunderbolt with. You know, the electricity everyone talks about. When you touched me for those few seconds, and the way our eyes connected... It took my breath away. All those feelings came rushing back when I saw you again a few weeks ago." She looks away shyly and focuses on a candle. "And I was a goner." Her eyes find mine again. "You smiled at me that day just like you are now. I savored that moment for months. Then I convinced myself it was only a stupid crush, a fantasy because you were an older, sexy guy. It's amazing how those two little incidents could make such an impact."

"Not even with Jordan?"

Her face turns somber. "Nope." She pops the *p*. "When I think back, I wonder if I was settling." *Just like Mick mentioned.* Her eyes squint. "Don't get a big head now."

"It'll be my goal to always give you that thunderbolt you mentioned," I tease her. *In and out of the bedroom.*

"No complaints here. I love the way you make me feel and how you smile at me. Will I get to see that all the time now?" She leans her hip against the railing, facing me.

"Be careful what you wish for. I know where you live. You'd better watch out." She drops her head back and laughs. What I wouldn't do to pull her closer again and kiss her supple neck and lips all night. But I have to take it slow with her... if that's even possible at this point.

"Now that I know what it feels like, I don't think I could get enough of your touch, your handsome face, or your bright blue eyes. You might find *me* on *your* doorstep."

"I'll take what I can get. We can go slow—I know your life has been turned upside down and your priorities are new and different. You can set the pace. I don't want to be a bad distraction or scare you away."

"You? A *bad* distraction? I don't think so. Since we're asking questions, did you ever have a serious girlfriend? Wasn't someone with you at Dad's funeral? A few minutes ago you mentioned a woman named Chelsea."

My chest tightens remembering the hurt written on Chelsea's face. I spend the next couple of minutes telling her what happened between us. "I loved her. But not enough because my heart belonged to someone else. It was pretty rough when she moved out."

It'd be so easy for me to tell Charli I'm in love with her. That her beauty brings me to my knees. That I've felt more alive in the last two weeks than I have for years. Now that I've opened up, I have the urge to tell her everything. Almost everything...

She squeezes my hand. "I'm sorry. It's never easy to break up with someone, even if it's the right thing to do. She did a good job decorating. I've wondered about the feminine touches I saw here and there. I like her style."

"Dara helped out a little too. Chelsea took a bunch of furniture with her." We stand in silence as Charli looks up at the stars. "Are you cold? Do you want to go in?"

"Maybe we should. I need to explain my situation too. Get everything out in the open so we can move on."

Out in the open. Guilt burns through me. I press it back into the dark corners of my mind where I want it to stay.

We carry the candles in, still lit, and place them around

the living room. I notice we didn't eat anything. I'd rather starve than stop talking to her.

"Are you hungry?" I ask, placing the full bowls of snacks on the bar.

"Not really." She takes a sip of her water, then places the bottle on the kitchen counter.

I walk over to her, and our eyes lock. She grabs my shirt and pulls me to her slowly. She backs up so she's leaning against the counter. I lose myself in her big blue pools. I can't believe she's here. Wanting me. Touching me.

"I need a break from talking." She pushes up on her tiptoes and brushes her lips against mine like a feather. Testing my willpower. "Want another taste?" *Damn.* Blood shoots right to my dick.

"I'm starving. But not for food."

"What are you hungry for?" She slides her jacket off her arms and shakes her hair back, revealing her sexy shoulders. I take it and toss it on the counter away from us. She pulls me back to her so we're chest to chest. Her questioning eyes wait for my answer.

"Hungry for you. Only you. For these tempting lips." I trace my thumb gently across her bottom lip. Without warning, I scoop her up and set her on the counter. Then plant myself between her legs. "And this." I kiss and nip down her neck to her sexy bare shoulder. She angles her head back, giving me better access. I flick my tongue along her collarbone, coaxing a moan from her. And that makes me even harder.

"Yes," she hisses, her breathing heavy. Magnetic energy crackles around us. I will never take this feeling for granted.

I grab her hips and pull her flush against me. "Do you feel what you do to me?"

She nods, her eyes hooded, then captures my lips. Tasting, sucking, teasing until I'm breathless. Her hands drag mine to her heaving chest. "Touch me," she commands. She's going to kill me, but I'll die a happy man.

I circle my thumbs around her pert nipples through her top. She drops her hands to the counter and leans back. Her breasts jut forward, inviting my touch. I pull her top down so it pools at her waist, revealing her perfect, swollen breasts. I'm in heaven.

"You're breathtaking," I murmur against her skin.

"I—"

I draw her pebbled rosy nub into my mouth, cutting her off, winning more deep moans from her. Her head drops back.

"What are you doing to me? Every touch feels so good," she murmurs, her breathing labored.

"I want you so badly," I whisper, kissing the silky skin between her breasts. Then I draw the other one into my mouth. I could do this for the rest of my life. "There's no denying it anymore."

Her hands fist my hair and pull me up to take my mouth with hers. Our tongues tangle and twist, trying to make up for all the years we've wasted. *I've* wasted. I pull her to me and shift my hands to her tight ass as she slides off the counter and wraps her legs around my waist, rocking even harder. I'm going to explode any second.

This goes on for minutes until her stomach grumbles loudly, making us burst out laughing. We pull apart breathlessly.

She covers her mouth. "I'm so sorry."

"Don't be. You're so damn beautiful, especially when your lips are swollen because of me." Her mouth is on mine again like she can't get enough of me. I stop us and I press my forehead against hers. "And if we don't stop, I'm going to blow in my pants like a teenager. I could eat you all day."

Her delicious lips transform into a sensual grin. "I'll take that as a compliment. I thought I lost it a long time ago."

I kiss her neck. "You definitely didn't. I'm living proof."

"That's a relief." I help her fix her top, and she hops off the counter. "I guess we should eat something," she huffs with a smile. "I was eyeing those Reese's Pieces when we were outside."

"My favorite. Everything's on the bar. Go sit down on one of the barstools and I'll bring us more water."

She rubs my chest. "I'm going to use the bathroom first. I'll be right back."

Once she's out of sight, I rake my hands through my hair, then adjust my pants. I'm so fucking hard, I'm going to have to sit on the couch with a pillow on my lap. This night has got to be a dream. I've imagined this so many times and the reality doesn't compare. She's lucky we weren't near my bedroom because I would've stripped her bare and thrown her on my bed.

"I'm back," she announces a few minutes later. "Do you have a cleaning lady or something? Your bathroom is spotless. Actually, your entire house is impeccable. This place is off limits once Noelle can crawl."

I wrap my arms around her waist. "I'll babyproof the shit out of it, so you two can come over here whenever you want. I'll even cover it in bubble wrap if I have to. No excuses."

She leans back with squinty eyes. "Even when she has one of her meltdowns? Or poops through her clothes or spits up…?"

"Even then. I'm not going anywhere, Charli."

"Jordan stayed at Sandy's house the night before the wake," she says. I lift an eyebrow. "He slept on the couch. He was such a dick about the house and Noelle crying. I couldn't wait until he left."

"Speaking of Jordan. It's time for *you* to talk and me to listen." I crook my finger for her to follow me. "Let's go."

"Where should I start?" she mumbles, sitting sideways on one of the stools.

I sit down next to her so we are knee to knee. "Begin anywhere. Make me understand your relationship and your life in Barton. And why you didn't tell me sooner that you split up."

She sips some water, then puts the bottle to the side. "Him being at the funeral was an act. He didn't want to be there, and I didn't want him to be either. I almost didn't tell him Sandy died. After you left, Mom told him to leave." She giggles. "My mouth almost hit the floor. Mom didn't even know what was going on between us at the time, but she obviously didn't like the way he was acting."

"I love Tricia. She's a force to be reckoned with. I definitely have to watch myself." I smile, trying to imagine her telling him off. "Did something happen after I left?"

"He confronted me about you."

I pull my head back. "About me? *Me?*"

"He said you had feelings for me and he'd seen it at Dad's funeral too."

"At your dad's funeral, I talked to you for about a minute before he pulled you away." Talking about him is starting to piss me off.

"We had a big fight outside the funeral home to the point —" She taps her fingers on the counter. "I smacked him across the face."

I stand up quickly, almost knocking over the stool. "Did he touch you?" I growl. She grips the edge of my shirt with both hands and pulls me between her legs.

"Calm down, tough guy. No. He was being himself... selfish. He couldn't stand that I was talking to you. Not because he loved me. Because he thought you were competition. A threat. It was a blow to his ego and that's all."

I skim her cheek with the back of my hand. "I hated myself for how I acted when I saw him. But I couldn't stand the way he treated you. And I'll admit I was jealous. I wanted to be the one at your side. And he pushed my buttons. Dara reamed my ass when we got in the car, and that's when she put two and two together about my feelings for you. I didn't tell her. She figured it out."

Her mouth drops open. "Really? Dad's the only one who knew?"

"Yeah. Besides him, it was my little secret, and it was eating me alive every single damn day." Now the accident has replaced that feeling.

She taps my stool. "My neck hurts, looking up at you." I sit back down, then pop some Reese's in my mouth. She dives in too. "Y'know, Mom and Dad were ten years apart in age. Seven years isn't so bad."

"Now it isn't. But when you were, let's say, sixteen, and I was twenty-three or something like that…"

"Eww." She crinkles her nose. "Okay, I get it."

"Come on. Finish your story."

"You remember that I was at my place in Barton before I went to your house, right?" I nod. "When I got there, I found Jordan in a… compromising position… with one of the producers. A much older producer."

"Fuck." I rub my hands through my hair. "What a piece of shit. He's lucky he's not here. You don't deserve that."

"I know," she says. "Don't get mad. Our engagement has been long over."

"I had a feeling. Do you think I'd be around you as much if I thought you were still with him? But I was waiting for you to tell me."

She rubs her foot up one of my legs. "Sorry. I should've told you right away. I just wanted to forget about him. About that part of my life. I'm glad you know now."

"Me too."

"Anyway, when I caught them, I found a way out."

"A way out?"

"Yeah." She explains to me everything about the show

and their contract, what she'd dealt with, and how their relationship had broken apart.

I shake my head. "How are you so calm?"

She shrugs her shoulders, slides off the stool, and steps closer to me. "Because I'm free now. I can do whatever I want. Like hug and kiss you." She rests her arms over my shoulders, pressing a kiss on my lips. I want to kiss her, but I need to hear the rest of her story.

"Who else knows?"

"About the show or about our breakup? Other than my mom, I have no clue."

"Is he still living in your house?"

I nod. "I told him he has to be out by December thirty-first. The house is in my name. That's a different story to tell at another time. I'm going back that day to make sure he's out and to change the locks."

"I'll go with you."

"You don't have to."

"I'd feel better if someone were with you. We can take my truck in case there's something you want to bring back. I can help change the locks too. I'd like to see the world you lived in."

"Okay. Anyway, after the shit went down with Jordan, that's when I decided to renovate the house. I have all the experience I need to make it happen, and I don't have to run it by the show first."

"I can't wait to help you. I'll have to remember to not press any of your buttons. Well, not the bad ones anyway."

29

CHARLI

I roll over in bed and stretch. My eyes grow wide when I glance at the clock. Nine already! *Shit!* I jump up and whip open the bedroom door. Did I close it last night? It's usually open during the night so I can hear Noelle. I rush to her room, but her crib's empty. I'm on the verge of a panic attack when I hear Mom ask Noelle for help with her daily newspaper crossword puzzle. Noelle babbles away as if she knows the answer. Relief rushes through me, followed closely by guilt because I slept in.

I trot down the stairs, amazed at how much brighter, warmer, and dryer this house is than Sandy's. No wonder I slept so well. I round the corner to the kitchen. "Good morning." I kiss Mom on the cheek, and then Noelle. "Why didn't you get me up? Did Noelle wake up during the night?"

Mom puts down the newspaper and pen, then removes her glasses. "You deserve to sleep in once in a while. She woke up one time while you were still out, but she slept the rest of the night. By six-thirty, she was up and raring to go." Mom leans over and taps Noelle's nose. "We're going to need to buy new clothes for her. Some of the onesies and pj's are getting too small. Her little toes are going to pop out soon." Mom tickles the bottom of her feet.

"I must have been exhausted. I didn't hear a thing. I'm sorry."

"That's why Grandma's here. So I guess you had a good night." She smirks, folding the newspaper in half.

I pour myself a coffee and grab a strawberry yogurt from the refrigerator. "It was more than fun." Searching cabinet after cabinet, I finally find a bag of granola. Moving into two different houses within a month is screwing with my brain. I don't know where anything is.

"Do I get details or are you going to make me suffer?" Mom huffs with her hand on her hip. "I know I'm your mom, not a girlfriend, but I need to live vicariously through you."

I slide into the chair next to Noelle with a big smile on my face. But I'm so much happier than one smile can reveal. "It was magical, fun, and exhausting. I met a lot of new people. Several knew about Sandy since they're from here, including a reporter from the *Sunnyville Post* who had no filter." I roll my eyes. "She asked too many questions, which put a damper on my mood. A couple people recognized me, thought I looked like Charlize from the show. Funny, I wasn't prepared for that. It wasn't easy. Kellan had to save me."

I tell Mom about the girl who kept raving about Jordan.

"Was she drunk?"

"Yes, or close to it. The more she said about Jordan, the more uncomfortable Kellan and I became. For two different reasons."

A slow smile forms on her face. "And those reasons would be?" She leans in attentively.

"I didn't want her to know I actually was Charlize, and Kellan didn't like her talking about Jordan as if we were still a couple. But I guess that's what we needed."

"Needed?" Her forehead crinkles.

"For me to confirm that Jordan and I are through and for him to finally kiss me." My smile reappears.

"Finally!" She cheers. "I was ready to lock you two in a room."

"Mom!" I exclaim, laughing. "He laid his heart out last night. I felt like I was dreaming. It was amazing to hear him talk about me the way he did. Our chemistry is off the charts."

I trace my sensitive lip, remembering his delicious mouth against mine, his scruff that tickled my skin, almost melting into my chair. When it was time for me to leave his house, he walked me out. We ended up having a hot-as-hell kissing session against my car. My entire body was on fire and my lips stung after. The passion was so strong we almost couldn't stop. My stomach twirls with delight.

"Oh, no. You've got it bad." Mom's looking at me with a giant smile. "Check out that dazzled look on your face."

A blissful sigh escapes me. "You were right. He acted the way he did because of his relationship with Dad and because of our age difference."

"Age difference? Look at me and your dad. Ten years! What's the age difference between you two? Six? Seven?"

"Seven. He apologized over and over again and told me he wants to be with me. To finally show me how he feels." I shake my head. "I'm not used to this. I love it, but I need some time to adjust to this whole new life. Can I jump into a relationship on top of everything else going on?" Because it's Kellan, the answer to that is yes. There's an ease and familiarity because he's known my family for almost twenty years.

"I hope you two talked about Noelle."

I nod, sipping my coffee. "Yes. I was very honest and firm. It's a no-go if he can't accept her. He said he does, and you and I have already talked about how much he adores her. It's almost too good to be true."

Noelle grabs my attention, banging her hand on the table and babbling at me.

"And what's there not to love?" I croon. "Look at your adorable face." She grins like she's posing for a picture.

"Now don't start questioning it," Mom warns. "It's finally out in the open. Let yourselves enjoy each other with nothing in the way."

"Kellan told me something last night about Dad," I say, twirling a spoon in my coffee.

"He did? About what?"

I look down, chewing on the side of my mouth, making sure I want to bring it up.

"Charli?"

"Did you ever talk to Dad about me and Kellan?"

She purses her lips to the side. "Maybe once or twice a long time ago. Before you were with Jordan and he was with Chelsea. Nothing after that. I didn't want to cause problems. I told you I had my hunches, though. Your dad didn't say much. But you know how men are. Why?"

I tell her what Kellan told me and am shocked when we both have tears in our eyes.

"The morning he died?" she asks, her lower lip quivering. I jump up and sit in the chair next to her, pulling her in for a hug. "I can't believe he didn't say anything to me about confronting Kellan. We hardly discussed you two at the time. I didn't know about Jordan either. This is a lot to take in."

"Dad supposedly said he was going to tell you about their talk when he got home that day."

"Wow. I don't know what else to say." She leans back and wipes under her eyes. "I can't believe Kellan kept that to himself all this time. He guarded himself a lot. It breaks my heart for him. But now there are no more roadblocks for you two." Her hand cups my cheek. "I'm really happy for you. I couldn't ask for a better future son-in-law."

"Whoa, whoa." I raise my hands. "Nobody is talking

about the M word." I can't even say it myself, but the thought does make me giddy. "That's the furthest thing from my mind. Let's talk about something else."

"Right." She grins. "I'll let you off the hook now, but I want more details later on."

"We'll see. Hey, I asked Kellan about his plans for Christmas and invited him over for dinner. I told him to ask Dara too. Noelle should get to know her since she'll be starting daycare soon. Their mom usually comes to visit this time of year, but she had surgery and can't travel. So I thought it'd be nice to have dinner here, since they grew up in this house."

Mom's face lights up. "What a wonderful idea. I'd love that! Let me think about what we can make. I know I usually make a turkey, but... I don't think I'll ever do it again."

I squeeze her hand. We're so wrapped up in other things, but we're both still hurting. We're also blocking it out. We've been putting off looking through Sandy and Abigail's things. I take a breath.

"Mom, I have an idea. Just hear me out before you say anything. You know we have to empty the house before the renovations start. We need to do that soon—my goal is to have the house ready and gutted by the end of January, even if we don't have all the permits yet. I'd like us to go from one room to the next and agree on what we keep and what goes." We've already said we'd let a lot of the furniture go because it's not our style. Thankfully they didn't have much.

"I thought we could spread the word to the neighbors that we'd like to share the things we don't want. We have more money than we need. I might even bring some stuff from my house in Barton. We can also ask for help to remove every-thing from the house in exchange for what they might want. We could make it a town effort since we met numerous people who met Sandy and Abigail. And we can donate whatever's left.

"I was even thinking we could ask the local newspaper to write an article about how we're doing this in memory of them. The reporter I met last night gave me her card. I could ask her about it. What do you think?" I scoop up some yogurt and enjoy the sweetness when it hits my mouth.

She's quiet. I turn and ask again, "Mom, what do—"

Her eyes are full of tears and her shoulders are shaking like a leaf. I drop the yogurt cup on the table, spilling the contents, and wrap my arms around her. "Oh, Mom."

She shakes her head and uses a napkin to wipe her nose. "I'm fine."

"No, you're not. Talk to me," I beg, squeezing her tight. She whimpers.

"It's a big reminder that Sandy's never coming back. I keep thinking we're just babysitting Noelle, and she'll walk through the door any minute. But she's really gone. Gone!" she sobs. My eyes pool as she falls apart in my arms.

"It's okay. Let it out. You've been so strong for all of us. It's about time you let it out. Sandy was your daughter. Grieving her is natural. Necessary," I murmur, rubbing her back.

"I suffered losing your father, and I picked myself back up no matter how hard it was, because I had to. I still miss him so damn much it's hard to breathe sometimes, but this is worse. No mother should ever have to bury her own child. Sandy and Abigail had so much to look forward to and it was taken away from them.

"You and I are the ones who'll get to enjoy Noelle, to watch her grow, meet her milestones. She should be making them smile every second of every day. It breaks my heart so much. I dread going through more of their things because everything we give away… every piece is another part of Sandy, gone forever."

"But we'll keep the valuable stuff so Noelle has memories of them. We have tons of pictures from when Sandy was little. We'll make sure Noelle knows who her moms were. We'll stay in contact with Katherine too."

"But what are we going to tell Noelle?" She jerks away and stands up, her voice rising to a pitch I haven't heard in a long time. "We didn't even know Sandy anymore. We don't know anything about Abigail. Sandy deprived us of being a family while she was off making a family with someone else. Do you know how much that hurts me as her mom?" She balls her fist on her chest. Tears stream down her face like a waterfall, splitting my heart in two.

"After your dad died, I imagined that I'd walk my girls down the aisle on their wedding day. When Noelle was born, I should've been in the hospital waiting to meet my first grandchild. Is it my fault that Sandy and I weren't close anymore? Could I have done something better?"

"Mom, look at me." She drags her eyes up to mine. "You need to calm down a little bit. You're scaring me, and don't forget Noelle is here." She glances at Noelle then her face drops.

"I'm so sorry. I've been holding it in for so long. Your idea really hit my heart."

"We don't have to do it." I embrace her again.

"No. Not in a bad way. It's really beautiful what you want to do. You make me so proud." She strokes the side of my head. "I love you so much. Let's promise to stay close. I'll always be here for you and Noelle, no matter what you decide to do or where you choose to live. I don't want to miss another day out of your lives."

I didn't think my heart could ache anymore. She's been suffering more than I realized, and not only because of losing Dad and Sandy. I hurt her too because I was hardly around. She's been alone for years. It's my turn to be strong for her.

"I'm sorry too, Mom. I've been so selfish and obsessed with what's happening to me, that I haven't paid attention to what you needed too."

"Don't apologize. Your life has changed far more than mine. Sandy's death ripped me apart, but look what I've gained because of it. It brought you home and gave us Noelle. I'll admit I'm a bit selfish too. I've enjoyed every second being here with you and spending time with Noelle. It's helped me so much."

My stomach twists. It's my fault. I asked for this. I wanted a change, but I didn't want people to suffer for it.

How did I end up the winner in this situation?

I don't deserve it.

30

CHARLI

"What about the basement?" Kellan asks, leaning closer to the screen.

"What do you mean? Haven't I shown you?"

He shakes his head. "You focus on the upper levels most of the time."

"Oh. Well, it's simple. Gut it and make it a finished basement." I pull up the basement on the screen and point at a section. "I want to add two walls here to split it into three rooms. One room for storage, one a laundry room, and the third could be a game or exercise room. It's such a waste of space in its current condition.

"I want to make this house about family and friends. Family gatherings in the kitchen, big holiday parties, barbecues. The house everyone wants to visit," I express with a giant smile.

I glance at Kellan to see what he thinks and do a double take. His chin is propped on his hand, and he's displaying a sweet grin. The basement is furthest from his mind. It's the same for me when he gazes at me like that.

"I love watching you work. You press your sexy lower lip between your fingers when you concentrate. Your blue eyes dazzle when you discover something new or an idea pops into your head. And when your hair's up like now, I want to kiss your neck... like this." His soft lips tickle under my ear, and I chuckle.

"Behave. We're supposed to be working. I need to send these scaled drawings to the engineer by tomorrow." I'm trying to be serious but failing epically. "Timelines, mister. I really want to finalize the blueprints." He doesn't stop, and I shiver with excitement.

This is only the third time we've been alone for more than five minutes. Noelle is in bed. Mom went home, and we're in the dining room working with my laptop. When we're alone in the same room, the electricity thrumming between us could light up the entire town. It's hard to concentrate.

"You're such a temptation. Just a little taste. Then we can get back to work." His mouth smiles against my lips.

"A little bit? Is that possible?" I tease him. I don't trust myself because whenever I taste him, it's hard to stop, and he knows it. He's become my favorite weakness.

"Try me." He wiggles his eyebrows with a challenge.

"Tempt me enough that I can't refuse you."

"Oh, I like the way you play." Without warning he swoops me off my chair and plants me on his lap so I'm straddling him. A loud squeal flies out of my mouth. Thankfully Noelle's on the second floor. "Is this a good start?"

"Maybe, but we need to be quiet." My body is already humming with my legs spread around him.

I gasp as he pulls me closer so my core presses against his hard length. "Every time I'm near you, I have to control myself. The smell of lavender and your shiny pink lips make me lose my mind. I want to touch your soft skin and sexy curves," he whispers, kissing my neck, making my pulse race.

I rub against him and watch his eyes close. "Hmm. You like that." He nods, grinding me against him harder. God, I want him more than anything. "I want to touch your warm, naked skin."

He yanks his Henley out of his jeans, then lifts his arms. I rid him of it and drop the shirt to the ground, then lean back to drink him in. "You're so sexy."

His eyes open and are a fervent midnight blue. I love how his eyes change color when he's aroused. I trace my fingertips over the perfectly sculpted muscles of his chest, then play with the soft patch of hair there before continuing down to the rim of his jeans.

"My turn." He quickly unbuttons my shirt all the way down and pushes it off my shoulders, exposing my silky white bra.

"Take them off me," I pant, my chest heaving, wanting his touch more than anything.

He yanks off my shirt and tosses it to the side, then removes my bra with speed and ease. I wrap my arms around him and brush my breasts against his chest, creating a magical spark. I swear I could come undone just from the friction between my sensitive skin and his. Finally his mouth is on mine, taking what he needs. I give it to him freely.

His rough fingers brush down my spine, leaving a trail of heat behind. Then his hands glide to the front. His thumbs find my nipples and pinch them lightly, making me groan.

"I want you." His voice is rough and needy. *Hell, yes.* "Floor or couch?"

"Couch." I'm living my twenty-two-year-old self's fantasy. He picks me up, and I wrap my legs around him. He lays me on the couch and places a pillow under my head... and then hovers over me like he's afraid he'll crush me.

His eyes caress my face and then lock with mine. Lines form on his forehead. "What's the matter?" I ask, raking my fingers through his hair.

"I've waited so long to be near you, to touch your perfect body. It's hard to believe it's real and we're together."

"You're not dreaming. Feel my heart?" He dips his head and peppers sweet kisses over my racing heart, making me wish I was completely naked against him. "That's what you do to me every time you're near me or touch me or kiss me." Slowly his lips find their way to my overly sensitive nipples. One by one, teasing them, licking them. "I love when you do that." My entire body is on full alert. Any touch lights a flame in me.

I spread my legs farther apart, wishing his hands would move lower. I'm not usually a vocal person during sex, but with him it's different. He slides one hand from my knee all the way up my inner thigh to my center, rubbing lightly against my pants. My breath leaves me, and I feel myself nodding my head. "Just like that," I mumble.

He lifts his head, his eyes connecting with mine, and touches the button of my pants. I claim his mouth, giving him silent permission. His fingers undo it and lower the zipper, then he pushes my pants and underwear down. But down is not enough.

"Pull them off," I plead. He quirks a smile, sits up, and slowly removes them. More clothes to scatter around.

Dark with desire, his eyes sweep my body from head to toe. My heart skips a beat with anticipation. "You're beyond my wildest dreams," he mutters huskily.

I fiddle with his jeans, but my hands are shaking. "You too." He stands up and strips with no inhibition. I push up on my elbows to get a full view of his spectacular naked body. His tight muscular physique and light tan lines from his shirt are products of his physical labor. My mouth waters, knowing he's mine. "I could stare at you all day."

He hovers over me again and kisses me softly. "When we're ready to have sex, I want you alone for hours so I can memorize every curve of your body. Then you can stare at me all you want. Right now, I just want to explore you and make you feel good. Tonight's a preview of what's to come."

When will that happen? With our busy schedules and Noelle, it feels like it'd be impossible to be alone for a long length of time. When I say alone, I mean with no one else in the house.

"Touch me, Kell. I can't take it anymore. It's been so long." He flashes me a sly smile, spreading my legs again as he kneels. His eyes watch as his finger circles my nerves and teases my entrance. *That's so hot.*

"Fuck, you're so wet and warm. I'm not going to last long just because of this." He slowly presses a finger inside me, still watching, and I buck into his hand. One of my hands squeezes his forearm, guiding him, and the other wraps around his pulsing erection, forcing a guttural moan from his sexy mouth. I love the feeling of him in my hand. Soft skin and hard.

He moves in and out of me faster, adding another finger. My hips move in sync with my hand pumping him. He hovers over me again, taking my mouth in a savage kiss as we move together like we can't get enough.

"Yes," he hisses, breaking away from my mouth. "More." His thumb circles the bundles of nerves, and I'm building, so close.

"Kellan," I gasp, my back arching. His mouth covers mine to mute our moans as I let go. Spasms of pure bliss rush through me and seconds later, Kellan's body freezes, then follows me explosively. Riding out the last euphoric pulsing waves, he collapses on me. I can't find the breath to speak.

I just did that with Kellan. *My Kellan.* And it was the hottest thing I've ever experienced. And I want to do it again.

He lifts his head and looks at me with hooded eyes. "What a mess." We chuckle together.

"Yeah, but it was worth it." I kiss him hard and fast. "*So* worth it."

"It sure was." He sighs, laying his head on my chest. "Christmas came early."

"Just to make sure I understand. My friend Kerry will write an article for the paper, and it'll go out around January third. Then a week later, you'll have an 'open house,'" Dara says, using air quotes. "And people can come and take whatever they want. Right?" She pushes her empty plate forward. "And Kerry will also write something on the day itself."

"Yes. First come, first served," Mom answers her.

"Between that time and January fifteenth, you want the house cleared out of furniture and anything else the people want to take. That way, by the end of January, everything is gutted in the house and it's ready to go," Dara concludes.

"Yep. I already went to the neighbors around Sandy's house, and they were excited to help. Most of the furniture is in decent condition. I'd rather give it away to someone who could use it than dispose of it. Not everybody is as fortunate as us," I explain. Kellan squeezes my hand under the table.

She leans forward on her elbows. "I'll send out an email to the moms at the daycare and my neighbors."

"Thanks. I'd like as much exposure as we can get," I say.

We've just finished Christmas dinner. Mom outdid herself —there are hardly any leftovers. The afternoon has been full of light conversation, happy memories, and what we needed most… laughter. It's the best Christmas I've had in a long time.

"Are we all finished? Looks like everyone enjoyed the feast. Your plates are clean." Mom beams and starts to clear off the table.

"It was delicious. You'll have to give me your recipe for that ham," Dara compliments her.

"Thank you." Mom gives her a quick hug. "If you're all finished, why don't you go into the living room and relax. I think I saw some Christmas presents still under the tree."

"I'll help you, Tricia," Dara offers, stacking the plates. "You guys go to the living room and play with Noelle."

Kellan walks over to where clean towels are, grabs one, and wets it. Then he comes back and cleans off Noelle's hands and face. I sit there in awe that he did it without hesitation or prompting, and my heart feels warm and fuzzy. Noelle responds by blowing raspberries, and Kellan mimics her. She lets out a true belly laugh that causes us to join in with her.

"Let me get my phone. That's something I want to make a video of. There's nothing like a good baby laugh." I find it and run back to the dining room. "Okay. Do it again." Kellan starts up again, and thirty seconds later, I stop the video with tears running down my face. "Oh, my stomach hurts. I swear she loves you, Kellan." *And I think I do too, or close to it.*

He would make a great father someday. Does he really want a future with us? What does that entail? Marriage? It's so early to think about that, but I can't help it when it's not only me anymore. Ever since the other night, things have been even more intense between us. And I'm not complaining. The magnetic pull is hard to resist, but we've been so busy; it's also hard to find time alone. And it's driving me nuts because I'm looking forward to taking this to the next level.

When Noelle stops entertaining us, I take her out of her seat and carry her into the living room. Sitting on the floor, I plop her in the middle of my legs. Kellan drops down next to me with some of her new toys.

"Hey, I didn't show you what I gave Mom for Christmas. It was a surprise." I point behind me. "Can you grab that envelope off the coffee table?" He crawls over and picks it up, then hands it to me. "You can open it." He takes out the contents and sifts through them.

"Wow. Your first professional pictures together. Mom and daughter."

I sigh and look away.

"What's the matter?"

"It's really weird to be called her mom because I'm not. I know that's basically what I'll be for the rest of her life, but it'll take a lot of getting used to. In the beginning, I was thinking she should call me Aunt Charli."

"I can see why and it's up to you, of course. But I think *Mom* fits you. It's hard to explain. The way you treat her and cuddle with her, I see a mom. You already have a strong bond. Not that aunts don't do that. Maybe I'm biased, but I'm pretty sure strangers would think you're mother and daughter."

"The photographer did. I didn't bother correcting her. The pictures came out better than I thought they would. I should do it every year so we can watch Noelle grow."

"I want a copy of this one." He flips it around.

I drop my head and blush instantly. "How embarrassing. She insisted I be alone in some of the pictures. I played along to make her happy."

He lifts my chin with his finger. "You look beautiful. I know I use that word often, but it's the one I connect with you most. You're gorgeous, sexy, pretty, hot... but beautiful matches you best because you're beautiful inside too." His words make me melt on the floor.

"I don't mind hearing it, especially when I don't feel that way sometimes. Thank you." Our lips connect and I enjoy every bit of it like he's going to be taken away from me. I know it's stupid, but after all that's happened, I can't help feeling vulnerable. "I love your kisses. Soft and yummy. You've been a part of this family for so long, but really, this is our first Christmas together."

"Mmm hmm." He caresses my cheek with his thumb. "And not the last."

Mom comes into the living room, all cheery. "Okay, time for some presents. It's only a couple. I know we said only gifts for Noelle but, oh well!" She turns on some Christmas music. "Dara, let's sit on the floor so we're with Noelle too."

Pretty soon, we're all seated with Noelle in the middle. Kellan reaches under the tree.

"Sorry, Charli. I couldn't resist. This is a little something that I think you'll like." He hands me a gift bag.

Inside is a triangular blue box. My eyes widen in surprise. "Swarovski! Is this what I think it is?" I lift the top. "Yay. I was right. This is like the ones on your tree, Dara. I wonder where he got the idea," I tease. Carefully I take out the gorgeous crystal snowflake and admire the intricate details. "These are so exquisite and heavy. I love it!" I lean over and kiss him sweetly. "Thank you so much."

"Dara said you liked hers, so I had to do it," he admits, rubbing my back.

Noelle grabs the little gift bag and shakes it in the air, then tries to put it in her mouth. I take it and place it far away. She whines because I'm no fun. "Nuh uh. You don't eat that. Bite on this." I pop her pacifier in her mouth, and she spits it out, making me laugh.

Mom gets up and retrieves a large gift from the side of the tree. She carries it over to Kellan and places it in front of him. He cocks an eyebrow and glances at me and Mom. "No presents, huh?"

"What could it be?" Dara says excitedly.

He goes to rip it open but I stop him. "Wait. Let me explain this first. Mom and I had a long conversation the other day, and this is something we thought you should have. It means something to us, so we hope it does to you too."

He hesitates, and Dara nudges him. "Well come on. Open it!"

I watch him intently, nerves kicking up in my stomach. What if he doesn't want it? Or thinks it's stupid? I guess I'll take it back from him because it's worth millions to me and Mom. Mom glances at me and grins, but I see the apprehension in her eyes. She's worried too.

With the paper off, he opens the box and then doesn't

move as he focuses on what's inside. *Oh no!* Is that good or bad?

"I can't believe you still have this," he croaks, pulling Dad's old tool belt out. Mom puts the box to the side. "And you want *me* to have it? I don't know what to say." His emotional gaze ping-pongs between me and Mom. *Phew.* He likes it.

"I didn't have the heart to throw it away. He had that belt since he started ColMa. You can't find them made like that anymore," Mom explains. "Mick would've loved for you to have it."

This was a big step for us, to give this to him. I've only been with Kellan a few weeks, but I can't imagine life without him now. Everything is moving so fast, but it doesn't scare me. He fits in, despite all the chaos in my life and family. Like a missing puzzle piece, he slipped right into place.

"Even if you don't use it on the job, maybe you can display it at the office or use it at home," I suggest.

"Or to finish my bench," Dara chimes in, then chuckles.

"Thank you. Really. It was one hell of a ride all those years, working together with him. I wouldn't be here right now for several reasons." He places it back into the box, then hugs me tightly and gets up to hug Mom.

Today couldn't get any better.

31

KELLAN

We're halfway to Charli's house in Barton, and I can feel the tension oozing out of her pores as we get closer.

"Are you nervous to see Jordan?" I ask, reaching for her hand across the console of my truck.

"If he's there," she responds, staring out the side window. She's been pinching her lower lip for a while. It has to hurt by now.

"He told you he would be."

"Yeah. But I don't believe anything he says. Maybe I'm worried he didn't take me seriously and hasn't packed up his shit."

"Are you worried because I'm going to be there too?"

"No. I want you there whether he likes it or not. But I didn't tell him you were coming with me or that we're dating." She lifts our clasped hands and kisses the top of mine, then presses it against her cheek. "That's none of his business."

"Oh. I thought you had," I respond lightly. "That could make things awkward. Not for me… for you." I glance at her from the corner of my eye.

"Any more awkward than me walking in on him screwing someone else in *my* bed?" she counters, her eyebrows raised.

"*Your* bed?" I growl. "You forgot that detail. I want to kill him even more now. And to think I didn't want to make things more complicated for you. But Charli, this is the end of a long chapter in your life. It's okay to feel uneasy or sad," I sympathize, squeezing her hand lightly. Even though my anger is churning inside.

"I don't know what I'm feeling."

"Is there something else on your mind?"

"Everything, I guess. There's a lot to do between now and the open house. Kerry keeps calling me about the article, which is annoying. I appreciate her enthusiasm, but it's a bit much. Her overbearing personality grates on my nerves."

Dara told me how Kerry had mentioned the article her coworker had written about the accident and that she'd mentioned doing a follow-up piece. That isn't sitting well with me because what if something leaks to Charli involving me and the accident? But I think my connection would've been out by now. My paranoia is getting the best of me.

"Take it day by day. Give yourself some flexibility. Don't make yourself sick if things don't go exactly according to plan. A couple days' delay or change won't make a huge difference to the whole. In our profession, we're hit nonstop with delays that we need to make up for later on."

"I know… I know you're right, but flexibility isn't my best trait. One of my major downfalls in this business."

"Mine either."

"Now that my life is like this, I've been forced out of my comfort zone." She shrugs. "That's probably a good thing, I guess. Anyway, let's talk about something else."

"Sure. I've been meaning to ask you something and keep forgetting."

"Oh?" She turns to give me her full attention.

"You've mentioned a couple of times that you'd consider

doing another show if you had the right offer. What kind of offer are you looking for?" A real smile tugs on the corners of her mouth. *There's my girl.*

"Do you remember the popular show *Extreme Makeover: Home Edition?* The one where they renovated a house in seven days?"

"Yes. I think I saw a couple of episodes. It's not running anymore, right?"

"Not for years now. I loved the concept of the show. There are so many people out there whose homes desperately need renovation, but they can't afford it because maybe one of the parents fell ill and have no income. Or a low-income family has a handicapped child who's in a wheelchair but the house isn't optimal for one. You get my point." Her eyes are bright and she's glowing, like she always does when she's excited about something. I nod to keep her talking.

"Well, if I had my way, I'd revive that old show, only with a slightly different concept. We'd renovate those houses, but we'd do it on a more modest, less flashy scale. I'd want the owners to be able to maintain it easily without high costs. And it wouldn't have to be done within seven days, even though I am Ms. Fast-Track herself." She stops and looks at me. "What d'you think?"

"It sounds amazing. You'd be perfect for something like that. Has your agent been trying to sell your idea?"

It is a good idea, but inside, I'm worried. What would she do if someone approached her to do it? Would she relocate? Would I lose her? No matter how much I love her, I won't ask her to give up her dream for me. Especially after seeing how she lit up just talking about it. I don't think she'd want me to give up my company, either. Especially with our shared connection in it through Mickey. I could expand to a new location, though. And what about Noelle? The more time I spend with her, the more attached I become. To both of them.

"Kay should be working on it for me, but I haven't heard from her. I need to give her a call. The holidays are almost over. It'd have to be an awesome offer for me to consider it after all that's happened. My life is different now. I have you and Noelle. Mom would be alone if I had to move." She flicks her hand. "I can't think about it. Let's get this year over and start the new year fresh. How does that sound?"

"Perfect." Now it's my lips that brush over the top of her hand. The love of my life, and I might lose her anyway.

A few minutes later, she tells me to slow down and points to a cream-colored modern country-style house on about a half-acre piece of land. There's a truck in the driveway loaded with furniture in the back. I guess he took her seriously. He makes good money; why didn't he hire a moving company?

"It's a beautiful house. But you didn't design it, right?"

"No. We bought it when it was a couple years old. We didn't have the time to build one of our own. It was on the to-do list." Her voice trails off. "Come on. Let's get this over with. I'm looking forward to celebrating New Year's Eve with you under the stars."

I cup the back of her neck and crash my lips on hers. "You're going to see more than stars." Her eyes sear into mine.

"I'm going to hold you to that," she taunts me.

"You won't have to." I wiggle my eyebrows.

She rolls her eyes and chuckles. "Okay, let's at least get out of the truck. We could sit here forever going back and forth."

"You started it."

She slaps my arm and jumps out. I follow and lock the truck. We both stand there looking at the house. I touch her lower back and urge her forward. She pulls the keys out of her pocket and quietly opens the door. We're welcomed with the sound of people laughing somewhere in the house.

Charli's face contorts, then she whispers, "Lizzy's here?" She motions for me to be quiet when we step inside.

"Jordan, we have to stop. Charli could show up at any moment." Charli tilts her head and puts her arm out to stop me. Lizzy's voice continues, "I don't want her to know about us yet." Charli's breath hitches, and I grind my teeth.

"Then you shouldn't have come with me," dickhead responds jokingly. If he's trying to be cute, he's an idiot. I can tell he's full of shit, and I can't even see his face.

Charli walks down a corridor toward the voices. I follow, knowing this is going to be another major shit show and blow to Charli. We round the corner to find them locked in a kiss.

"I'd agree with him," Charli snaps, tossing her purse on the kitchen counter. They split apart and wipe off their mouths. *Gross.*

Dickhead's eyes bounce between me and Charli several times. He'd better be very careful with what he says.

Charli's looking at Lizzy, her facial expression unreadable. "Lizzy, you can't be serious. How long have you been fooling around with him? Before my sister died?"

Lizzy's eyes cast down. *Holy shit.* Charli cackles.

"And what the hell are you doing here?" Jordan sneers at me, trying to draw the focus away from them. I laugh at him, and he clenches his fists at his sides.

"I'm helping Charli get rid of the last scraps of the life she hated. You're obviously one of them, and I believe Lizzy has now been added to that growing pile."

"Fuck you. I knew you wanted her."

"And what's your point? She hasn't been with you for months. I don't get this possessive streak of yours when it comes to her."

He opens his mouth to say something, but stops. It's obvious he has no comeback. But I do.

"Thanks for letting me be the man she deserves. The one who will make sure she knows how beautiful, smart, courageous, and generous she is every single day of her life. Something you lost the right to do a long time ago because you chose money and yourself instead. You made the biggest mistake, but I benefited from it. Now I get to spend the rest of my life with her." I glance at Charli. Now her face is reflecting something close to love. For me. I hope, anyway.

"So then what's the problem if I'm with Jordan?" Lizzy asks innocently. It's ridiculous that she's falling for his bullshit.

"The huge difference, *Lizzy*, is Kellan is an outsider. He has no connection to Jordan. Not his best friend or coworker. I could care less who Jordan's screwing as long as it doesn't affect me. And here, I felt bad that you were helping me by occupying him at Sandy's wake. Then helping with Noelle." She snorts. "I guess *occupying* takes on a whole new meaning, doesn't it? I don't even want to know if you fooled around in Sandy's house that night you stayed. And you were probably playing house here. The house that *I* own. You both disgust me."

She steps forward and opens her phone, searching for something. Dickhead's eyes spring open, and he steps between Charli and Lizzy.

"What's the problem, Jordan? Afraid I'll show her those lovely pictures of you?" Lizzy's head peeks over his shoulder. "I think she deserves to know who else you've been screwing."

"What pictures? *Jordan?*" Lizzy asks warily. "And you've been sleeping with someone else?"

My cheeks burn because I'm embarrassed for her. Charli's flicking through her photos, not even looking at Lizzy as she answers. "Pictures that prove the type of asshole I was with for several years... and the one who's manipulating you now."

Lizzy's eyes throw daggers at Jordan, and I can see a sheen of sweat on his forehead. *You're going down, asshole.*

"Oh," Charli says lightly. "Here it is. The lovely one I took of him fucking Penelope in my bed a couple weeks ago. Maybe you two have used my bed too? I guess I'll be lighting it on fire." She glances at me. "Babe, do you have any gasoline in the back of your truck?"

"No, but it'd be my pleasure to go buy some if you want." She winks at me with an evil smirk. I love this woman even more, and I kind of like her calling me *babe*.

Charli turns the phone briefly, and Lizzy's face pales. Then she pushes Jordan to the side. "Penelope Wrick? A couple of weeks ago? *Eww*. And she's so old."

That's all she has to say?

"Bingo," Charli responds calmly. "Do you want to see the rest of the photos?"

"Jordan, how could you?" Lizzy shouts at him, her eyes glistening from the tears that want to break free. "And you moved into my place a couple days ago."

Again, if he makes so much money, why does he have to move in with Lizzy? Something doesn't make sense. But that's not my problem or Charli's.

"No, Lizzy!" Charli snarls, pointing her finger at her. "How could *you*? I expected it from him, but not from you. You were supposed to be my best friend here, and all this time you've been screwing him behind my back. Agreeing with me that he's an asshole, but fooling around with him anyway."

"You called me an asshole, Lizzy?" he has the nerve to ask. They ignore him.

"Not until you said you were over him," Lizzy mumbles, her bottom lip quivering.

"You two have no idea what loyalty means. You could've at least waited until he was out of my house. And let me guess. You were hoping you'd get a show with him since you've filled in for me for the last few episodes. This gets even more twisted."

Silence. Then Jordan gloats. "We were offered a contract for a different show," he says. "There will be a press release in a couple of days about you and me going separate ways, and that our show wasn't picked up for another season."

"Wow, what a tangled web he weaves." She shakes her head. "You must have figured out a way to deal with Penelope. But you know what? *I don't care!* As I said, I'm done with you. Both of you now, and the network and this fucking town. Have fun dealing with his shit, Lizzy. Who knows who else he's been sleeping with. Make sure you get checked for STDs. But it's your fault if you walk out this door, sign the contract, and stay with him."

Lizzy hugs herself tightly. Jordan tries to put his arm around her shoulder, but she elbows him hard in the ribs, making him yelp and bend over. Too bad it wasn't his nuts. But he doesn't seem to have any.

"Jordan and Lizzy, you both exhaust me, so I'm done here. There's nothing else to say. If you haven't finished moving yourself out—" Charli twists around to scope out the area. "Well, it seems you took everything in the house—it's too late. Anything still here stays here. I want the keys, and I'm changing the locks immediately. Get out."

She walks over to me and wraps her arm around my back. I do the same to her and pull her tightly to my side, trying to express how proud I am of her.

Jordan tries to touch Lizzy again, but she shimmies away and storms toward the front door. He watches her go, then drops the keys on the counter. He doesn't even look at Charli. No one's perfect in a relationship, but he should've at least apologized. Not that it would make a difference.

After all this chaos, Charli deserves the surprise I have for her even more.

32

CHARLI

Well, that sucked. I rake my hands through my hair, and my fingers get tangled in the ponytail. I scan the empty kitchen and then the living room.

"He really cleaned this place out," I say, opening and closing the kitchen drawers. No silverware. Nothing. I don't need it, but still. I shrug. "Less for me to do. He better not have taken my expensive tools in the garage."

Kellan comes up behind me and wraps his arms around my waist, resting his chin on my shoulder. "That was a lot to take in. Sorry you had to deal with that. But I'm proud of you. You're sexy as hell when you're mad. I'll be sure not to piss you off, though. I don't want to be a victim of your wrath."

I giggle, then turn around. "It hurt about Lizzy. In a way I can't be mad; Jordan and I haven't been a couple for months, but… it's the principle of it. And going behind my back. People who I've cared for the most keep letting me down. I feel like I can't trust anyone." Kellan kisses me deeply like he's trying to erase the last couple of minutes. His familiar minty flavor is a taste I crave more and more. I melt into his warm embrace and enjoy every sweet sensation cascading through my body. When we separate, I murmur, "That was a nice attempt to distract me."

He caresses my cheek with his thumb. "I hope it worked. Now what do you want to do? Change the locks? Walk around to see what's left in the house?"

"Locks first. I don't think I even care what's left. In the middle of fighting with them, I decided to sell the place. The bad memories here far outweigh the good. I'm a different person than I was when I bought it. I don't want to be that woman anymore. Maybe I should've offered for them to buy it."

I look around, and it feels like I never lived here. It's deprived of life and love. The memories of me and Jordan, especially any good ones, are distant, like we were together in another life. Staying here would be like living with a ghost. Goosebumps run up my arms as I imagine being here alone with Noelle. Without Kellan nearby.

He rubs my arms. "It's a big decision to make while you're pissed off. Why don't you wait on it for a couple days?"

"I will, but I'm pretty sure I'll feel the same tomorrow. This is something I need to do to finally move on with my life."

Kellan releases me and says, "I'll get the stuff out of my truck. Walk around and see what the condition of the house is. Think about what you want to take." He kisses me again, hard this time, but steps away.

"Stop teasing me," I warn.

"I'd love to tease you even more, but not in this house. You'll just have to wait for the surprise I have for you."

"A surprise? What surprise?" Excitement brews in my stomach, making me smile.

"Let's get moving so we can get out of here faster. I don't want to get back too late." He turns to go to the truck, but I grab his hand and pull him back to me. I cup his face.

"Thank you for coming with me. I wasn't sure it was the best idea, but I'm glad that you did."

"I told you I'd do anything for you. If coming here helps you move on, you're wel—"

This time I kiss him, and my lips take him by surprise. He embraces me and pulls me tightly against his chest. Our tongues entwine and dance to a slow tune. A warm sensation fills my heart, and I know my feelings for him have quickly changed into something I'm afraid to admit. Is it too soon to have fallen in love with him?

We slowly release each other, and he rests his forehead against mine. "You're not playing fair," he growls playfully. "We won't get anything done if you keep kissing me like that."

"Fine. I can't help that I love kissing you." I trace my finger along his jaw. "I guess it'll have to wait until I can show you how thankful I really am." He grabs my ass and pulls me against him, making it clear how hard he is.

"Let's get to work," he demands.

I nip his neck softly. "Yes, sir."

I thought it'd be hard to walk out of this house. I'll have to come back, but this time has a finality to it. My heart hasn't been here for a long time. My life was so different back then.

When Sandy died and I held Noelle in my arms for the first time, I thought my life was falling apart. Now I realize I'm starting to live again. My heart will never be the same because I had to lose my sister to gain this happiness. That guilt eats me alive sometimes when no one is looking.

"You're really quiet. What's on your mind?" Kellan asks, casting a quick glance my way as we pull out onto the highway. "You look lost."

"Just wondering how I got to this point of my life. I've

been wondering that since Thanksgiving. And how am I still standing and not in a mental institution?" I scoff.

"You have a great support system."

"Mom is the best, isn't she? I hope she doesn't think I'm taking advantage of her because she's constantly watching Noelle. And I have you, of course."

"I think Tricia loves it. In a couple of days, Noelle will start daycare, and that will free up her time again. You know why I think she loves it?"

"No. Did she tell you?" I watch as a smile forms on his face.

"Yes. So much so that when I told her my idea about tonight, she didn't hesitate to offer to watch Noelle so you can celebrate New Year's Eve with me and stay overnight."

I perk up in my seat and cry out with excitement, "Really?" But then I deflate. "I can't do that to her. It's New Year's Eve."

"I said that to her too, but she said she's in bed before midnight, every year. She also knows that we haven't had much time alone."

"I told you… she has a weakness for you." I twist in my seat to see him better. "So this is my surprise." He nods. "What are we doing?"

"Hmm. Should I tell you now or make you wait?"

"Come on. Tell me. I'm too impatient."

"We didn't start this relationship in the typical way. Boy meets girl, they go on a date… you get the point."

"Hmm. That's true. We did skip over a few fun steps."

"I really want to do something nice for you. Since we've never been on a date, I'm taking you back to my house and would like to make you dinner. How does that sound?"

"Wow. I'm loving it already." It's impossible to stop smiling.

"Then I'm going to eat you for dessert because I'm really

hungry. I've been starving for you for years. You have no idea how hard it's been for me to keep things slow. You want to talk about testing patience?" He skims my inner thigh with his fingers, making my core clench... *Holy hell!* He glances at me quickly with fire in his eyes. I swallow hard, anticipation building in my chest. I check the time and curse under my breath. We're still an hour away from home.

"Wait. I don't have any clothes. Well, I do have the stuff I packed up from the house." I look over my shoulder to the bed of his truck, loaded with my stuff. "I'll have to find the right box back there, but I'd love to take a shower when we get to your place. Wash away this part of the day and start fresh again."

"Don't worry. Tricia packed a bag for you, and Dara dropped it off at my house. My house is your house. You can do whatever you want when we get there. Shower, take a bath…"

Super. Now Mom *and* Dara know we're having sex tonight. Hopefully *a lot* of it. It's going to be hard to look Mom in the face tomorrow without blushing.

"You really thought ahead. When did you ask Mom?"

"Christmas Day. Let's think of it as a late Christmas present."

I reach up over the console and whisper in his ear, tracing my hand down his chest, "Can we have dessert first?"

He growls. "So tempting but… no."

I fall back into my seat and pout. "Stop getting me all hot and bothered then."

"Okay. Let's talk about something else that gets you excited."

"And what would that be?"

"The renovations. Time's ticking. In two weeks, that house'll be empty. Have you thought about what color you want to paint the exterior?"

"I have, actually." I laugh. "Right now, all I know is I want a dark blue front door. So maybe slate-blue with white trim for the rest? I have time to decide so it might change."

This is a perfect diversion, but nothing is going to stop me from wondering if dessert will be sweet or salty.

33

KELLAN

"Charli, time to wake up," I call, caressing her shoulder. "We're at my house." Somehow, I got her to relax enough during the drive that she fell asleep. Man, she's out. That's good because I don't intend on sleeping anytime soon. I get out of the truck and walk over to her side. Once I open her door, she startles, blinking her eyes several times.

"I can't believe I fell asleep," she mutters, stretching her arms over her head.

"You said Noelle woke you up a couple times last night, and we've had a long day already. I'd be exhausted too."

"Where are we?" She glances around.

"I parked in the garage since your stuff is in the back." I extend my hand to help her out. "Let's go inside and get this party started."

She hops out and doesn't let go of me. I smile to myself. I love how she doesn't want to break the simplest of connections. Years ago—hell, months ago—she was a constant unattainable dream. And now she's mine.

She bounces on her toes with a beaming smile, waiting for me to unlock the front door. I let her walk through first. I close the door and turn, almost bumping into her. She's frozen, standing in the middle of the living room, with her hands over her mouth.

Dara and her meddling. Little tea lights are placed all over the living room. Not lit, of course. The kitchen table is already set with a tablecloth, candles, nice dishes, and crystal wine glasses that aren't mine. I'm a little afraid to see what she's done in the bedroom and bathroom.

"Did you do this?"

"I'd love to take the credit, but Dara seems to think I don't know how to be romantic."

Charli turns and grins suggestively. "Are you romantic?"

"I didn't used to be, but I think I'm turning into one. I keep thinking about doing all this cheesy stuff with you. Carving our initials into the big oak tree in Sandy's back-yard when it's finished, writing you little notes and hiding them so you'll find them when you least expect it. Things like that."

Her eyes spring open. "Have you done that? Written me little notes?"

"Maybe. Maybe not. The question is, where would I hide them if I did?"

She fists my T-shirt, pulls me flat against her, and looks up at me sweetly. "I'm falling so hard," she murmurs against my pounding chest.

"I hope so… because I'm already there." I claim her mouth with a searing kiss before she can respond, leaving her breathless. When I let her go, I smack her on the butt.

"Hey!" she protests. "You can't say something so beautiful to me and then act like it was nothing."

"Let me assure you, it's not nothing. You'll see. Do you still want to take a shower?"

"Yes! I feel so gross."

"Then let's go upstairs. While I'm preparing your surprise dinner, you can shower and relax. Whatever you want." She follows me, holding the rim of my jeans.

"Did you know I like it when you're bossy and that you have one of the nicest asses I've ever seen?"

I laugh. "I'm not being bossy, but it's good to know for the future."

We walk through the bedroom door, and I scan the room. Dara invaded here too. Charli's bag is on the floor near the bathroom. Flower petals are spread all over the bed. *Flower petals?*

"How many bags of tea lights did she buy?" Charli laughs. "She's crazy, but I love her for it. I guess she assumes we'll be spending a lot of time up here tonight." Charli approaches with burning eyes that spark something in me so hot, it's dangerous.

I take a step back. "You're a very tempting distraction, but not yet. Shower or bath?" Her lower lip sticks out and I'm so sucking on that tonight.

"I love your gigantic bathtub and the walk-in shower with that rain shower head. But I'll only use that tub if you're in there with me." She proceeds to unbutton her shirt, deliberately revealing her black lace bra. My jeans are getting tighter and tighter.

"It's not working. Well, it is," I confess with gritted teeth. Her eyes focus on the large bulge in my jeans, and her lips tug up into a knowing smirk. "But I'm not going to give in to your attempts to seduce me. I'm going downstairs now. You have everything you need in the bathroom. Fresh towels are waiting for you on the sink, and I bought some of your body soap. Your bag is by the door." I peck her lips really quick and jump out of the way just as she tries to grab me again. She huffs and walks to the bathroom, giggling. "Take your time."

"I'll be thinking of you while I rub the soap all over my naked, needy body and watch the rainwater rinse it off," she flirts again.

I cover my eyes. "Now you are just plain mean." She smirks, then I hear the door click.

Time to start. I take my phone out of my pocket while I trot down the stairs and call Dara.

"How did I do?" Dara whispers.

"Why are you whispering? She can't hear you."

"Oh. That's true. Did you like what I did?"

"Yes. It was more than enough. Thank you. Charli was really surprised."

"You know I love this. The tea lights are the eight-hour ones. I bought a shitload of them from IKEA. There's more in a bag in the hall closet. All the food that was on the list you gave me is in the fridge or in the bags on the counter. The wine and champagne are in the fridge too."

"Have I told you lately that you're the best sister?"

"I'm your only sister," she grumbles with a hint of a smile in her voice.

"It doesn't matter. You're the best."

"How did it go at her house? Was Dillon there?"

"Jordan!" I correct her. She cackles. "Total shit show, but Charli's a badass. I love it."

"And her too," she slips in there, catching me off guard because I want to say yes.

"Whatever. How was Tricia when you went to pick up Charli's bag? And Noelle?"

"You'd think you were proposing to Charli tonight. Tricia practically threw Charli's bag at me because she's so excited. You have the Brannon women wrapped around your finger. Whatever you're doing, keep doing it. Noelle was in the cutest mood. Seven months is such an adorable age. Anyway, go back to your preparations. Have fun and use protection. I put some condoms and lube in the side table next to your bed."

"You better be fucking joking," I warn, my hand tightening on the phone. She guffaws.

"I am. I love you, but there's no way in hell I'm buying shit like that for you. That'd be sick!"

"I'm going now. Thanks again, and Happy New Year.

Enjoy your party." I hit End and laugh to myself. What would I do without her? Then I think of Charli losing Sandy, and my good mood plummets. To busy myself, I take items out of the grocery bags so I don't have to think about that.

Since the candles can burn for eight hours, I grab the lighter in the kitchen and light them wherever Dara put them. Then I open the refrigerator and take out the ingredients I need. My idea for dinner might be a winner or it could be a total bust. It's nothing fancy but it's something she said she was craving, and it's something I'm known for cooking well. We'll see what happens.

A while later, I see movement from the corner of my eye. I turn and Charli's walking toward the kitchen with her wavy golden hair flowing over her shoulders. *Breathtaking.*

"Stop! I don't want you to see what I'm making yet. Stay over there and sit on the couch."

She points to her outfit. "Of all things, this is what Mom packed for me. A T-shirt and sweatpants? This is the sexiest I'm going to get tonight."

"Charli, no matter what you're wearing, I'm going to find it lethal."

Her forehead crinkles. "Huh?"

"To me, you are so damn sexy all the time. Even the night you were covered in Noelle's pee. You look beautiful as a mom, an architect, slumming it with sweatpants, wearing a tool belt, when you're pissed off like you were today, and when you call me babe. So those sweats? I promise you won't be wearing them for long. And I can't promise they'll be in one piece tomorrow morning, either."

"Stop doing that or I'm going to say fuck dinner and get naked upstairs right now, *babe*."

I guffaw. "Let's add that to the list of things you do that make you sexy. Let's call a truce."

She takes a deep breath likes she's meditating. "Okay.

Something smells like sautéed onions. I'm starving. I guess I need some food if I want to have energy for later."

"*Charli*," I warn.

"Okay, okay. I can't help it. It's so much fun watching you squirm."

"We're getting nowhere. I need to cook. Do you want something to drink? Dara brought over a bottle of that wine you had at her party. She said you liked it. Or were you only being nice?"

Her face lights up. "I loved that stuff. Yes, please, I'll take a glass." She turns and plops herself onto the couch. "It's amazing what candles can do to a room. It's so cozy in here."

I wash my hands and grab the bottle from the fridge, then take a glass from the table.

"Look how adorable you are with that apron on. Are you going to wear it later when you serve dessert?"

I stop in my tracks. "I think I'm scared of you."

34

CHARLI

"I'm sorry. I can't seem to stop myself tonight. Maybe it's because when I'm around Noelle, I have to watch what I'm saying. Now that it's just you and me, it's no holds barred."

"Give me until we finish dinner. That's all I ask." He places a wine glass on a coaster, then fills it halfway. "Deal?"

I lift the glass. "Deal. My lips are sealed."

"So let me finish preparing, then it's my turn to shower. And no peeking in the kitchen."

"Can't you give me a little clue about what we're eating tonight?"

He scratches his chin, deep in thought. "I have to use the grill."

"The grill? Yum! Is it—"

He throws up a hand. "Nope. That's the only clue."

We enjoy some easy conversation as he cooks, then he places a bowl of breadsticks on the coffee table for me to "nibble on." Seriously? It's not a breadstick I want to be nibbling on. I grin but keep the thought to myself. I watch as he heads upstairs, then massage my temples. "Do not think of him naked in the shower," I order. But I don't listen.

I love his bedroom and bathroom. There's a king-sized

bed with navy blue sheets and comforter in the middle of the room, directly beneath a giant skylight. He can lie there at night and watch the stars. How cool is that? The bathroom is the same way. Over the bathtub is another skylight, plus there's a large picture window. The walk-in closet is long and narrow, but for one person, it's enough space. Of course, all of his clothes are perfectly folded and hung as if he'd been in the army at some point. The entire house is pretty much free of clutter. He probably twitches when he's at my place.

I search in my purse for my phone and call Mom. "Hey."

"Hi, Charli. Is something wrong?"

"No. Why?"

"Because you're supposed to be having a romantic evening. I didn't expect a phone call."

I chuckle. "Oh. Kellan's in the shower. We're going to eat in a little while. I thought I'd call and thank you for tonight. It was such a surprise, especially after dealing with Jordan today."

"Oh dear. What happened this time?" I tell her the short version. "Good riddance. I'm shocked and disappointed about Lizzy. But now he's gone, and you can move on. You have a lot of things to look forward to. Focus on your future."

"Thanks, Mom. Did Noelle give her grandma a hard time today?"

"She had her moments, but most of the time she's kissable. She loves to snuggle right now. I love it. It reminds me of when you girls were babies. She was bouncing away on her hands and knees today. Before you know it, she'll be crawling. Then we'll be in trouble."

"I don't want to think about that. I'm glad she's behaving. I'll make sure I'm back early tomorrow morning so you can go home."

"Take your time. Enjoy Kellan. Let him dote on you."

"You make it so obvious."

"What?"

"How much you approve of him. Love you. See you tomorrow."

"Happy New Year."

I keep forgetting it's New Year's Eve. "You too. Time for a fresh start." Speaking of fresh, Kellan stands to my left, and he looks mouthwatering. *Time to go.*

"Mom, I'll see you tomorrow. Call me if you need me." I hang up and put my phone on the table.

He steps forward, pointing to his clothes. "If you get to be comfy, then I do too."

"You're looking mighty fine from over here with that tight T-shirt and those low-hanging gray sweats. Can we eat soon before I lose my mind looking at you?"

He struts over and pulls me up to him. "Here's an appetizer to hold you over until dessert." His soft lips brush against mine, starting off slow. I'm thinking he'll stop, but no. His hands begin to roam my body, brushing over my breasts, teasing my nipples, which he knows I love, then down my body, cupping my ass... and all the while, he's kissing me senseless. He ends by sucking on my lower lip.

"When you were pouting in my truck and upstairs, that's what I wanted to do with your lip. Now, do you want to know what's for dinner?"

I straighten my shirt and adjust my sweats. "Yes. I can't wait to eat."

He grabs my hand and walks to the kitchen. "You recently mentioned how much you were craving something. I made a mental note because it so happens, I'm known for making the best."

"Cheeseburgers! Am I right?" It's so easy to make me happy. "My mouth waters just thinking about biting into one."

"Yep. I have tons of toppings, so you need to tell me what you want on yours. Grab your wine, sit at the bar, keep me company, and watch me prepare them. I can make fresh

French fries, or we can have chips with them instead. It's your decision."

"Whatever's easiest. I don't want to eat too much or I won't be able to move later, and we don't want that to happen."

"No, we don't."

"Can I help with anything?"

"Nope. This is your night off. Get your wine and sit your gorgeous ass down." He pulls out a barstool for me.

I don't want this night to end.

35

KELLAN

I gaze through the candlelight, watching Charli lick off her fingers, wishing she were licking something else. She's turning me on already. What am I saying? I've been turned on all day, but now that dinner's finished, I'm looking forward to the rest of the night.

"Want another one?" I ask. She stops licking her fingers. That's too bad.

"Are you kidding?" She leans back in her chair. "I'm full. The burgers were so delicious. Soft, juicy, perfectly pink inside… the list goes on and on. Maybe I'll eat one for breakfast. I'm glad you didn't make fries."

"If you want, or maybe later if we work up an appetite again."

She props her elbows on the table and places her chin on her hands. "You're putting a lot of pressure on tonight. I hope you aren't disappointed."

"That wouldn't be possible when I'm with you. We could just watch the ball drop on TV later, and as long as you're in my arms, I'd be happy. I've lived too long without you. Sitting on the couch with you is more than I could've asked for."

Where are these words coming from? I feel like I'm

reading Hallmark cards. It's like I'm throwing up anything that goes through my mind. I should shove another burger in my mouth.

I stand up and take my plate to the kitchen, feeling almost embarrassed. Gathering the plates, I open the dishwasher. A few seconds later, Charli's arms wrap around my waist, and she rests her cheek on my back.

"Thank you. For tonight, for everything. I agree with you. There's nowhere else I'd rather be than right here with you. In sweatpants, watching your hot self make dinner. Mmm. There's something so sexy about a guy who can cook. And listening to you empty your heart without restraint and filling mine with your loving words—" She squeezes me tighter. "I'm so afraid I'm going to wake up and find this was all a dream."

I turn in her arms and look into her glistening eyes. "You will never lose me. Now that I have you, there's no way I'll let you go. I'd fight until my last breath." *I love you* is right at the tip of my tongue, but I still don't say it. It's not the right time yet.

A tear runs from the corner of her eye. I wipe it away with my thumb. "Don't cry."

"I can't help it. I love the way you talk to me. It takes my breath away because deep inside the broody Kellan is the best man I know. If Dad could see us from heaven, he'd be really happy. Or maybe I drank too much wine."

"I promised him, and look where we are." I lean down and nuzzle her neck. "There's more of that to come. But let me get the kitchen cleaned up first. And don't offer to help. I'll say no." I glance at the clock on the wall. "We have three hours until midnight."

"Why does time run so fast?" She kisses my chest, then lets me go.

"That's why it's nice that you don't have to go home. There's no rush." I lead her to the couch and turn on the TV for her. "Here, you relax. Do you want another glass of wine?"

"Sure, why not?"

I refill our glasses and place them on the coffee table. "I'll be done in a few minutes."

"Okay," she says, curling up on the couch.

"No sleeping," I warn.

"Then get your butt in gear. It'd go a lot faster if I could help with the kitchen." She twirls a piece of hair around her finger. "Please?"

"Okay, when you look like that, you win. Let's go."

After the kitchen's clean, we stretch out on the couch, watching TV. My finger traces small circles on her stomach, and she shivers. Slowly, I travel south and do the same to her inner thigh. Her breathing quickens, and she squeezes my hand.

"Don't start what you aren't going to finish." *That's my cue.*

"Oh, I'll finish this time. Stay put. Give me a few minutes." I get off the couch and walk toward the stairs. She listens and doesn't follow me.

Back in my room, I light all the candles here and in the bathroom, then brush my teeth. I leave the flower petals on the bed, even though I know eventually they'll end up on the floor. Then I turn off the lights and go quietly back downstairs.

The TV is off, and Charli is playing with her phone on the couch. She's on her back, and her hair fans around her head. The powder-blue shirt she's wearing is pushed up, revealing her slender stomach. One leg hangs over the side; her foot rests on the floor. I love how relaxed she is here and how sexy she looks like this. I love *her*.

"How long are you going to stand there and watch me?" she murmurs, sliding her phone in her pocket. "Not that I don't like it. It turns me on, actually."

Without a word, I walk over and intertwine my fingers

with hers. She stands up and follows me up the stairs and into the bedroom. My heart pounds in my ears. Her dazzling eyes scan the room then fix on me.

"Wow. It's beautiful in here," she says softly, placing her phone on the dresser. Her eyes blaze, then roam my body, stopping to focus on the tent in my pants. My temperature spikes.

I walk around her, so her back is facing me. She doesn't move other than her heaving chest. I push her hair to the side, revealing her enticing neck. "You smell so good." With one finger, I pull the collar of her shirt away. My lips connect with her warm skin, and she shudders. I kiss, lick, and nip where her neck and shoulder meet, wishing I could leave a mark.

I grab the bottom of her shirt and pull it up over her head, letting it fall at our feet. She aims for the back of her bra, but I gently push her hands away and unfasten it myself while showering her back with kisses. She shakes it off her body.

My warm hands slide over her hips and up her smooth stomach. She lets her head drop back onto my shoulder. Our breathing comes in short pants. I find her sensitive peaks and massage them. She arches her back, then lifts one arm and wraps it around the back of my neck, pressing her ass into me.

I hook my thumbs beneath the elastic of her sweats and slowly push them down, along with her underwear, letting them pool at her feet. She kicks them out of the way. I yank my shirt off and pull her back against my bare chest, wrapping one hand around her waist. My other hand travels down her hip and along her inner thigh, making her inhale sharply.

"Do you like that?"

"Yes. I love when you touch me. Every brush of your fingers amplifies the sensations that travel through my body," she breathes. She arches her head back so her lips are near my mouth. "Kiss me."

I capture her mouth with mine, slipping my tongue through her needy lips. I take my time, enjoying the taste of her and the little whimpers she releases.

She breaks from my hold and turns around. Her lips brush across my chest while her fingers caress my stomach, making the muscles tighten. Seconds later, my sweats fall to the ground, exposing my hot desire for her. She steps back, and we enjoy the sight of each other.

"You're so beautiful with the candles reflecting off your skin and eyes," I murmur, stepping forward until the backs of her legs hit the bed. One of her hands travels along my back and lands on my ass, squeezing it, while the other wraps around my erection. I shudder when she gives it one long, slow stroke, teasing the head. "Fuck."

She kisses my neck and then nips at it. "Do you like that?" she mimics, smiling against my skin, taking me higher with every slow and steady motion.

"Mmm hmm."

"I do too. Seeing you so turned on by me makes me ache for you. What are we going to do about it?"

My patience finally snaps.

"Get on the bed," I say through gritted teeth. She sits on the edge, flashing me a sizzling smile, then scoots back, giving me a perfect view of what I want. Not even in my wildest dreams have I been as turned on as I am now. My entire body pulsates.

Kneeling on the bed, I crawl up to her, rubbing my hands slowly from her thighs all the way up to her breasts then back down again, spreading her wide open. Slowly, I lick and kiss her wet center, and her quivering thighs clench around me. She writhes after every slide of my tongue on her burning skin, releasing low moans that I love. I'm getting high on her taste and scent.

"Kellan, I want you inside me when I come," she says, her voice full of desperation. I tease her further with my fingers and a lash of my tongue, and her back arches. "Please!" she begs.

One more stolen taste, then I crawl up her quivering body, kissing along her petal soft skin. She pulls me to her and devours my mouth, rocking my body against hers with her needy hands. I reach over to the side of my bed for a condom.

"No, I'm on the pill and clean."

"I'm clean too," I mutter, biting my lip when her hand dips below and rubs me against her slick entrance.

"Nothing between us. Ever." I can't help to wonder if she means this physically and mentally. No secrets or lies… *Nope. Not going there.*

I position myself between her legs and slowly slide into her, my eyes locked on hers. My tongue finds hers in an open kiss.

"Oh, yes," she moans into my mouth. "All the way. Deeper."

"Fuck. You're…" Every muscle in my body quivers with delight as I sink in, feeling our connection. "So warm, so soft, so tight, so perfect…" I mumble through ragged breaths, willing myself not to go over the edge.

"And I'm yours," she whispers.

"All these years, you're all I've ever wanted. You, us, this… We were worth the wait."

36

CHARLI

Our breathing comes in heavy pants as he moves faster. I spread my legs wider and clench his ass in my hands, pulling him deeper inside me. He lets out a feral moan. My nipples brush against his chest, magnifying the flame inside me. It's so intense and so beautiful the way we fit together when he slides in and out. I want to stay connected like this forever.

Our mouths reconnect as I lift my hips to meet his powerful strokes, and he hits a spot inside that makes me see stars. Loud moans take over as our bodies spiral out of control. I pull away from his lips to catch my breath. "That— Don't stop. I'm—" He captures my nipple in his mouth, zapping my core with electric jolts.

"Yes. Let go for me."

My body clenches around him and I yell out his name as waves of hot pleasure swim through every part of me.

He grips my hips, driving into me twice more, riding out my orgasm like he can't get enough of me. One last deep thrust, and my name bursts from his lips as his body convulses. His hooded eyes connect with mine, and I wrap my arms around his back. Slowly his movements lessen, and he relaxes in my hold, nuzzling my neck.

We lie there quietly, basking in the afterglow. Once our breathing levels out, he pulls out of me, rolls onto his side, and pulls me against his chest. Feather-light kisses from his soft lips drift along my shoulders.

"Charli," he murmurs softly, wrapping his arm tighter around me.

"I know." There are no words.

After hours of worshiping each other's body, eating, and celebrating the New Year, I lie here gazing at the stars through the skylight. Tea lights are still flickering around the room. I'm exhausted, but I can't stop replaying every delicious detail and dreaming of what's yet to come. This has been, by far, my favorite day in a long time. Minus the Jordan issue.

Kellan sleeps peacefully on his back next to me. I flip over and hug my pillow while I admire his irresistible physique. The navy blue sheet lies low on his hips, making me shudder. He's so damn sexy. One hand rests on his chest. His soft lips are slightly parted, looking kissable. My fingers ache to run through his ruffled hair, but I don't want to wake him.

I'd watch him all night, but I need to pee. Without making noise, I go into the bathroom and close the door. The bathtub is very enticing. The view through the large picture window must be fabulous at sunset or sunrise. Shades aren't even necessary—there are only trees and fields around this house.

I flush the toilet, hoping it's not too loud, and wash my hands. Carefully, I open the door and jolt.

"Charli! No! No! You can't leave me!" Kellan yells. Weird whimpering follows, like he's in pain. "Charli!" he shouts again, curling up in a ball. He's dreaming.

I'm not sure if I should wake him up. He's sweating

profusely. I perch next to him and place my hand on his arm. He jerks awake.

"Kellan, you were dreaming, shouting my name. You scared me." His eyes move erratically.

He looks away, then gets out of bed and goes to the bathroom. What the hell was that? The shower turns on a minute later. I don't know if I should do this, but what if he needs me? I'm already naked.

I enter the bathroom and approach the shower. One arm braces him against the wall and his head hangs low as the water runs over his muscular body. I open the shower door and slip in. He doesn't move. I wrap my arms around his stomach from behind and rest my cheek on his back.

"Do you want to talk about it? Do you remember what the dream was about?"

Seconds go by.

"Yes. I lost you in the car accident." His voice is so quiet, I almost didn't hear him.

"I'm here and safe with you," I assure him, pressing little kisses along his back. He straightens and turns around, grabbing my face with his hands. His mouth crashes on my lips, taking what he wants like he's so desperate to feel me, to convince himself I'm alive. My body hums again from his touch.

He picks me up, and I wrap my legs around him. Seconds later, I'm pressed up against the wall, aroused beyond belief. His stormy eyes collide with mine.

"Charli, without you, my soul would be empty. You will always be the love of my life."

"I lied to you before… I've already fallen in love with you," I confess, my voice thick with emotion.

He slips inside me with a groan, knocking the wind out of my lungs. I grip his back and tighten my legs around his waist as he thrusts deeper and deeper, creating delicious friction. His pace quickens, igniting a flame within me. When our mouths connect hungrily, that's all it takes for continuous shocks of pleasure to ripple through us seconds later.

After we catch our breath, he lowers me to the floor and rinses us off. He grabs a towel and wraps it around me, drying me off like I'm a delicate flower. I don't say anything because I don't want this beautiful moment to end.

Once we're dry, we go back to the bed, hand in hand. He lies on his side, facing in. I slip in onto my back. He pulls me close to him and drapes his arm over my torso, burying his face in the crook of my neck.

"I love you," he murmurs.

With a large smile on my face, I observe the twinkling stars above us and dream about my future with Kellan and Noelle.

"I love you too. Always."

37

CHARLI

Several times a week, Kellan stays at my house until late in the evening. Sometimes he sleeps over too. He helps me with Noelle, and we hang out like we're a family. Once in a while I think he knows Noelle's routine better than me. Since he's a neat freak, he goes around the house cleaning up. It annoyed me in the beginning, but then I realized that's him and that's where we can balance each other out.

At random moments when I'm busy doing something in the house, I hear her belly laughing as he's playing with her. It's the most adorable thing to witness. This big man joking around with this tiny person. A couple nights ago, he fell asleep with Noelle snoozing on his chest. I stood there and watched them as my heart expanded two times its original size. My heart is so full of love for them, it's overflowing. I want this for the rest of my life.

We didn't talk about the dream he had. I tried to bring it up the next morning, but he brushed it off like it was no big deal. I didn't press the issue because he woke up happy. He focused more on telling and showing me how much he loved me. I couldn't complain. And anytime he's been with me since, he hasn't had another dream.

The day has finally arrived. Mom and I have worked our butts off, going through all of Sandy and Abigail's belongings. Most of their jewelry, we kept for Noelle, along with their wedding dresses and tons of pictures. It was bittersweet when we finished. Whether there was closure, I've yet to decide.

"Charli, are there enough baby wipes for today in the diaper bag? And what about diapers?" Mom hollers from upstairs.

"Let me check." I grab the bag off the chair and open all the pockets. Five diapers. I think that's enough. There's one full package of wipes. "We're good to go," I call out.

Mom is going to take care of Noelle during the morning at the open house. Kerry's bringing a photographer to take pictures to go along with the article. I think Noelle should be there, since she's part of the story. We have no idea how long this day will be, so after noon (or sooner, if Noelle decides she's had enough), Mom will bring her back here.

This diaper bag is a mess. I remove the contents, then shake it upside down over the garbage to get out the crumbs and other junk. A folded-up piece of orange paper falls out onto the floor. When I open it, I smile like I've won the lottery. It's one of the notes Kellan told me he'd hidden some-where. Trying not to laugh, I read it out loud. *You're like Reese's Pieces. I can't get enough.* He is so damn sweet.

I slip it into the back pocket of my jeans. That'll get me through the day.

"Mom, I'm going to pack the car. We need to get going."

Half an hour later, I pull up on the street near Sandy's house. Kellan's already there. Two large industrial dumpsters, delivered this week, take up the driveway. The sky is blue like Kellan's eyes, and the temperature is perfect for a day like this. Rain would put a real damper on it.

Kellan walks out of the house, and we meet on the side-walk. "How are my girls this morning?" he asks with a big smile.

I cup his face with my hands. "I'm floating on air after I found a little note from you. It was a nice surprise. Perfect for today." My lips caress his. He smiles against them.

"Which one was it?"

I cock an eyebrow. "There are more?"

"I told you there would be."

"The one about Reese's Pieces."

He smiles sweetly. "It's true. I can't get enough of you. You're too hard to resist." He licks his lips. I glance over to where Mom is. "Don't worry. She's not paying attention." I slap him in the gut, and he laughs. "Ready for today?"

"As much as I'll ever be. Anxiety is bubbling underneath my skin. Hopefully I'll be too busy to worry about anything."

He wraps his strong arms around me. "We'll get through today knowing it's one more thing that frees the path to us fixing this house."

"Want to help me over here?" Mom yells from the street. *Oops.*

"I'll help her. Go in the house," he offers.

"Maybe not," I grumble, sagging in his arms. "Here comes Kerry with her tag team. Why is she here so early? She said she wouldn't be here long, but I don't believe her."

"*Charli,*" Mom says again.

"Go deal with Kerry, and I'll help your Mom with Noelle. Dara and some of the guys will be here soon."

"Same with the Hendersons who live across the street."

"Okay." He pats me on the butt, then nudges me in the direction of the overly excited Kerry, who looks like she's waving down a ship.

Give me strength to get through this day with her.

We open the doors around ten, but fewer people stop by than we were expecting... until, suddenly, at noon, the entire town shows up. Including a news crew for Channel One.

I walk down the driveway to ask what they're doing here, but Kerry intercepts me.

"I called them," she admits. *Why won't she leave?* "Now, don't be upset. Your story is one that needs to be told. Something that started off with tragedy has a happily-ever-after ending. Doesn't it amaze you that you ended up the winner in this situation?"

My stomach turns, and I'm ready to puke. The anxiety that was bubbling earlier might boil over soon, and I don't want that to happen in front of people. All I want to do is give stuff away. It was stupid to let Kerry do this. I don't want this kind of recognition. The focus should be on Sandy, Abigail, and Noelle. We're doing this for them.

"The cameramen are going to ask you a couple of questions about what you're doing here. You know what it's like to be in front of a camera, so knock 'em dead. Maybe some will ask you to help with their own homes. Great advertising."

I furrow my eyebrows, but she walks off before I can say that I'm not trying to get work out of this. It's no use with her. She has a one-track mind and has no clue how she comes across in front of people.

"Charli." Kellan walks up to me with a smile on his face. "It's amazing. Someone even wants the kitchen appliances. I warned him how old they are, but he still wants them." On cue, a man pushes the oven past us on a dolly. He stops to say thank you several times. I admire his hair. When he leaves, I turn to Kellan.

"Are you going to get gray like that?" I ruffle his hair.

"Maybe. My dad was about my age when he left us, and he was pretty gray already… from what I remember, anyway. I'm lucky because mine's taking longer to get there. Remind me to show you the couple of pictures I still have of him." He doesn't talk about his dad, so this is unusual.

"Well, I find your gray really sexy, Mr. Salt and Pepper."

He lifts my hand to his lips. "And your opinion is all that matters." I grin at him, then turn toward a sudden commotion. *Ugh.* Should've known Kerry would be involved.

"Can you believe she brought a camera crew here?" I growl. "I'm glad Mom already took Noelle home. I don't want her on TV. I let them take photos for the article, but that's enough." It's been hard for me to talk about Sandy and Abigail today. I know it was my idea to do this, but I didn't expect to be so emotional about it. And Kerry wanted me to rehash, in detail, Thanksgiving Day, getting Noelle from the hospital, suddenly being a single mom, the funeral—

"Charli," Dara calls. "Someone has a few questions about the bedroom furniture. Can you come in the house?"

I raise my hand. "Sure. I'm coming."

"Hey, we'll talk later," Kellan says, kissing my forehead. "If you need a moment to yourself, take it. We have enough hands to help out. I love you."

"I love you too. Thanks."

I'm going to need it.

"That's everyone. Dara just left with some of the guys. They're going for a drink." Kellan walks into the living room and looks around. "Look at this place—it's practically empty. I can't believe so much of the stuff is gone. You were lucky."

"I'm not lucky," I mumble.

"What did you say?"

"I'm not lucky. It wasn't luck that got us here today. Sandy and Abigail died. You wouldn't believe all the people who commented on how I've come out the winner in this. It makes me sick." My heart rate spikes, and nausea sets in.

"Charli, I—"

"No. And in a way, it's true, too. I lost my only sister in order to gain a beautiful, healthy baby girl. Then it comes out that I've inherited everything of theirs, including some money. So to some people, it does seem like I lucked out. To me, I feel guilty every damn day." My voice breaks, and I turn away from Kellan.

His hands squeeze my shoulders, and I step away.

"Why do you feel guilty?" he asks. "This wasn't your fault."

"Yeah... I think it was. I asked for this to happen. I hated my life. I felt so trapped. The day before Thanksgiving, as I was leaving Barton, I wished that something would happen to keep me here so I wouldn't have to go back. Well, something sure did. But why did it have to be this? I didn't mean for them to die."

Tears pour down my face as the words continue to fall out of my mouth. "Noelle, that beautiful girl, is now mine. What did I do to deserve someone so precious?" I pound on my chest. "Sandy and Abigail wanted kids so badly, and I hadn't even thought about having a family. How is that fair?

"So now, here I am—I'm out of my contract, I've inherited money and a house, Noelle's my daughter, and on top of everything else, I fell in love with you. All of this in exchange for the death of two people? I'm so furious with myself, at life, because it shows we have no fucking control over anything. No matter how hard we try to get a grip on it and steer it the direction we want, it hits us from the side, pushing us in a completely fucking different direction. So tell me, Kellan, how that is fair? And the really fucked up thing is, I am happy now. Happier than I could've imagined. And that makes me feel guilty too. It's one vicious cycle."

"Hang on a minute. I think you need something. It's in my truck." He doesn't wait for an answer as he runs out the door.

I go into the bathroom and grab some toilet paper to blow my nose. I look in the mirror, and I want to shatter the glass when I see my reflection. Snot is coming out of my nose, mascara is running down my cheeks, and my hair looks like one big knot.

The front door opens and closes.

"Charli, where are you?"

"In the bathroom. I'm coming." I wipe off my face and head back out to the living room. I stop short when I see Kellan standing there with a sledgehammer in his hand. "What's that for?"

"I think it's time you get some of that anger and pent-up energy out of your system. Why not do it with a sledgehammer? Which room do you want to start in?"

Suddenly I find myself smiling. "The kitchen. Or maybe one of these disgusting bathrooms?"

"It's your choice. Please wear this face shield and gloves. I wouldn't forgive myself if you got hurt. I've got some too. But this is all about you. I get to watch my favorite person beat the shit out of something. I'm glad it won't be me."

His favorite person. He's the only man who can cause butterflies in my stomach when I'm pissed off. He secures the shield over my face, then hands me the gloves.

"I'm ready," I say, pulling the gloves on my hands. I pick up the heavy sledgehammer with one hand and walk into the kitchen. This is going to feel good. "I haven't done this in a long time."

"That's okay. It's like swinging a baseball bat. Well, kind of. The bat is lighter."

I spin in the kitchen, looking for a good place to start. Ah, the bottom cabinets next to where the fridge was. I glance at Kellan, then at the cabinet I want to smash. One side of his mouth quirks up and he nods his head, quickly moving out of the way.

Deep breath in and then out. I roll my shoulders while adrenalin gives me the strength I need. *Don't hurt yourself.*

I lift the hammer and swing low. *Crack!* It smashes into the cabinet door, creating a giant hole. I yank it back to set it free, and the door pulls off its hinges and tumbles to the floor.

"Perfect. Again!" Kellan shouts.

I swing again, screaming, until the head hits another cabinet.

"Again! Let it all out."

Crack!

Minutes go by, and I keep at it. Screaming and crying repeatedly to Sandy and Abigail, wailing, "I'm sorry." Pieces of the kitchen fly around from each impact. Kellan opens the drawers, and I destroy them too. One last swing, and I almost fall over. I drop the hammer on the floor, and Kellan wraps me in his arms, letting me release the last of my tears.

38

KELLAN

"Feel better?" I ask, stroking her hair while she's still wrapped around me.

"Exhilarated. I didn't realize how much frustration I was holding in about everything. But now I'm completely exhausted. It's been a long time since I've destroyed something with a sledgehammer." She loosens her arms and steps back. With her eyes closed, she removes her gloves slowly. "I'm sure I'll have blisters from the death grip I had on that handle."

I take her hands in mine and kiss her palms. "Nope. Only red marks. Nothing major."

"My arms feel heavy, and my shoulders and back are going to be screaming tomorrow. I think I'll feel muscles I forgot I had," she says, stretching her shoulder muscles and then her triceps.

A lightbulb turns on in my head. "I have a cure for that. Let me make a phone call." Her brows furrow. When I walk toward the front door, I can feel her heated stare on my ass. She must not be too tired.

With my phone in hand, I dial Tricia's number. She answers after one ring. "Hi, Kellan. How'd it go?"

"Terrific. The house was almost cleared out. Listen, Charli had a little breakdown a few minutes ago."

"Oh, dear! Is she okay? It was a long time coming."

"She's better now. She's destroyed part of the kitchen with a sledgehammer."

Tricia laughs. "Mickey let me do that a couple times. It definitely gets the anger out."

"She might feel better, but she's exhausted. I hate to ask this, but can I take her to my house for a couple of hours to let her soak in my tub? She's going to be hurting tomorrow, if she's not already."

"Of course. I've heard about that enormous tub you have. I'm glad you're there for her, Kellan. It eases a mother's heart. Thank you," she says sincerely.

"I'll take good care of her, and I'll make sure she's home before Noelle goes to bed." I'll make sure *we're* home... I like the sound of that better. "See you soon."

I tuck the phone back into my pocket and go inside. "Charli? Where are you?"

"I'm still in the kitchen, babe."

"You know what happens when you call me babe."

"Yeah, you get all hot and bothered. And that makes you even more enticing."

"Uh huh. So let's go," I say with a gravelly voice, urging her out of the kitchen.

She stops in her tracks. "Wait. Where? I need to go home."

"I'll get you home in a couple hours. Right now, I'm taking you back to my place."

She shakes her head adamantly. "Noelle's been with Mom all day. I need—"

I place a finger on her lips. "I know. But I asked Tricia, and she said it's okay. We'll be home in time to put Noelle to bed."

"*Tsk tsk*. In cahoots with Mom again. But, okay. Twist my arm. What are we going to do at your house?"

"We're going to take a bath."

"We?" she screeches. I chuckle at her excitement.

"Yes, we. You said you wouldn't use the bathtub in my house unless I'm in there with you." I shoot her a suggestive grin.

"Enough said. Time to go."

"I think we could both use some R and R," I admit.

"My body will sigh in relief after the beating I just gave it." She intertwines our fingers and pulls us toward the door. "We can leave the rest for tomorrow. Let's get out of here."

In record time, we're walking through my bathroom door. This is why I love living in a small town. Everything's so close.

I rummage under the bathroom sink and pull out a bag of Epson salts. "I hurt my back in September, and the only thing that helped was taking long baths with this stuff."

"Alone, I hope." She squints her jealous eyes at me.

"I kinda like it when you're jealous, just don't become a psycho. That's not how I dreamed of you all these years. Don't ruin the fantasy," I quip. I tip the bag and pour a generous amount in, then close the drain and turn on the faucet. "How hot would you like the water?"

"Well, think about how hot my showers usually are."

I chuckle. "Right. I hope my skin doesn't melt off."

She wraps her arms around my waist like she loves to do. "You've survived just fine when we've showered together. And if I recall, you thoroughly enjoyed it."

"Okay. You got me. I love showering with you." I wander over to the window to close the shades.

"No. Don't. The sun will be setting soon. I'd love to see it from this view. No one will be looking in."

I press her to my side and kiss her temple. "Only for you. It'll take a few minutes to fill up. How about a drink? Water, wine, beer?"

"I'd love a cold beer."

I peck her lips. "Good choice. And this"—I squeeze her firm ass—"is mine later."

"We don't have a lot of time." She pushes me out the door, giggling.

"There's always your house," I yell back.

It's like we're horny teenagers when we're alone. We can't keep our hands off each other. The more we're together, the more I want her at my side. I want her face to be the last thing I see at night and the first thing I see in the morning. Forever.

It crushed me to see her so defeated earlier. Today was her breaking point. I had no idea she was carrying so much guilt, but I know how it feels. My own guilt from not telling her everything is similar, and it gets worse as the days go by. After she witnessed me having a night terror weeks ago, I should've told her then. Maybe it's my turn to throw the sledgehammer around.

I take two beers out of the fridge and pop the caps off, then head back upstairs. "I'm back." She's been busy. Candles are lit around the tub, and towels are waiting on a stool next to it. "It looks nice in here." I hand her a beer and we clink the bottles, then put them on the stool next to the towels. I dim the lights in the bathroom. "Did you test the water?"

"It's perfect."

"We'll see," I joke.

I stand in front of her. "Lift your arms." She does what I say with a sexy grin. Gently, I pull her T-shirt out of her jeans, then slide it over her head.

Slowly I strip her bare, kissing different parts of her body, focusing on the parts that turn her on the most. I had intended for this to be a relaxing bath. I'm beginning to think it won't end up that way. No… I know it won't.

"Why am I the only one naked?" she asks, one hand on her hip. "Strip."

"Patience, beautiful." I help her step into the bath and watch as she submerges herself beneath the water. The big smile on her face shows she's enjoying it already.

"I love this bathroom. Look at that orange glow of the sunset, shining through the window."

I grunt appreciatively and strip out of my clothes. "Is there room in there for me? Or do I have to wait my turn?"

She traces my body with her appraising eyes. Then she scoots forward and lets me slide in behind her. Once I'm comfortable, I pull her back to me. I grab a washcloth, squirt some body soap on it, and lather it up. She rests her head on my shoulder, and I gently wash her arms and chest.

"How's that?"

"Nice," she murmurs, sounding sleepy. "Thank you for today. I was a little scared with how my emotions took over. They hit me like a freight train. I felt it building all day long—really since Thanksgiving, I guess—but I kept ignoring it. Once I thought everyone had left and I was by myself, my nerves snapped like a rubber band. I didn't want you to see me break down like that, but then I thought, what kind of relationship would it be if we don't accept each other even at our worst."

I let go of the cloth and rest my cheek against the side of her head. "I want to see all of your moods, your quirks, your pet peeves, your desires. I want it all because that's what love is."

She sits up and turns toward me. The love in her eyes reflects my own. I pull her up so she's straddling me, and water splashes against the sides of the tub. Then I turn the faucet off.

"My love for you runs so deep, Charli. When you crumble, I'll be there to pick you up. When you're hurt, I'll carry your pain on my shoulders, and when you're excited, I will do everything in my power to keep you flying higher. I was an idiot for pushing you away all those years. But it doesn't matter because I have you now."

"You sure do," she says, rubbing her nose against mine. "But I have a lot of baggage. Sometimes I wonder why you'd want to be with me."

"Everyone has some kind of baggage or past that weighs us down. Time will go by and things will get easier for you. And I have no doubt there'll be a time that I'll need you to hold me up." One by one, I kiss the tips of her fingers. "But either way, I can't express how my life has changed and how much happier I am with you in it." Her face lights up with the smile that I love.

"I thought I was in love once, but it doesn't compare to how I feel about you. You're the best man I know, and I'm the lucky girl who gets to fall in love with you more and more each day."

I press soft kisses along her jaw. "My soul recognized yours when I looked into your bright eyes for the first time, way back when. Nothing will break our bond. You're stuck with me forever."

"Oh, really?" She laughs and the mood changes immediately. "I think you need to prove that." She nips my earlobe.

Untamed desire takes over. "It'd be my pleasure."

39

CHARLI

"I still can't believe this house had no insulation. No wonder it was so cold and damp." I shake my head as Kellan and I walk through the house again. "And the amount of mold on the walls and under the carpets in the bathrooms and kitchen—it's so nasty. I've seen worse, but—"

"Yeah, me too. It's not healthy to live in a house like this. I'm glad you were only here for a short amount of time."

"Well, now is when the fun starts." I rub my hands together with excitement. "Watching a house transform along the way is probably my favorite part of the process. I took a ton of pictures so we can post before and after shots. Starting an Instagram page was a great idea so people can follow the progress. I posted these this morning." I open the app on my phone. "Wow, look at how many likes and followers we've gotten already."

He chuckles as I scroll through the pictures. "I'm sure people love to see black mold everywhere. They're now wondering what's hiding behind the tiles in their bathroom."

I shrug. "It's the reality of old houses if they aren't taken care of." My phone begins to vibrate. Kay's number shows on the screen. "Let me take this."

"Go outside where it's quieter," Kellan says, opening the front door for me. "There's too much noise in here."

"Such a gentleman." I shuffle out the door before he can smack my butt.

"Hi, Kay. I haven't heard from you in a while. How are you?" Shit, it's just as loud out here. I step off the porch and into the yard. She says something, but I can't hear her. I cover my left ear and keep walking. "What? I'm at the house, and it's a little loud. It's our first day on the job."

"Congratulations," she shouts. "How's it going?"

"It's always a thrill to see what's behind the walls and under the floors."

"Please spare me the gruesome details. Hey, listen, do you have time to talk?"

"Sure. What's up?" I stop at the end of the driveway where it's finally quieter.

"Brace yourself." *Holy shit! No way!* Goosebumps cover my body. "I have an offer on the table." My mouth drops open, and I'm speechless. "It's not exactly what you want, but it comes pretty close. Living the Life Network read the story about you and Sandy and saw the coverage on the news from the other weekend. I had approached them before Christmas, but I didn't hear anything back. Something about that coverage impressed them. The executives want to meet you. Sooner than later."

My arms feel heavy and numb, almost like I can't hold my phone. "I don't know what to say. Give me a second to catch up. This is the last thing I expected today." After not hearing from her for so long, I've been assuming none of the networks wanted me or appreciated my ideas. I'd kind of given up. "When do they want to meet me?"

"Wednesday in Los Angeles." My lungs harden like concrete. I'm surrounded by fresh air, but nothing goes in. *Count to ten and breathe.*

"Wednesday in LA?" I repeat. "That's in two days. What's the ru–rush?" I can't stop shaking.

"If you agree to the conditions and sign the contract, they want to start the process rolling right away. Charli, this is what you've been fighting for. Your dream is about to come true. I think you need to say yes to the meeting. You can fly to LA in the morning and be home by the end of the day. They offered for me to be there with you. Just say the word and I'll do whatever you want."

"Sorry, Kay. I need to let this settle in. I'm completely blown away." I turn around and see Kellan coming out the front door. My stomach twists with excitement and dread. How will he react when I tell him? I can't even figure out how I feel about it. "Can I call you back in a few minutes?"

"Sure. I'll be here. Congratulations. You deserve it. I'll forward you the draft contract right now."

"Thanks." I hit End and stuff my phone in my back pocket. Kellan walks up and kisses my neck.

"Who was on the phone?"

I rub the back of my neck and look away, then down to the ground.

"Charli, talk to me. Did something happen? Was it Lizzy again?"

Lizzy has been calling and texting me for several days now, but I haven't bothered to respond. I'm not in the mood to deal with her. Her messages are full of apologies. In one, she said she's not doing the show with Jordan and he's not living with her anymore. Again, not my problem.

"No. That was Kay," I respond, not making eye contact. "Guess what."

"Holy shit. You got an offer," he says with what I think is excitement in his voice. *Huh?*

I glance at him uneasily. "That was my reaction too."

"Really? A network wants you?" His smile is contagious.

"Yep." I yelp when he picks me up and twirls me around.

"Congratulations! I'm so happy for you." He puts me down and leans back, scanning my face. "So what's wrong? Isn't this what you wanted? Is the offer good?"

"I don't know. I haven't seen it yet, but Kay says it's pretty close to what I've been shooting for." *Honk!* My heart jumps out of my chest when my neighbor passes in his car. Kellan and I wave to him. My nerves are shot at this point.

"Charli, I'm not following," he says, propping his hands on his hips. "What's the problem? Why the long face?"

"It's a lot to think about. It's amazing but terrifying too. We're just getting started here. They want me to fly to LA in two days." *It'll change everything.*

"Two days?" Realization kicks in, and his face crumples.

"I know. It's fast. If I sign, they want to start right away. I don't even know where they'd want to tape the show. Let me read the contract first."

He rubs my arms. "Don't worry about us here. This house is in good hands, and you know that. You have to go to the meeting. You'll regret it if you don't."

"I don't understand why you're so calm when I'm freaking out inside." I step back. "Doesn't it bother you that Noelle and I might have to relocate?"

He exhales roughly and rubs the back of his neck. "Of course. But this is the chance you wanted. It's once in a lifetime that your dream could come true. I should know because I've got you. And I'd never keep you from what you want." *I want us.* "We'll figure it out. Listen to what they have to say and take it from there. Maybe the offer isn't what you want and there's your answer. I don't want you to regret not checking it out at least. Don't think about us right now."

Easier said than done. It's not just me anymore. "I don't know if I should love you more or worry because you aren't upset."

"Charli, believe me, this won't be easy for me. I'm doing

everything in my power not to push my eyebrows together right now," he jokes, forcing a smile from me. How can he do that when I'm so confused? "But I can't worry about it until it's time for you to make a decision."

"Shouldn't it be *our* decision if we're in a solid relationship?"

He squeezes my shoulder. "Maybe it's the offer of all offers or maybe it's not. Read the contract before you get upset or make any decisions."

"Okay." I huff louder than intended. "I'll call Kay back and say yes to the meeting. It's probably stupid because I haven't seen anything in writing. But I trust her, so I'm sure it's worth it."

"We were already going to McGregor's with the crew tonight for a drink. This gives us another reason to celebrate."

I can't believe he's taking this so well. Isn't he worried about what will happen to us? Are we strong enough for a long-distance relationship? Mom will be heartbroken.

"Hey, stop worrying," he urges, running his thumb over my forehead. "Now it's your eyebrows that are stuck together. I'm a bad influence. We'll attack it when a decision has to be made. Enjoy going to LA. Enjoy that they want *you*." He taps my chest with his forefinger. "They're smart. They'd be lucky to have your talent."

I wrap my arms around him and squeeze him tight. "Thank you for believing in me and for being so supportive. I love you so much. But we're only going to celebrate the meeting in LA, not signing a contract. Go back inside. I need to call Kay back."

He kisses me the soft way that he knows makes me melt, then walks away. How could I live without seeing or touching him every day? Once he's out of sight, I deflate against a dumpster, far away from where anyone can see me. Tears pool in my eyes, and my heart pounds in my throat. What is wrong with me? If this is an offer of a lifetime, why am I not jumping out of my skin with excitement?

～

I called Mom and asked her to babysit again. Then I picked up Noelle from the daycare and went home to wait. I sent Kellan a text saying I'd be late to the bar, then I sat Mom down and told her about the offer from LTL. She responded more positively than I expected, similar to Kellan. I wonder if they're only acting that way for me, because it's my dream job. But the question I have for myself is, is it really what I want right now?

I read through the draft contract quickly, only skimming through to the critical sections and the small print. The biggest issue is that they want to film the show in neighborhoods around Los Angeles. There's no way I could commute or only be home on the weekends. I know a lot of people do it, but I don't want to. Maybe if I didn't have Noelle, it'd be different. Maybe the location is negotiable.

The plane tickets are already in my email box, and Kay will be accompanying me. I've decided to leave tomorrow afternoon so I can meet her at the San Francisco airport, and then we'll fly together to LA Wednesday morning. Mom's agreed to watch Noelle while I'm gone.

I haven't told Kellan any of this yet. Maybe he'll be disappointed that I didn't ask him to stay overnight with Noelle. Just when I think my mind has quieted down, this happens. Now I feel more scattered than ever.

I never expected to find love in the middle of this chaos. And that's what I am—completely head-over-heels in love with Kellan. After we spent the night together at his house on New Year's Eve and then my meltdown, I surrendered and gave him my heart without another thought. And he loves

Noelle like she's his own daughter. Kellan would risk every-thing to protect us. He'll always put us first, and I'd do the same, right? I shouldn't analyze it because I know I'm the luckiest woman in the world to be loved by him and I won't give him up for anything or anyone.

"So why the hell would you want to leave if everything you want and need is right here in Margo Grove?" I grumble to myself out loud, then deflate in my seat. "I don't fucking know!"

My head is not in the right place to celebrate tonight, but I promised I'd meet up with everyone. Dara will be there too. I'll make an appearance, pretend like everything's fine, have one drink, and then run outta there. My phone rings, and I answer, assuming it's Kellan.

"Hey, babe. I'm almost there."

"Um, Charli. It's Kerry." *Gulp.*

"Sorry, Kerry. I'm in my car and assumed it was someone else."

I swear this woman is driving me nuts. If it's not Lizzy calling me, it's Kerry. She tried to contact me a couple times today, but I didn't pick it up and I haven't listened to her messages either. It has to be about another article, I'm sure.

"No worries," she says cheerfully.

"Sorry I didn't call you back today. I haven't had a moment to myself. What can I do for you?"

"You've been holding out on me. I had no idea. I can't believe you didn't mention it. It would've made things even more exciting."

"You already knew what day we were starting." I sigh and roll my eyes.

"No, not that. The *other* secret you've been hiding." Is she talking about Kellan and me being together?

"Ah, yes. You figured it out. Kellan and I are a couple." Why would this be exciting to strangers?

"That was obvious at the open house. It was written all over your faces. You are so in love. I'm jealous. He's such a catch! But then today I found out that Kellan was one of the heroes at the accident." *Kellan? At the accident?*

"Kerry, I'm getting a little annoyed. Spit out whatever it is you're hinting at." I glance in the rearview mirror to see if someone is behind me.

"Wow, you're really going to make me pull it out of you." She chuckles.

"One more time. What are you talking about?" I growl, ready to hang up.

"Why don't you tell people that Kellan was the person who saved Noelle? He and some other man took Noelle out of your sister's car when it was crushed in the accident." *Okay, she's finally lost it.* "Is that why you and Jordan split and you're with Kellan now?"

Focus on the road.

"Kerry, I don't know who told you that, but it's not true. Where did you hear this? It's completely ridiculous."

"That's strange. I was talking to my coworker who wrote the original article about the accident, and we were looking through some of the pictures on file. There's one of Kellan in action. His face is clear as day."

This cannot be possible. Why in the world wouldn't he have told me and Mom? How could he have kept it a secret? And why?

"Is this some kind of sick joke? I don't find it funny at all," I hiss.

"Oh shit, Charli... you didn't know?" she whispers. "He didn't tell you. I–I'm so sorry."

"Where's this damn picture? I want to see it. Text me the image." Rage bulldozes through me.

"Sure, I'll send it right now. I'm really sorry."

I disconnect the call and park in the bar lot. It couldn't have been him. She must be mistaken. *Ping.* My hands shake, and suddenly, I'm filled with fear like I've never felt before. I open the text and can't believe what I'm seeing.

A smashed car, almost flat. People standing around with their phones. A man holding a car seat. My heart stops.

Omigod. It's him.

40

KELLAN

The bartender slides two beers in front of us. "Thanks, Alex." I glance at my phone on the bar when it lights up. It's a message from Charli that she's on her way.

"Wow. That's tough," Dara sympathizes, sipping her beer. "Shitty timing. So do you think she'll sign the contract?"

I lift my beer, then put it back down without taking a drink. Alcohol isn't going to change anything. "I don't know. After she told me about it, she was super quiet. Kept herself busy around the house. Sometimes I thought she was walking in circles, not really doing anything. I don't even know if she's read the contract yet."

"You didn't ask her if she was okay?"

"No, because I think she doesn't need me to hound her. She needs space, and I'm giving it to her."

"How are you feeling about it? And tell the truth." She nudges my arm.

"I'm fucking terrified," I confess, watching the beer foam decrease in my glass. "What if I lose her and Noelle? What if she doesn't choose me... or us?"

"Maybe she won't have to choose. Maybe the contract is

better than expected, and she won't have to leave. Would you be willing to follow her?"

"Give up everything here? It'd be hard to give up my business. *Mick's* business. But if that's what I'd have to do to be with her, then I'll... yeah, I'll do it. Or we could have a long-distance relationship, I guess. That's not what *I* want, but... I want all of Charli, not little bits and pieces." I look at the beer in my hand and swirl it in the glass. "It sounded like an offer would never come, so I believed it like she did. She warned me from the beginning that her being here was temporary, but as we got closer, I thought she changed her mind. I didn't worry about it."

"And now you're together and it's serious..." She points her finger at me. "I know you're thinking marriage. Don't deny it."

"Of course I am. I want the whole damn thing with her. I'd ask her now if I could."

"Then love will conquer all. Think positively and be supportive. You need to be honest with her, and she needs to do the same."

I nod in agreement. This is supposed to be a night to celebrate. "Listen, Charli will be here any minute. I'm going to wait outside for her and get some fresh air."

"Sure. I'll watch your beer and save your seat. Maybe I'll find someone to flirt with." She wiggles her eyebrows and glances around the busy bar.

I shake my head and wander to the door. I walk out, and a strong, cool wind slaps me in the face. I zip up my coat and walk down the steps.

"Look who it is. You've been dodging my calls, man." It's Grady Malone, and his brother, Gray, is next to him. "Where the hell've you been? I wanted to see how you were doing after that accident on Thanksgiving. That was one of the worst wrecks I've seen in a long time. And I couldn't believe it was Sandy Brannon who died."

"Hey, guys," I say, shaking their hands. I look behind me to check if Charli is coming. I don't want to have this conversation. "Sorry I didn't get back to you. It's been a crazy bunch of months and, I'll be honest, I've been trying to forget about that day."

"Understandable. It was a shock to see you there. I saw you on the news about that house renovation. It's amazing what you're doing, especially after you witnessed that accident. Aren't you one of the guys who got the baby out before we arrived?"

"So it seems," Charli's bitter voice answers from behind me. My entire body stiffens. *She knows. I'm totally fucked.* Grady and Gray glance behind me, and their faces still.

"Guys, I need a few minutes alone. I'll catch up with you inside."

They nod and disappear.

"Is it true?" Her voice cracks. "You were there? You're the one who saved Noelle?"

I turn around, and my heart breaks when I see the shock and anger written on her face. Her chest heaves as she raises her phone with a picture on it.

"Is this you? And the answer better be yes or no," she snaps.

I don't look at it. "Yes."

Her arm drops and she covers her mouth with her shaking hand. Tears stream down her face.

"Please. Let me explain."

"No. How could you possibly explain this?" She turns and walks back toward the parking lot in long strides. I follow her until she gets to her car.

"Wait, damn it," I shout.

She whips around and gets in my face. "No. You don't deserve my time. You've had over two months to tell us."

"I didn't tell you because I wanted to protect you."

She cackles. "Yeah, right. I don't think I'll believe any

excuse you give. Hiding that information from me and Mom is unforgivable."

"Unforgivable? Because I wanted to protect you? Whether you like it or not, I'm going to explain myself. Then you can decide what you do next."

She crosses her arms, signaling she'll listen.

"I swear I did it to protect you and Tricia. My truck was higher than the cars around me. I had a movie-theater view of every damn thing that happened. Things that I'll never forget. Every single day, that accident finds a way to replay itself in my mind. Every detail comes to life again. I didn't know it was your sister until I got to the car."

"The dream you had that night... it was about the accident?"

"Yes. It happens a lot, only it's you who dies, not Sandy."

"But why? Why didn't you tell us?" she yells.

"Because you would have asked..." I stop. No, she wants to know? Okay. "Would you have wanted me to describe in detail how I found your sister and her wife in their car? How the steel pipes had flattened it? How the windows were shattered? All the tires were blown out?" My voice rises; building anger boils out from deep inside.

She shakes her head, tears streaming. "No."

"Don't lie. Eventually, you would've asked. You'd have wanted to know. It's human nature to be curious, no matter what it is. I know you said you didn't want details, and that's why you didn't read the papers or ask so many questions. But deep down, I know you wonder."

She looks away.

"Do you want to know about the blood and destruction I saw? Do you want me to tell you right now? I'd rather carry that burden on my shoulders for the rest of my fucking life, Charli, than let it torture you and your mom every damn day like it does me. And if that makes me the bad guy, so be it."

"Don't you think we would've wanted to know that you're

the one who saved Noelle? That you were there with my sister during her last minutes or seconds? Don't you think that would've made us—me—love you even more?"

"No."

She stills, surprised by my firm response.

"No, Charli. Because when I saw your sister, I thought it was you. My life crumbled in front of me. I thought I'd lost you and that you'd died not knowing how much I've loved you all these years. That you were the only woman for me.

"And then I looked at her again and realized it was Sandy. And you wanna know what makes me the bad guy, the asshole?" I stomp forward, startling her. I almost don't recognize my own voice. "*I thanked God it wasn't you.* I felt relief! I–I was almost happy that it was Sandy. That's what makes me a selfish prick. I knew I still had a chance to see you again. And that's when I vowed I wouldn't hide my feelings for you anymore.

"That's what kills me inside, not that I didn't tell you I was there. It's because of what I thought. It eats at me every fucking day. You aren't the only one suffering from guilt.

"Sandy's death gave me the chance to see you again. I saw that things weren't working with you and Jordan, so I took advantage. I don't know what would've happened if she hadn't died. Maybe I would've seen you anyway. But I don't care, because I can't change the past and I'll have to live with the consequences.

"What's even more fucked up is that I shouldn't have even been there. I missed the exit I was supposed to take and a minute later the accident happened."

She steps forward, shaking her head. "Why didn't you tell me the day I confessed to you? When I was crying in your arms because I felt so guilty. You could've told me then. And what did I ask for the night of Dara's party? *Pure honesty* from then on. No secrets between us. That was a perfect opportunity for you to tell me. And then again, after I found out about Jordan and Lizzy!"

"I was tempted to, every time. It killed me not to tell you, but I couldn't. My focus was on you. It wasn't my time to confess." I mutter that because I know she doesn't want to hear it.

"Always me. Everything was for me." Her tone is mocking and bitter. "I trusted you. What else are you hiding from me, *Kellan*? Let's see, there's the accident, saving Noelle, your feelings for me, the conversation you had with my dad the day he died, *three years ago*... How much longer is the list?"

"Please look at it from my perspective, why I didn't tell you. Please forgive me. Don't let this ruin us. If there's one thing to take away from this, it's that I love you more than anyone, even myself. I want to have a future with you and Noelle. I want you to be my wife someday and the mother of my children. I want fucking everything with you."

I step toward her to touch her, and she backs up. This time not for fun. My shoulders droop, and I take my own step back.

She's shaking her head. "I need to be alone so I can think. I won't be at work tomorrow." She whips her car door open.

"Don't you dare walk away from us. We're strong enough to get through this. I believe in us, Charli. But do you?"

Her eyes dart away, causing the ache in my chest to increase.

"I'm meeting with Kay in San Francisco tomorrow afternoon. We'll fly to LA together and come back Wednesday night. What happens from there, we'll see. What I thought about us an hour ago has changed, and yeah, it breaks my fucking heart." With that, she gets in the car and drives away.

Leaving me here with my heart in my hand.

The one I gave her.

The one I think she just gave back to me.

~

I couldn't sleep last night, and Charli wouldn't answer my calls. I was close to showing up at her house in the middle of the night, but I was sure it wouldn't have helped. Besides, I was too drunk to get behind the wheel. Dara called this morning and told me Charli didn't bring Noelle to the daycare. So now I'm in my car, driving to Charli's house, hoping to catch her before she leaves.

My gut plummets when I see her car is gone. I park my truck in the driveway and rest my head back. I don't know if there's a good way out of this. I jolt in my seat when there's a light knock on my window. It's Tricia with Noelle in her stroller. My heart beats a little faster when I see a sympathetic grin.

She moves away so I can get out of the truck. I walk up to Noelle and kiss her forehead. I want to take her out of the stroller and give her a hug, but after last night, I don't know if I have the right to do that anymore. I stand still instead, waiting for Tricia to break the silence.

"She told me everything when she got home last night," Tricia says. "She was a mess."

"Everything?"

"Yes. You, the accident, Noelle, the meeting in LA. I was going for a walk with Noelle. Come with us." I nod, and we amble down the driveway together.

It's quiet here. The only noises are the scraping of the stroller's wheels along the road, the birds chirping, and Noelle's intermittent babbling. That's a noise I've missed even after one day of not seeing her.

I stop walking. "I'm truly sorry, Tricia. I should've known it'd get out somehow. I never meant to hurt either of you. You have to believe me."

Her worried gaze fixes on me, then she turns away and continues to walk. "I know. It was hard to hear last night.

There were a lot of ugly tears and anger, not just hers but mine too. I'm surprised Noelle didn't wake up." She sighs.

"Things were starting to calm down around us after Sandy's death, and this gets dumped in our laps. I am disappointed in you, but the more I think about it, the more I understand why you did it. You were right to say that we'd ask questions even though the answers would hurt us. And knowing you were there for Noelle, that is the strangest of coincidences. It warms my heart." That gives me a sense of hope. "I can't say it was okay, but it's not enough to push you out of my life. You have a long history with this family, and you thought you were protecting us."

Noelle tosses her stuffed baby elephant onto the street. This girl's got one hell of an arm. I trot over and pick up the toy. I wiggle it in the air as I walk back to her. She starts kicking, and her sweet giggles come out. When I hand it to her, she wraps her arms around it.

That's what I want to do to Charli and Noelle. Hug them tight and never let them go.

Tricia looks sad. "Now, what Charli decides to do is up to her, and she may have a different opinion about it. I tried to talk to her this morning but she refused. She'd only talk about her trip."

"I can't lose her, Tricia. I won't survive. Going back to the old me, to my old life… it isn't an option. What can I do to convince her to forgive me?"

"Give her time. She's so in love with you, Kellan. It's been so wonderful to watch it develop. You didn't come together after all these years to end after the first real challenge to your relationship. A love as deep as yours isn't easily severed. I can't imagine that she'll walk away from you. Frankly, I'd be pretty disappointed if she did, giving up that easily. But that's me talking. I don't have control over her heart or her decisions. Leave her alone while she's gone. Give her the time and space that she needs right now. Try to understand why we're upset and disappointed in you."

Stuffing my hands in my pockets, I drop my head. "I've waited almost twenty years to be with her. I can't let me, being in the wrong place at the wrong time, break us apart. I'll find a way to fix this."

She pats me on the back. "Good. I can't wait to see what happens. There's one thing I've always had, and that's hope."

41

CHARLI

Kay and I sit in the massive modern waiting room at LTL headquarters. Last night, we had dinner together and went through the contract with a fine-toothed comb. The only red flag is the location. To be honest, two months ago, I'd have been in heaven.

My nerves are at an all-time high, and I'm exhausted. My head isn't in the right place to be here either. Why did I have to get the contract and find out about Kellan on the same day? When it rains, it pours in my world lately. I hope I can at least come out a stronger person in the end.

Kellan has tried to call me several times, and he's left a few messages but finally he stopped. And that killed me. It's his fault we're in this mess, but it's my fault I left him so easily and have refused to talk to him.

I know I'm acting childishly, but I have every right to be mad. *Don't I?*

Mom has been quiet about what happened. She texts me updates on Noelle but doesn't try to call. I know she's giving me space. But the quiet I thought I needed is stifling. It makes me second-guess my anger toward Kellan. I understand his guilt. He's seen me suffer with it myself.

I don't hold it against him that he was relieved. If anything, it proves how much he loves me. And I really do love him. So what am I thinking?

"Ms. Brannon, Ms. Korner, please follow me." An older woman with large gold glasses greets us. Kay and I glance at each other, then stand up.

"Here we go," I whisper.

"Good luck, Ms. Brannon." Kay smirks, then winks.

We follow the woman toward black double doors. She ushers us inside a large empty room, then closes the doors behind us. Suddenly I feel claustrophobic. We choose our seats, and I search through my leather bag for the contract and my notes. A yellow piece of paper falls out onto the table. It must have been stuck between the folders. I unfold it, and butterflies start an aerobics class in my stomach. A giant smile forms on my face.

"I'll say it again. That was an amazing meeting. Great job keeping your cool. The salary alone should push you to sign on," Kay rattles on. I'm partly not listening.

"You know the money isn't the only thing I'm interested in."

"I know, and I think you're crazy. I'm going to go to the bathroom before we land." She unfastens her seatbelt and walks down the aisle.

There were no messages waiting for me when we left the meeting. It was a shitty feeling, not being able to pick up the phone to call Kellan. He's the first one I wanted to talk to. This is the longest flight ever!

I open my hand and play with the yellow piece of paper tucked inside. This note made the decision for me. Such simple words, but they rocked me to my core. I trace them with my fingertip. *Never doubt my love for you.*

Kay's back, and she's still talking. "God, do I hate airplane bathrooms. I should've waited until we landed." She shivers as she sits down, pulling hand disinfectant from her bag.

"Kay, we need to talk."

A long hour later, I'm rushing to my car in the massive airport parking lot. Once I'm inside, I check to see if I finally have a signal. I'm shocked when I see I have four missed calls and several text messages from Mom.

I don't bother reading the messages and call her instead. The phone rings twice. "Charli!" Mom cries. "Finally!"

Chills run up my spine. "What's the matter? Is Noelle okay?"

"It's Kellan. There was an accident at the site."

No! No! "Wh–what? Is he okay? Please tell me he's okay!" He has to be okay. It can't end like this.

"He fell off a ladder while doing something on the roof. Or so they told Dara. Dara's at the hospital now. He's in surgery—he broke his arm and a couple of ribs. And there's something with his shoulder."

Tears blind me. With shaking hands, I push the button to start the car.

"Where are you?" Mom asks.

I pull the note out of my pocket and place it on the dash-board where I can see it.

"Charli, where are you?"

"Sorry. I'm leaving the airport. How am I supposed to drive after this? I'm a nervous wreck."

"Please don't drive fast. We need you here, but you need to take care of yourself. I'll keep you posted if I hear anything. Charli?"

"Yeah," I croak, wiping tears away with the palm of my hand.

"He's going to be all right. Do you hear me? He'll be fine. Have some faith."

Sniff. "I have to believe that. I'll call when I get closer. It'll take an hour and a half, maybe two. I love you, Mom."

"I love you too. Remember, we'll get through this together."

"Yep," I agree, then end the call. Sobs burst out of me. I'm so tired of crying! Mom said he'll be fine, and I have to believe it.

Please let me get there before he wakes up.

This'll be the longest drive of my life.

42

CHARLI

I slam my car into park and jump out. Mom called about an hour ago to tell me he was out of surgery. My head's pounding, and I'm dying of thirst. I run to the hospital entrance, ignoring my phone as it rings on the chain around my neck. I'm sure it's Mom.

Bursting through the emergency doors, I spin around, looking for anyone I know. Noelle's crying leads me to them. It's past her bedtime. I round the corner and find Dara and Mom, looking haggard.

"Charli. You're here!" Mom stands up, Noelle in her arms.

Before I say anything else, I take Noelle and hug her tight to me.

"How is he? Is he awake?" My eyes ping-pong worriedly between Mom and Dara.

"The surgery went well, but he's not awake yet. Hopefully soon," Dara says, patting my arm. "He'll get through this, Charli. It could've been so much worse."

I nod, then breathe in Noelle's baby powder scent, finding a sense of peace in it.

"Sit down. I can take Noelle again," Mom offers.

"No. I've missed her." I take the seat next to Mom, and Noelle lays her head on my chest, sucking on her pacifier. I rub my cheek against her soft hair.

"How did your meeting go?" Dara asks with a touch of caution in her voice.

I shake my head. "Sorry. I can't even think about that right now. I'm too worried about Kellan and how I left us on Monday night. What do you always say, Mom? Never go to bed angry? I should've said more. I had a right to be mad, but I should've handled it better." I drop my head in my hand and close my eyes.

"By the way," Dara whispers behind her hand. "I told the hospital that you're Kellan's fiancée so you could see him when he wakes up."

I crack a smile when she winks at me. "Thanks... future sister-in-law."

"I'd love to have you as a sister. Finally, another female. Well, I'd get three more females in the family. You, Tricia, and Noelle. Four of us against Kellan. He doesn't stand a chance." We all crack up in laughter, disturbing other people in the room.

Kellan's fiancée. Never in a million years would I think I'd fall in love with Kellan and maybe become his wife. A sudden burst of happiness washes over me.

"Dara Kierney? Charlize Brannon?"

We both stand.

"Kellan is awake. He's a little groggy, but he'll be fine."

I step forward. "Can I see him?"

"Yes, but only for a little while. He might fall back asleep. Follow me."

"Should I take Noelle?" Dara asks.

"No, thanks. Wait. Yes. That might be better." Dara carefully takes her from my arms.

I follow the doctor down a hall, worried about what Kellan will look like. The doctor stops at a room and stands to the side. With a little hesitation, I walk in. My stomach twists when I see him with casts and a ghastly, pale face. But he's awake, and his eyes lock with mine.

"There's my favorite girl," Kellan mumbles in a rough voice. That's all he needed to say for me to break down into tears. I run to the side that's free of casts and bandages. I lean over and kiss his lips softly.

"Thank God, you're okay. I don't know what I would've done if—" I sit down on the chair next to the bed, then grab his hand and kiss the back of it.

"I'm here. It hurts like hell, but I'm not going anywhere. I'll be out of commission for a little while."

"Who cares? You have tons of contractors to work for you. It'll get done. And it's my turn to take care of you. I need you healthy." Tears run down my face again.

"Don't cry. I'll be fine."

"I can't help it. So, tell me, what happened?"

"I went up on the roof to help the guys start breaking it apart. When I went to climb down, I lost my balance and the ladder fell over. I landed on my left side and shoulder."

"Is your shoulder broken? Did you hit your head?"

"No, just my arm and two ribs. My head's fine. I had a helmet on. They had to put metal rods in my arm." *Metal rods.* That gives me the shivers.

"I'm so sorry for how I left you in the parking lot." I run my fingers through his hair. "I should've talked to you about it instead of leaving you there. But I was so shocked and confused."

"Don't apologize. It was all my fault. I should've been honest with you from the beginning. You wanted honesty, and I didn't give it to you."

"It doesn't matter anymore. I love you so much, Kell. I can't imagine my life without you."

"I love you too. And no matter where you go, I'll follow," he says.

"You won't have to. I declined the offer. When I sat down in the meeting room, I found this note from you." I pull it from my pocket and read it aloud. *"Never doubt my love for you.* My heart had already made the decision before I even went into the meeting room, but this made it even easier. I choose us. I want to renovate this house with you, and I don't want to sell it." His lips quirk up in a grin. "I want us to live here as a family."

"Marry me then. I know it's fast, but I've loved you for so long, I can't wait any longer. Being away from you for two days has been a complete nightmare. Please be my wife?"

"Yes! Yes! Can we get married tomorrow?" I blurt excitedly, showering his face with little kisses. He chuckles and winces, then breathes through the pain.

"Eager, are we? But no. We're going to do it right. Big party in the backyard of Sandy's house when it's finished."

"You mean *our* house," I correct him.

"Right. Our house. I love the sound of that."

"Me too."

EPILOGUE

KELLAN

7 Months Later

"You still have time to run if you're having second thoughts," Dara says, straightening my tie. I roll my eyes, and she chuckles.

"There's no way in hell I'll walk away from Charli again. She's stuck with me, whether she likes it or not."

"Well, she said yes, so I guess she does. She's been walking on a cloud for months. You deserve your happy ending. Don't forget, you're getting up there in the years."

"Shut the hell up. I'm not even forty. I can run circles around the twenty-year-olds."

"If they're drunk," she sasses.

A light knock on the bedroom door interrupts us. My heart pounds, knowing that it's finally time to marry my best friend and favorite woman in the world.

"Ready?" Dara asks with a wide grin.

"More than ever." I tighten my tie again. "Come in."

The door opens and my mom peeks in, then walks

through. "Oh, Kellan. You look so handsome. Finally, one of my kids is getting married."

"*Mom*," Dara warns.

"It's time. Charli's ready." Mom waves us to the door, smiling brightly.

"So am I. Let's go before you two start bickering again."

Mom opens the door and checks that we're in the clear. I've been hiding downstairs in the guest room while Charli gets ready in the main bedroom upstairs. When we step out the back door, emotion takes over. The backyard is beautiful. I helped do it, but it means something different right now. All Charli wanted was a lot of colorful flowers. I probably financed a two-week vacation for the florist, but that's okay.

Flowers, ribbons, and tulle decorate the deck railings, the rows of chairs near the aisle Charli will walk down, the wedding trellis I built for her, and the large white tent ready for the reception. Hanging from our favorite trees are white lanterns that we'll light after the sun goes down.

"Come on, big guy. Charli's ready, and I'm hungry." *Shocker.* Dara pushes me forward.

Charli and I decided not to have a bridal party. We wanted a small ceremony and a reception in the backyard. Our house has turned out more beautiful than we could've imagined. It took longer than we thought it would, but that's because we didn't have to do it in record time like Charli had originally planned. We made some minor changes to her original design, and now she has the house she dreamed of. One ready for family and friends and maybe a brother or sister for Noelle one day. I told her when we started dating that she'd love it so much when we finished, she wouldn't want to sell it. I was right. I rub it in from time to time.

I make it to the end of the aisle and wait patiently while the photographer clicks away. Music begins to play as Dara walks with Noelle, dressed in powder pink, down the aisle, encouraging her to throw red rose petals. She tries to eat them instead, then plops herself on the ground. I chuckle at my daughter along with the guests. Not too long after I got out of the hospital, I adopted Noelle. Charli wouldn't wait until we were officially married. I'll be honest, I didn't want to wait either.

Then I see Charli on the deck with Tricia. Tears push at the back of my eyes. Her smile shines as bright as the sun. It feels like yesterday that I saw her striking eyes and her mouth full of braces for the first time. Yet it took an eternity to get where we are today. In a couple of minutes, she'll finally become my wife.

As she comes closer, I'm undone by her natural beauty. Her hair is down, just like she wore it for the prom. Her breathtaking, sequined, strapless dress follows the sexy curves that I love, flowing out gradually toward the bottom. A gentle breeze blows her delicate veil softly out behind her. It's Charli's borrowed element—the veil Tricia wore when she married Mickey. Charli's bouquet is a mixture of the white roses she wanted and the lavender that makes me think of her.

A couple more steps and our hands join. Chuckling, I pull tissues out of my pocket and hand her one. Then we wipe the tears from our faces.

Minutes later, my heart swells when I finally hear, "I now pronounce you husband and wife."

"Does that mean I can kiss her now?"

"Ye—"

I cup her beautiful face in my hands and kiss her like everyone else has evaporated into thin air. Dara clears her throat to get our attention. Charli giggles into my chest. Then Dara lets little Noelle run up to us.

"Dada," Noelle calls sweetly, running to me with her arms open wide. I sweep her up in my arms, and Charli and I kiss her chubby cheeks. The photographer better have captured that.

"Wrapped around your finger," Charli murmurs. "Just like

it should be." That makes my smile spread even larger, because I've been truly blessed with the family I've always wanted.

An hour later, the sun is setting in glorious orange and red hues. Charli and I are wrapped up in our own world as we dance our first dance to John Legend's "All of Me". As the last notes fade away, the guests slowly find their way out of the tent.

Charli looks around. "Where's everyone going?"

I press a kiss under her ear, then murmur, "I have a surprise for you."

"Really? Is it in our bedroom?" She kisses down my neck.

I pull away and grab her hands. "I've created an animal! Not that I'm complaining." I sneak a kiss on the corner of her mouth. "But no. I do need to blindfold you, though." She cocks a curious eyebrow. "Don't worry, I'll make it up to you later." Her eyes widen with anticipation.

I cover her eyes with a satin white ribbon, then walk her out of the tent.

"Where are we going?"

"You'll see."

I lead her to our favorite tree and wait while our guests gather around. Tricia hands me Noelle, and I balance her on one arm. With my free hand, I remove Charli's blindfold, and her breath hitches.

"Kellan... it's amazing. You mentioned it once, on New Year's Eve. I thought you'd forgotten about it." Her delicate fingers trace the heart I've carved into the tree with our initials and Noelle's.

"You don't know how hard it was to hide this from you and Tricia. And look, I left some space for more initials if we decide to have more kids."

Around us, guests chuckle, but Charli pokes my side. "Let's enjoy being married for a while."

"We can practice, right?" She pokes me again and laughs. I tug her hand. "Now come over to this side of the tree."

She follows me around, then covers her mouth. Her eyes glisten as she sees what I've done. "Oh! You made one for Sandy and Abigail. And it has Noelle's initials too. Just when I think I couldn't love you more, you do something like this to prove me wrong again." She wraps her arm around my waist and rests her head on my chest. "And stop making me cry all the time. I have cried enough in the last year to last a lifetime."

Noelle points at the heart with Sandy and Abi's names and says, "Mama."

Next to us, Dara, Tricia, and Katherine catch their breath. Charli and I are rendered speechless, and my eyes tear up.

"That's right, baby girl," Charli finally responds, rubbing Noelle's back. "Every one of your mamas loves you."

Tricia dabs her eyes with a tissue. "You two and Noelle are making me cry," she says. "Thank you so much, Kellan. This is absolutely perfect."

"They deserve to be remembered," I explain. "They're the ones who brought us together."

"And gave us Noelle." Charli's adoring blue eyes lock with mine. "We're the luckiest people in the world."

"We really are."

The End

EVERYDAY HEROES WORLD

Want to keep up with all of the other books in K. Bromberg's Everyday Heroes World? You can visit us anytime at http://www.kbworlds.com/ and the best way to stay up to date on all of our latest releases and sales, is to sign up for our official KB Worlds newsletter.

BOOKS BY KRISTINA BECK

COLLIDE SERIES

Lives Collide

Dreams Collide

Souls Collide

Collide Series Complete Box Set

FOUR SEASONS SERIES

Snowflakes and Sapphires – Winter

Passions and Peonies – Spring

Colors and Curves – Summer

Maple Trees and Maybes – Autumn

STANDALONE

Into Thin Air

Trapped

Key To His Heart

ACKNOWLEDGMENTS

Thank you, Kristy Bromberg, for granting me the wish of participating in the Everyday Heroes World. Trapped is my tenth book! Woo hoo! I can't believe it. Sometimes I lost my way because of the worldly events surrounding us, but I prevailed. I've enjoyed every minute of this journey and have learned a lot along the way.

During the plotting phase of this book, I had a few people help me along the way to make sure my facts were straight throughout the book. I would like to thank my brother, Ron, who owns his own construction company and my sister, Deanna, who has renovated many houses.

Thank you, Kate and Kevin Scott, and Lisa Hemming for answering my questions regarding the involvement of firefighters and police in automotive accidents. I appreciate that you took the time out of your day to help me.

And big hugs to Lisa Hemming (again), Rachel Childers, and Jamie Buck for being my beta readers again. Your enthusiasm for my books helps me get through the grueling editing process. I value all the feedback you send me. It's priceless. Beta readers are so important for the creation of a new book and I'm glad I have you.

I couldn't be happier with the Trapped book cover. Usually I don't have models on my covers but it was required this time. For my first one, I think it came out pretty good. When I found the image on depositphotos.com, the model fit Kellan's description perfectly. Thanks, Jody Kaye, for making the cover creation process so easy. You always do a fabulous job.

Rachel Overton, I know the editing process wasn't easy this time but I think we wrapped this book up into a beautiful package. Thanks for being patient with me and guiding me in the right direction. You are the only editor I trust with my books. I look forward to our next adventure.

And to Helen Pryke... my lovely proofreader. The two-step review process that you offer is very valuable because you find all of those little mistakes that I'm blinded to by the end. Your eye for detail is a benefit for any author. Thank you for your support as a friend and fellow author!

Thank you, Amy Rhodes, for helping me pick my hero's name. Kellan was a perfect fit.

Ilona, where would I be without you? You are my shoulder to cry on, someone to laugh with, and my book buddy wrapped all in one. I'm so thankful for our friendship and for us bouncing ideas off of one another when we're writing our books. Even though I'm moving, I'll always be a phone call away.

And of course, to my husband and kids who dealt with me writing during several lockdowns. With homeschooling, no time to myself, fears of the future, and moving again, I'm surprised I was able to finish this book. Thank you for letting me hide in the corner to finish my tenth book.

Hugs to my readers! Thank you for following me and encouraging me to keep writing. That always helps me get to the finish line. Without your love for my books, I wouldn't be where I am today. I hope you enjoyed Trapped.

ABOUT THE AUTHOR

Kristina Beck was born and raised in New Jersey, USA, and lived there for thirty years. She later moved to Germany and now lives there with her German husband and three children. She is an avid reader of many genres, but romance always takes precedence. She loves coffee, dark chocolate, power naps, flowers, traveling, and eighties movies. Her hobbies include writing, reading, fitness, and forever trying to improve her German-language skills.

For updates on her new releases, book news, and sales, check out her website. Sin up for her newsletter and receive a free ebook. Want to chat about everything books, join her Facebook group, Krissy's Captivating Reads.

www.kristinabeck.com

facebook.com/krissybeck73

instagram.com/krissybeck96

amazon.com/author/kristinabeck

bookbub.com/authors/kristina-beck

goodreads.com/kristina_beck

tiktok.com/@simplykristinabeck